Grey Matter Series

The Story of Mark Trogmyer in the World

of the Unknown

Written by Anthony S. Parker

Illustrated by Brendan Alicea

Edited by Laura Le Baron and friends

Grey Matter Series Volume 1:
The Story of Mark Trogmyer in the World of the Unknown

Written By: Anthony S. Parker

Copyright © August 2021
By: Anthony S. Parker

All Rights Reserved. Published in the United States by Kdp.amazon.com
Printed in Milford, Delaware

No part of this publication may be reproduced, distributed, or transmitted in any from or by any means, including photocopying, recording, or other electronic or mechanical methods, without the prior written permission of the Author, except in the case of brief quotations embodied in critical reviews and certain other noncommercial uses permitted by copyright law. For permission requests for the text or artwork in this book please email the Author, addressed "Attention: Anthony Parker," at:

Grey Matter Series
Regarding Copyrights
Email: authoraparker@gmail.com

ISBN-13: 9798462213007

Imprint: Independently published

- Fiction > General
- Fiction > Fantasy > General

First Edition for Dyslexia Font. Volume. 1

Dedicated to those who are lost, so that they may find themselves....

Love for the Series So Far:

"A fantastic easy read that can be related to anyone's situation in life where they may have to fight true evils, in the end, it's unique." - **Randy Rodriguez**

"Though you may not be a fan of the fantasy genre, the fact that you are a human being makes this book a must-read. The author utilizes many of life's situations and events that we face almost daily and displays the positive perspective of such events. While reading Anthony Parker's book, you will find yourself reflecting on your own life while being entertained! What more can you ask for a book!" - **Toni Enriquez**

"Such a great book, definitely a must read!" - **Chris De Leon (Niteshockers)**

"An adventure away from reality. A well thought out story for which a boy can discover his power of impact just by sticking to what he believes in. If you are looking for a great escape from your world, then step into the World of the Unknown by flipping through these pages!"
- **Leah Garcia**

Love for the Series So Far:

"I just started reading the first few chapters of the series and was captivated from the start! I love the descriptiveness of the characters and the setting! I look forward to reading more of the series!" - **Matt Sweet**

"The story takes you on a thrill ride. It's easy to fall in love with the characters. The story's message conveys the true meaning of friendship, loyalty, and bravery." - **Kate Sweetman**

"It's a great story with well-constructed characters in a world, all, of its own. It has a sense of familiarity that draws you in and keeps you wanting to know what happens next. It's easy to get into and even if you put it down, it's that much easier to pick back up. You won't have to start over. I really enjoy the cast of characters involved in the story. Many of them play mentor to a character that is trying to understand his purpose in two worlds that he has yet to fully understand." - **Gaby Bucci**

Love for the Series So Far:

"For fans of C.S Lewis and J.K Rowling, this is a very fun coming of age story and adventure with strong characters and a lot of heart. A very promising start from an up and coming author!" - **Josh Snyder**

"Mark Trogmyer gives hope to the future in this amazing book. Anthony S. Parker developed the story and its characters in such a relatable manner. This series has introduced me to the World of the Unknown and I never want to leave it." - **Dunken Lopez**

"As soon as I started the book I was anxious to finish it. Now I am equally anxious to finish the series and learn more about the amazing World of the Unknown that Anthony Parker created in which I can escape to." - **Adrian Enriquez**

"Fantastic Story, easy read and descriptive with great characters. A real page turner, always leaves you wanting to know what's going to happen next! If you are looking for escapism, read this book! Can't wait for the next one! 4/5 stars. - @read_with_cc (Instagram) from UK

Love for the Series So Far:

"When reading this book from the start the first chapter grabs you immediately and sparks your curiosity and you don't want to put the book down. This ought to be a must-read book especially if you are into fantasy fiction. Anthony Parker uses the genre to reinvent real-life situations while in the realm of the World of the Unknown, which makes it easier to understand and for the readers to relate to in their own lives. Overall the author Anthony Parker has some unique writing skills. If you enjoyed this book as I have, then I am sure book two is bound to be a success, I can't wait to read on!" - Maria Ana Sanchez

"An adventure in time, if you enjoyed Harry Potter this is for you!"- **Cassandra Gonzalez**

"I don't read a lot of books but when I do I am very particular about what I grab. I picked up the first copy of this book and it was great. I didn't want to put it down the suspense was killing me. I can't wait for the next one, I am sure it's going to be even better! The author Anthony Parker, really put a lot of time into writing the first book and I can't wait to see what else is coming from him!" - Tina Bellon

Love for the Series So Far:

"I'm enjoying the book series quite a lot so far. I'm a huge fantasy fan so already, the book is right up my alley. It engrosses and pulls me into a new world I can get lost in as I read and was captivated by the world painted for me in the book. If I wasn't so busy, I honestly might have binged the whole series already." – Christian Alexander Billingsley

"Thank you for giving me book one signed. My son loves it and he has not put it down since I gave it to him. It is 2 am and I had to take the book from him so he would get to sleep. He is fifteen pages in and he already loves it! Thank you so much for getting my son to start reading again with your books! I look forward to reading it myself after him! - Tony Caruso, Delaware

"Right from the start, when I was first told about the book series, I was interested. I read the first book and it was fantastic. The characters were memorable and likeable, my favorites were Burgesis and Barty. I got my hands on the second book, and after reading it, it was phenomenal! There was SO much action in the storyline and interaction with all the characters! I really can't wait for the next two books!" -Maureen Phinney

Love for the Series So Far:

"When you open this book, you will step into a world of wonder, hope, and magic. A world where anything is possible with understanding and faith in in the good of people. You will feel as though you are walking along with Mark Trogmyer, feeling the wonders and emotions as he does. Anthony has created both a world and characters that pull you in and make you care for them. He has given insight into how many of them could have been made to feel like the path they have chosen seemed like the right one, even if it is not. I laughed and cried with and for the inhabitants of the World of the Unknown. Their story has gripped me from the very first paragraph to the last. I cannot wait to delve deeper and see how this journey and our heroes progress! - Christina Astrid Ferrante

"Awesome Book! I loved the way it was written and could be easily read. The story was thought provoking, and unique, filled with action, mystery, and intrigue that left me hanging all the way to the end! Loved this book and recommend it to all lovers of the fantasy genre! My Favorite scene was when Mark Trogmyer was introduced into the World of the Unknown, it left a lasting impression that made me reflect on things in my own life! This book was a real joy to read the likes of which I haven't read in the long time, it was refreshing! Thank you so much for the opportunity to allowing me to read your book!"- Jarvis Baxter, UK

Love for the Series So Far:

"Volume 4 of Grey Matter Book Series has begun to test the boundaries that have until now been crossed in the genre, as this compelling riveting story has become extraordinarily popular these last few months." - Daniel Spaizer, Massachusetts

Hi Anthony, Me and my girlfriend both equally love your book. We honestly couldn't put it down. After the first few days we made it to Chapter 5 and honestly we couldn't wait to read more. My girlfriend, Ella, loved the thought of Whiskers, being a cat lover, and sad, as, well you know, but we love it! We stayed up last night finishing the first volume of your book, we both can't thank you enough for sending us your book and the joy we have experienced reading it together. As we are already fans of the hobbit and lord of the rings, books and films, this book was already an easy catch for us and caught our eyes almost immediately after reading a few chapters. We have always said that we should start reading more books, especially together, and now during the current conditions that we are faced with, your book helped to be a distraction to our lives and to what is going on in the world. We will without a doubt be reading your next volume very soon and can't wait to see what happens, what a cliffhanger... - Scotty Jockey and Ella from Wales, UK

Table of Contents

Chapter	Name
1	In the Beginning (Primitus)
2	Frank Burgesis and Susie Que
3	The Adventure
4	A Path Less Traveled
5	A New Magical Being
6	The Basic Elements
7	Fire and Air/Wind
8	Water and Earth
9	The Challenge
10	The Others
11	Morals and Virtues
12	On the Run
13	The River of Peace
14	The Rebels
15	The Protégé
16	The Guard
17	Harmony Meadow
18	The Guard Continued
19	Hope
20	Pam and the Family Decision
21	The Transfer
22	The Family Connection
23	… and the world grew dark…
24	WANTED
25	The Guards Decision
26	The Traitors

27	The Trial	
28	The Tunnel	
29	The Verdict	
30	To Mend a Broken Heart	
31	The Light of Forgiveness	
32	An Issue of Loyalty	
33	The decision to keep moving	
34	The Loss of a loved one	
35	A Change of Heart	
36	The Path of Fortune and Misfortune	
37	Friend or Foe	
38	Whiskers and his Wife Gretta	
39	In the Beginning: The Seven Guardians, Seven Virtues, and Seven Deadly Sins	
40	The Book of the Known	
41	The Nightmare of Dreams	
42	A Weakness of a Great Leader	
**	Coming Soon/ Sources	
**	Illustrations of the Characters	
**	Character Chart	
**	Bookmark for Volume 1	

Autograph Page:

"Dreams are not to be brought to the cemetery of the Unaccomplished. They are meant to be achieved no matter the cost, no matter the pain, no matter of your fears! Push yourself to greatness and no one will or should be stopping you from reaching your full potential to live in complete and utter happiness!!"

- Anthony S. Parker

"I am the master of my fate; I am the captain of my soul." - William Earnest Henley, Invictus

Introduction:

Have you ever taken the time to deeply think about how the world is today? Maybe you don't care... Or maybe you have noticed the pressing issues and turmoil that people struggle with daily. Maybe this struggle that you see people go through keeps you up at night and you stress constantly about it. Then you wonder how this world could get any worse... Keep in mind how the world is today while reading this book. There is more to this story in depth than what immediately meets the eye, for nothing in the World of the Unknown is as it seems....
WARNING!!

The Earth and the World of the Unknown in 3176... It is with a heavy heart that I fear that your troubles have only begun when you opened this book today. You were probably thinking that you might be opening a book about a fantasy story of the brain and its wonderful changes and advances in the future. Sadly, this is not the case, in fact, Mark Trogmyer (the main character of this story), wishes to ensure two things before you start this journey with him.

First, that you are not Nerogroben or a supporter of his ruthless army because even being in possession of this book could be considered treason.

Finally, if you enjoy adventure, magic, and faraway places, you have picked up the right book. You will be taken to new depths of thought as you ponder in depth, the story of Mark Trogmyer's deep and at times dangerous adventure.

When you are ready to give this book a whirl, I recommend that you have the bookmark in the back of this book cut out and folded in half. This way you can keep track of where you are in the World of the Unknown. It's been known that people have gotten caught and put in mortal danger if they are found with this book in hand by the wrong person from the World of the Unknown ....

Chapter 1
In the Beginning (Primitus)

<u>Earth 3176 – Suffolk, VA</u>

"Mom, is he going to be okay? TELL ME WHISKERS IS GOING TO BE OKAY!" I shouted at my mom as I heard yowling from my cat in the cat carrier next to me as I started wiping my tears away as she slowed down for some cars in the lane.

"I don't know sweetheart, we have to see what the doctor says," my mom whispered as she stepped on the gas going around the cars into the next lane over. We finally had arrived at the veterinarian's office after what seemed like hours.

I rushed into the office and brought Whiskers to the technician. As soon as I handed them Whiskers, they brought him at once to the back as I tried to follow them. I was at once stopped by another person from being able to pass through the double doors as I saw them place Whisker's on the table and hook wires and tubes up to him and take his blood.

"WHISKERS!!!" I shouted in fear as I started to cry. Other people were in the office watching me cry, but I didn't care.

I had reflected on the days that I had first laid eyes on my cat Whiskers, he was my cat. But he had adopted the three of us four years ago. He was the talk of the neighborhood kids, he was unloved, unwanted, and untouched. He was a scraggily old thing and appeared to be looking for the two things that no one would seem to be able to give him: comfort, and a little tender love and care. I had wondered how far and how long he had traveled before he came into our lives.

I felt sorry for this cat, and every night, his persistent meowing for food made my adolescent heart compassionately want to care for him. At night, I would sneak downstairs to our refrigerator, pull out a hot dog from the package, one at a time. I then would cut it into small pieces for him and would go outside, to keep him company. I would watch him, gratefully eat the hot dog pieces off the napkin, savoring them, as if this was his last meal.

At first, he was very timid and unsure about me, but the hunger pains had taken over his mind and gradually, he came around. Whiskers after a while, finally got used to being around me. One night before dinner, my mom wanted to serve hot dogs and she had noticed that they were almost all gone. She had asked if I had touched them.

It was at that time, that I had told my parents I wanted to adopt him into our home. After telling them that I had been feeding Whiskers, I had told them that he had been coming to our home nightly for food out of habit now.

At first, my parents objected to allowing Whiskers into our home. For some reason, I had felt a connection to him, and so after a few more days of persuasion, my parents had bought cat food, adopted him, and he grew on us all over time. Whiskers would play with me with his toys, and he seemed happy, and content at our home for the last few short years we had him. But this autumn day, was the day that it all changed for us all and nothing was ever the same again after I realized how fragile our lives are.

After waiting for what seemed like hours, I stood up and started walking to the double doors.

"Mark," said my mom called out to me as I ignored her. I looked through the double doors and there I saw vet techs rushing around the room around the table where I saw him fighting for his life. I had then felt the comfort of my mom's hands on my shoulders. "Come on Mark, we have to let them do their job, they will come out as soon as things change."

I nodded silently and walked back to the chair and sat next to my mom burying my face in her.

"He is my cat, mine, and nothing was supposed to happen to him!" I cried in frustration, as she rubbed the back of my head and kissed it in comfort.

After waiting for what seemed like an eternity longer, the veterinarian came out through the double doors and into the waiting room.
She sat next to me and my mom and shook her head silently.
"I'm sorry, we tried everything we could, there was nothing else we could do for him," the doctor had said.
"NOOOO!" I shouted as I ran through the double doors and pushed through people who were trying to keep me from going to the back.
It was then that I saw him, my Whisker's lifeless body there on the table. The scene was surreal to me. There was blood everywhere, but I didn't care. I didn't believe he was gone, and I didn't want to believe it until I saw him lying there on the table. He looked like he was in peace, as if he was no longer in any pain. I wanted him back, to tell him once more that I loved him. I had felt horrible as if a part of me was dead. It felt like the entire world stopped around me and it was no use going through with it anymore, as I had started to feel in shock.
It might seem strange to you, but this cat of mine was not only a friend, but he was also a comfort to come to when I was stressed or when I had felt alone. But now, he was gone, and there was nothing I could do to bring him back. The Veterinarian had said Whiskers had died of old age and that his heart

had stopped, but I knew that my heart would *never* stop beating for him.

We started to drive home in silence, my mom called my dad and told him the bad news. I sat in the back seat and had started crying on top of the white box which held Whisker's lifeless body. As I hugged it I was trying to accept that Whiskers was in a better place now, he had to be.

As soon as I went home, I ran upstairs to my room and laid on my bed face down in my pillow hugging it in comfort, crying my eyes out. I felt alone, and that there was now a void in my life that could no longer be filled. My heart ached for him as I felt my stomach knot up from all the crying and stress.

A few moments later a knock came at the door. "Mark," said my mom's voice, through the closed door. "If you want to talk, just know that we are here for you."

"I just want to be left alone," I said aloud, I then heard

footsteps walking away from the doorway.

I just continued to cry and cry wishing his return, wishing that things would be easier to deal with. An hour later I heard my dad pull up and as I looked outside, I could see my mom and dad hugging. Within a few minutes, I could see my dad with a shovel, starting to dig a hole in the flower bed next to the tree by my window as the box of Whiskers was placed into the hole with his favorite blanket placed over it. Then my dad covered the hole and placed a painted rock over the grave site with WHISKERS name placed on it. He then looked up at my window, and he waved at me as I nodded in thanks and then I went to lay back down on my bed. I was so thankful for my dad doing that for me. It was from that moment on that I knew that I could never forget November 5, 3176. Less than an hour later he knocked at my door and opened it. "Hey buddy," said my dad sadly as I sat up and looked at him silently. "How are you feeling? I know you don't want to talk about it right now, but just know that we are here for you."

I nodded and then laid back down on the bed and turned to face away from my father. He pulled the covers up over me as he hugged me and said: "Goodnight, your mother and I love you."

That night I went to bed frustrated and a little angry. Why would God allow this to happen to me? I thought. What did I do to God that he would do this to me? Why would he want me to be alone? Didn't he want me to live my life happily and with purpose? Why didn't he take my life instead of the cat's life? Why couldn't God see the goodness in me and spare him? God had taken the one thing I had grown to love, and now it had made life unbearable...These frustrations continued into the next day as I kept to myself while my mom was at work. She had come home late after I had already eaten dinner and had already gone to bed.

Chapter 2
Frank Burgesis and Susie Que

<u>Three days Later</u>
"Mark Trogmyer, it's been three days since Whiskers has died. You should try to move on, and start helping out around here more," my mom said to me as she was dusting the living room coffee table. I looked at the exact spot of where I had remembered where Whisker's body was, which was a few feet away from where my mom was. My eyes teared up as I ran upstairs, closed my door, and started crying in my bed wishing he was here. I could still remember him in my arms as if it were yesterday and feeling him purr. I could see my reflection in the mirror of my room. My dark blue eyes were wet with the tears and my hair was wet from sweat.

My mom knocked on my door and opened it, "I am sorry Mark," she said as she sat next to me on the edge of my bed.

She rubbed the back of my head and said, "You have to understand life isn't forever, sometimes death comes to us all like a thief in the night."

"It's not fair!" I yelled angrily as I cried on her shoulders.

I leaned on her looking at the empty bowls on the floor, wiping my tears with a tissue that she handed me.

"I know Mark, sometimes it isn't until we have lost a loved one in our life, that we then realize, how much of a difference or impact that they had made on our lives. Sometimes it's at that moment, that it's too late. Whiskers' time had come, and all of our times do, when we have to leave this world and go on to the next," said my mom who stopped patting my head.

The doorbell rang from downstairs as I tossed my tissues in the trash can next to my bed. My mom stood up and left the room to answer the door. I stayed sitting down on the bed staring into space. It was from that moment on, that I realized that life, in general, was as fragile as you need to be when you are carrying a glass vase. It was also at that moment, that I had the urge to look at the two-empty bowls on the floor again as if hoping he would come back to me.

As I thought about what my mom had said I considered it. I thought maybe I didn't need to forget about him, but just accept the fact that he is gone, and make the most out of life as it happens.

"Mark!" shouted my mom up the stairs.

"Yes, Mom?" I replied as I stood up and moved closer to the doorway to hear her better.

"There is a man who wants to talk to you at the front door," my mom explained looking up the

stairs at me. "Can you come down here and talk to him, I will be making dinner if you need me."
"Okay Mom," I responded. Then I nodded my head in agreement with my own thoughts thinking, "Yes... I will try to move on," as I picked up the bowls, stuck them in a shoebox, and placed the box in my closet.

I then went downstairs, opened the front door, and I saw that there was an old man who was standing in the doorway. He was eagerly smiling and staring at me as if I was some amazing one-of-a-kind roller coaster. I would say this old man was in his late 50s, early 60s and he did not dress like he had a lot of money. Wearing a gray and yellow striped sweater over a yellow collared shirt and brown pants. He also had some old, styled converse type black shoes. What had stood out about him, was his long graying beard that fell all the way to his waistline. I looked up at him and even at fifteen years old, he was still as tall than me. I noticed his neck had a tattoo of a bald eagle on it, for some reason. I just stood there after observing him, and after a while, it had become awkward between us. I had felt strange around this mysterious guy, and I couldn't put my finger on it.

"Well, are you going to invite me in? I am not getting any younger!" the old man said laughing. I didn't know the guy, but I laughed, nodded, and ushered him into our decent, presentable living room. We never had much, but what we did have, we were grateful for.

"It seems to me that something may have recently happened that has changed you," he said looking around the room cautiously. He then walked into the room noticing where things were and smiled at our flowery wallpaper.

"What do you mean by that?" I asked wondering what he was talking about as I dusted off the grey cat fur off my blue shirt and black jeans as I sat on the couch across from the man. He sat on a love seat chair and looked at the coffee table in front of us deep in thought. "Well, I mean... you seem like you don't know what to do you with your life. I mean, I have recently noticed a change in your daily routines, from across the street. I have been meaning to introduce myself to you, my name is Frank Burgesis," he said hesitantly in a deep voice, as he held out his hand across the coffee table to shake mine. "I know your name is Mark Trogmyer and your parents are David and Kathy Trogmyer." I was amazed because he seemed to be reading my mind, as I was about to introduce myself to him and he just smiled as I shook his hand.

"What brought you to the conclusion that things have changed for me at all?" I asked feeling somewhat concerned that he knew who my parents were and that he had been watching me. At first, he just stared at me in silence, then he tilted his head and put on a thoughtful face as if debating with himself whether to answer me.

"So, what do you do on your free time?" he asked deciding to avoid answering my question.

"I love to read. The school has told me that I am advanced for my age since I've been reading high school level books for a while now," I said proudly.

"I figured. You do seem rather intelligent for your age. Um, how old are you?" he asked, looking at me genuinely interested and sat with his fingers touching each other and was sitting at the edge of his seat as if expecting to leave suddenly.

"I am fifteen turning sixteen years old within the next few days," I replied looking intently at his green eyes.

He had remained silent for a while as he observed me, and as he looked straight down to the floor, he then said in an almost inaudible whisper, "He is still too young to understand," said Mr. Burgesis thoughtfully.

"I am not too young to understand anything!" I spoke loudly staring at his face in frustration.

He looked up at me surprised that he had said what he was thinking aloud. His mouth started to move as he was debating whether to say something.

Then he suddenly stood up and started to walk off towards the front door. He then turned around and looked at me. I was still sitting angrily on the couch as my eyes followed his every move.

"We shall see then," said Burgesis now smiling. "Tomorrow night, after your parents have gone to sleep, step out of your window. Then climb down the tree and meet me at the bottom. Dress warmly because tomorrow night is supposed to get really cold out," he instructed.

"Why are you meeting me at night? Why can't you just tell me right now?" I asked rather frustrated crossing my arms.

"At night, it's easier to explain everything to you," said Burgesis hurriedly looking at his watch from under his long-sleeved shirt. "Oh, and by the way, no matter what happens... you *must* know that everything is going to be all right!"

"I am not too young to understand anything," I repeated to him. "Tell me what you were going to explain to me. How do you know things have changed for me? What is it that you say has changed about me?" I demanded angrily as he started to walk towards the door. I hated not knowing things.

Burgesis turned and walked back into the living room and calmly as if nothing had happened, he

said, "I will tell you between tomorrow night and early morning, good day,"
he said as he then let himself out and I sat there shocked.
Two minutes later, mom came into the living room from the kitchen which was in the back of the house and asked, "Who was that?"
"Our neighbor," I replied, feeling somewhat irritated. I got up from the couch, stretched, and followed her back into the kitchen.
"Funny, I don't recall us meeting him when we moved in, what is he like?" she asked as she was just finishing making dinner.
"He's strange, and he's not very talkative," I responded as my stomach gurgled in hunger.
"So, what did he want?" Mom asked as she looked at me grabbing my stomach. "You okay?"
"Oh yeah, just hungry, he just wanted to introduce himself as Frank Burgesis," I replied as she looked up at me as I was avoiding her eye contact as I grabbed a cup from the cupboard and got a glass of water to drink and drank it.
"Can you go wash up and set the table? Don't worry dinner is almost ready," she said dismissively as I nodded, turned, and walked to the bathroom. I started thinking about the conversation that we had in reflection, thinking about what I already knew. What was I too young to understand? Why

did he want to meet me at night instead of meeting me during the day? How would that make it easier to explain things to me?

After setting the table, mom finished dinner and was now serving them on plates as I helped to put them on the table in the family room. I heard the screeching of rubber tires, as I turned and looked out the window in the kitchen. The window was above the kitchen sink, I went to the window to hear who honked, and I saw it was my dad. He was finally home from a long day of work. He was wearing his business suit and was carrying his briefcase. Dad works in an executive sales firm and as part of the board of directors and is partnered with his friend who sells batteries all over the world. These batteries are energizing things from computers to advanced music players, to holographic cell phones, and gaming systems. These products were powered by the battery cells that my dad oversaw, which hold nuclear power. Dad had come inside and changed into comfortable clothes just in time as mom had finished putting the food and drinks on the table. We all sat down and after a while, Dad turned on the TV to the daily news station.

"As you know folks the weather outside is hot and going to be humid for the next few days. Don't worry, if you sleep all day, the next few nights we will be in the 50s and 60s by the evening," said the weather broadcaster laughingly as my dad shook his head in silence. Next, a reporter started talking about crimes in the area. I noticed how much it had changed just over the past few years, by getting worse. I shook my head feeling disappointed. There was a lot of evil happening in the world. I only wished that things were different, that people were a little more honest, respectful, and got along better by being more understanding of each other. I wished that they would stop hating each other and argue over things in life, that didn't matter. I mean every other night there was at least a murder, robbery, or a kidnapper that hadn't been caught yet. We would hear about car tires being slashed in the city or drug busts that had occurred. There was really, no sign of it stopping at all anytime soon, I thought to myself as I finished eating my burger. After watching the news and eating dinner, my mom and dad took us all out in the car, and dad told us about his day at work. I sat in the back of the car by myself and listened to the music down the familiar back roads of our town. Occasionally we traveled down back roads we had never been on as the gas from our car exhausted into the night air.

It was only six pm, so my parents and I were not worried about the time. Nor, were we worried about the people around us, who were all honking impatiently and angrily as if the end of the world was near. This was Washington, DC that we had ended up traveling to, and of course, people would act like what they had to do, and where they had to go was more important. Tourists in all cities alike are always easy to pick out. We stopped at a stop sign, and people with cameras around their necks were on the side of the road, taking pictures of the Washington Monument or The White House. It was then that I had noticed that within the crowd of tourists that were walking away, someone had just stolen a purse. A police officer who was nearby whistled at the guy, but he ended up getting away. I shook my head in disappointment. Though the cities in the United States are huge, and security is strong for the most part, they are still two times worse with crimes. There is a larger population of people that has grown significantly over the years that crowded the streets. Fights break out all the time, over political issues, etc. Protests and violence that had occurred in the past have been more frequent and not only in Washington, DC but everywhere. As of late, it just seems like people just feel like the world owes them success and happiness, and that they shouldn't have to work at all for it. Everywhere it seemed people had gotten killed daily due to religious beliefs, racial and working backgrounds, and even just innocent by-standers who were in the wrong place at the wrong time. Water shortages had happened a few years back and masses of people migrated from all over the world to the United States. Overall things have gotten worse on Earth over the last thousand years as our technology has increased. People have forgotten how to have a normal conversation and a normal relationship with each other.

While I was lost in reflection on these thoughts, I hadn't realized that my dad had turned down the radio and was trying to talk to me as he pointed out his open window.

"What Dad?" I asked

"I was trying to tell you that I walk down this road to my office every day from that parking lot!" my Dad said proudly pointing to the parking lot attendant waving as he passed. The parking lot attendant recognized him and waved back. He then continued having the conversation with my mom regarding how work was, as I was not paying full attention.

I continued to observe what was going on outside around us as I saw the various street vendors selling their products like President Tripolis's bobbleheads off their wheeled carts along the sidewalk to tourists on the side of the road. We had been traveling for a while and my parents decided that we should stop at Sam's Burgers and Steaks for ice cream sundaes, which was down the road a little further.

We parked and walked in. I could smell the familiar scent of burgers on the grill and French fries. I saw people standing in the doorway scanning their arms on their way out to pay for their food they had ordered from the waiter.

"Take a seat, anywhere," said a black-haired man impatiently from behind the counter pointing to the dining area as we walked in.

We sat near the door, and my parents sat across the table from me. I sat in silence looking around to see how many people were also seated at the different tables. Across from us, I could see that there were two parents and they had two younger kids with them. It was sad to see that the parents were on their phones instead of paying attention to their kids.

There seemed to be about ten tables in total occupied, it wasn't completely full, but all the other servers seemed to be keeping busy with their tables. After waiting for about three minutes, my parents looked around.

"Where is our waiter or waitress?" my dad asked impatiently as he looked around.

"The place is a little busy, so give them time," said my mom looking at me and then to my father firmly, as he nodded and looked at me.
Then an African American server came to our table. She was medium weight and height. She had a name tag on her apron that said, Susie Que.
"Well, what do you want?" she asked with attitude, looking from my parents and then to me.
"Whatever you do, don't waste my time. I have other tables to deal with, so don't take all day deciding on things. What do you want to drink?" she continued roughly, popping gum that was in her mouth.
"What do you have?" I asked Susie Que inquisitively.
"Oh, so you wanna be one of *those* customers today?" she said looking at me shaking her head. "The drinks are listed in the back of the menu."
I turned the menu over to the drinks noticing that they had sodas, teas, and various other drinks.
"I will have a water then," I said firmly.
"Oh, so you just want a water, after wasting my time asking me what we have to drink?" she said shaking her head again at me.
"You already know we have water, no use asking what we have to drink if you were just gonna get water, come on man," she said to me impatiently writing down water.

"I am sorry, get me a coke then," I said looking at her apologetically.

"Man, hm, hm, hm, hm, hm, junior... I just wrote down you want water and now you want to change your mind, so now I gotta use a new page just for you all because you can't decide on what to drink... hm, hm, hm, hm, hmm, my what has this world come to?" she said angrily shaking her head as she went to the next page on her pad and wrote coke.

"We would both like water," said my mom looking at my dad.

"Hm, hm, hm, hm, hm, got it, so I won't get much of a tip

now," she said quietly to herself writing down their drinks

as she left the table shaking her head.

Two minutes later, she came back with a coke and two

glasses of water, and she said, "What else are you getting today?"

"It isn't any of your birthday's, right?" asked Susie Que pointing at us all quizzically. "Cuz, our birthday parade came and left. We ain't got no time to be singing no Happy Birthday, or Happy Anniversary, or any Congratulations to anybody today."

"Oh no, we are trying to cheer up our son with an ice cream sundae since our cat died," said my father looking at Susie Que's long black hair that was dyed blond.

"Oh good, well boy, better get used to death, this happens every day on the streets around here. Just be happy you're alive and that your cat died instead of you," said Susie Que rather rudely looking at me. "You gotta tough life as it is out there, it's not all sunshine, daisies, roses. If you want something in life, you gotta fight for it. You gotta prove not just others, but to yourself, that you want and deserve success! Your parents are basically treating you like a pig for slaughter." She continued looking at them as they were open-mouthed and shocked at what she was saying. "I'm sorry, but kids today need to know how bad life is out there, and how fragile it is, and that life needs to be respected. You can't be naïve in life, it's better to be strong and know what you need to do to survive and what you are up against! Your parents need to realize that if something happens to them tomorrow, they can't go and buy you an ice cream to make you feel better. You know that they shouldn't be doing this right? I mean, every time someone or something you know in your life leaves or
dies, that you shouldn't just go out and buy an ice cream,"

said Susie Que pointedly. "Otherwise, you will turn out to be one fat tub of a kid!"

"I would appreciate it if you would just get our ice cream sundaes," said my mom rather angrily as she was worriedly looking at me after she had regained her composure from shock.

"Oh, I'm sorry did I make you hurt more son? Well, you should get used to it. No use sugar coating things. With life being so short, you gots to enjoy life while it's given to you, I will be right back, I forgot your straws," said Susie Que looking at me and then to my parents shaking her head as she walked away.

"What a horrible woman," said my mom then looking at my father who then frowned.

"You know, I think she is right," said my dad looking at my mom who raised her eyebrows surprised. "He needs to toughen up, if something happened to us we hope to have him survive without us eventually, he needs to be stronger in this crazy world."

"What do you guys mean? You both will always be, here right?" I said worriedly looking from my mom to my dad as they looked at each other.

"Of course, we will," said my mom as Susie Que came back with the straws.

An old man a few tables down started whistling at our server and was snapping his fingers at her. She gave him the, "I don't think so," face. He continued

to snap his fingers. She then turned to face us and said, "Would you please excuse me again."
My parents nodded at her in silence as she then went over
to the other table and said aloud, "Do I look like ur dog, sir?"
The guest turned red.
"I don't appreciate you calling me over here just to *serve* you when I was at another table and the guests there. That was very *rude*! You know what, I am going to continue to help those kind guests over there, you can wait for your ur turn," she said to the man as she pointed to us as he got up and asked for her manager.
"Go ahead, talk to my manager, you old fool!" she said to the old man walking away from his table and towards us.
"Where are our sundaes?" I asked her jokingly as she came back to us.
"Mark!" said my mom with a mad face.
"Oh, so now you are being impatient because you want ur ice cream," she said looking at me as I reached out for my coke and smiled as I started sipping it while looking at her. "Well you know what I want, I want a vacation, but you don't see that happening around here now do you? How many sundaes do you want Mr.?" asked Susie Que looking

impatiently at me and then to my father who stayed silent.

"Just three Ma'am," said my mom looking at Susie Que.

"Now what kind of ice cream sundaes do you want?" she asked sarcastically nice to us.

"I would like a mint sundae with sprinkles, and chocolate syrup please," I said looking at Susie Que who was half paying attention. There was a family sitting next to us who had two younger kids who had started throwing spitballs at her. All the while, their parents were on their cell phones, still not paying attention to what was going
on. The kids laughed, and the parents finally looked up.

"STOP it, or I will have you thrown out of here so fast,"
Susie Que said, and the kids jumped and then the parents got after their kids.

"Thank you," Susie Que said to the parents as they nodded, and she then turned around to us. "My goodness, anyway. I don't know if we even have sprinkles, and I know we do have chocolate syrup. But you want me to walk all the way to the back, just to get you chocolate syrup from the fridge. Then you want me to walk to the ice cream set up and pour it on your sundae? What do you want, a cherry with that now? What about you two?" she said shaking her head at me and looked at my parents.

"I don't like cherries," I said looking at her sternly "and I will have chocolate syrup on that, if it's, at all, possible."

"We would like to have vanilla ice cream sundae's and maybe some chocolate syrup just on mine as well," said my dad smiling at the server.

"It would be easier if all three of your sundaes had the chocolate syrup and they were all vanilla," she said as she then made a humph noise and walked away.

After we had ordered our sundaes at our table with Susie Que, my parents and I just look around at the people around us and how rude and disrespectful they were being to each other. Mom talked about her day and what she had done that day and how she had noticed that I spent the whole day in my room.

"Your mom told me that you have been upset about Whiskers, Mark," Dad said from across the table looking at me. "We noticed that you put his bowls away after they had been out for the past three days," he continued looking at me observantly.

"We are worried about you, are you ok?" Mom said stepping in while looking at dad cautiously and then she turned her head to look at me.

"I'm fine. I just don't understand why life is so short and so, I am trying to accept all of this. That is why I put his bowls away because I am trying to move on as you said I should try to do so..." I said looking at dad then to my mom reassuringly as they looked at each other. Susie Que returned to our table with the ice cream sundaes.
"I found the syrup in the back of the fridge and we ain't got sprinkles..." Susie Que said as we thanked her, and she walked away.
"As I was going to say before, we will always try to be there for you," said my dad slowly looking at my mom. "But what you have to understand is that life isn't forever. There may come a time when we may not be able to be there for you. Life on Earth is so unpredictable and we never know how long we are going to live. For all we know, your mom and I could die tomorrow. Susie Que was in many ways right, life is not a joke, but it's what makes the world work. The point of life is to try to live it to the fullest, with no regrets," he continued as Susie Que placed the check on the table, smiled, thanked us politely, and walked away.
I looked out the window and saw that there were grandparents outside with their young grandchildren, crossing the street and holding hands. I finished my ice cream sundae and wiped the chocolate off my face and drank the rest of my

coke. It was at the point that I realized, whatever Burgesis had in mind, I needed to be there. I didn't want to miss a lost opportunity. I was sure that he didn't intend to kill me. Obviously, if he had wanted me dead, he would have done so already. I just wanted to understand, what it was he wanted to tell me. What would I have been too young to understand?

We were on our way home, and I put my face to the open window of the car as a nice cool breeze hit my face, and I enjoyed the scenery taking in every breath of it. Once we were home, I had said "Good night," and thanked my parents for the dessert and went into my room. I then opened the window and laid in bed anxiously waiting for my parents to go to bed. I waited until all that could be heard in the house was the central air conditioning in the house kick in. I decided to stay longer in my room as I turned silently towards my alarm clock to look at the time. It was 2 am, I was surprised that my mom and dad had stayed up so late, but I realized that they didn't have much time together. I was thinking of my dad's busy schedule every day Monday to Saturday 8 am to 6 pm. It was frustrating to me to realize that although life was so short, we had so little time to enjoy it because as adults we seem to be working all the time. Whatever time I had left with my parents, I had

learned from that day on to learn to enjoy it. As I had waited, I started to get impatient because I wanted to know what Burgesis wanted. I wanted to know what could be in store for me, the opportunities endless as my stomach churned in excitement ... 2:59 AM. One minute left I thought to myself, 30 seconds.... 10 seconds....
5....4....3....2...1... 3 AM.

Chapter 3
The Adventure

Silently, I slipped out of bed in my blue short sleeved shirt, and sweatpants. I then put on my blue hoodie, which I zipped up halfway. Then I slid down the tree by my window as I felt the cold night air brush across my face. Carefully, I climbed down the tree and my sneakers touched the cold wet grass that soaked through my thin shoes and into my socks as I shuddered.

Looking around, I had heard a rustling noise nearby, so I nervously whispered, "Hello? Anyone there?" Then suddenly someone grabbed me from behind and covered my mouth as I squirmed in fear.

"Don't move, it's okay, it's only me," whispered someone from behind me into my ear. I turned around and saw Frank Burgesis.

"You must keep constant vigilance around you boy! Next time look before you climb down. Someone could have easily killed you from behind!" said Burgesis looking at the surrounding darkness grumpily making sure no lights had come on from the surrounding houses.

"Killed? What?! What are you talking about?" I asked looking at him alarmed and scared.

"Not now, it is too dangerous for us to talk right now. Follow me, and we *mustn't* be overheard," said Burgesis firmly as we walked quickly from the side of my house to the sidewalk. "I was starting to think you forgot, or that you had gone back to sleep," He continued quietly looking ahead as we passed a neighbor's house.

"I haven't stopped thinking about this morning since you told me that "I was too young to understand," whatever it was that you wanted to tell me. I was just waiting for the right moment to leave my house," I said quietly in a whisper following closely behind Burgesis as we started to take a left and walked stealthily down the road.

Burgesis started to look behind and around us cautiously as we went down several blocks in the moonlight in silence for what seemed like hours. A few moments later, he looked around again before we turned into a barely visible wooded area that was lit by a dim lamp post. For some reason, I had noticed that it was quite foggy, around this lamppost, which I didn't think anything of it at the time. No one would have noticed it being out of the ordinary. Burgesis walked up to the lamp post and bowed to it and then he pressed a small button on the lamp post. After he did, a path revealed itself up ahead as the fog moved. I frowned at this odd gesture he made to the lamppost as he looked at me.

"It's a sign of respect to the clan leaders who you might meet eventually. Now tell me everything that you observe from this point forth as best and well described as possible," instructed Burgesis as he walked at my side.

"Ok, I see the path we are now walking on, is a dirt road or pathway, I can't tell, but it is lined by trees, bushes, and shrubs," I described aloud to him as he pointed his finger at me.

"Exactly, exactly, now look ahead and tell me what you see with your heart," said Burgesis whispering calmly smiling as he looked ahead avoiding my eye contact as I had looked at him while continuing to walk down the path.

"I can't see anything, it's just darkness around us," I said confused. As we walked on, we got to see a light ahead. I said to Burgesis as he had picked up a walking stick that was placed against one of the bushes on the side of the path. "I see a light, a light at the end of the path ahead. Now the path has changed, it is made of stone. I can see more clearly what is going on ahead of us and around us," I explained as I looked ahead and saw stones ahead that were as huge as boulders. "I do not understand, now the stones look as though they are getting bigger ahead as we walk further along here. It looks like we might have problems climbing them," I told Burgesis worriedly who just smiled and kept quiet as we walked on.

As we walked closer, we got to a slightly steep incline, this originally was where I had thought was where we saw those seemingly big boulders that I thought we would have problems getting over. In the end, when we were closer to them, were very little. They were the littlest pebbles that looked like they formed into huge boulders in the distance.

"I am confused," I told Burgesis. "What is the purpose of this? Why am I here?" I asked him.

"Don't you see? Sit down here," he said, a bench had appeared along the path, almost as if it was out of nowhere but apparently, it was just hidden very well. "Take time to think about what you just observed."

"Can you explain to me what just happened?" I asked and was surprised I was already out of breath.

"This path," said Burgesis as he hit the stones with his walking stick. "Represents life and the change of the paths gravel represent the choices we make in life. The stones represent problems that come up after we make the choices in life. You noticed when you saw that the stones seemed huge in the distance, your fear kicked in and your deductions told you that you might have problems up ahead. Just like the problems of your future that you might see yourself have in your life for example. They may seem like such a huge problem with consequences, yet, as you got closer to the stones they ended up being the pebbles that were just keeping the path in shape. Just like when you come closer to deal with the problems in life they aren't as seemingly difficult to handle. Then they aren't necessarily as big of a deal as the end of the world," said Burgesis smiling.

"I feel sad suddenly," I said still sitting on the bench next to Burgesis. "Why is it that every day during the week it seems like it is the same as the next for me at times? At many times, I have felt bored and disappointed with my life."

"If life seems boring and disappointingly like the day before, it is because you fail to realize the good things that enter your life each day the sun rises and sets. If you want changes you can't just expect them to just happen, sometimes you must make some changes of your own in your own habits to get the changes in life," Burgesis explained. "For example, how much you love others in your life, or things right in front of you in life, like your cat, Whiskers. He was an unexpected change but through it, you learned many things. In the example, you learned that you can't take things for granted in life, and it is crucial to be thankful for what you have. Most people don't have as much as you do materialistically, they aren't as fortunate. You don't realize that you have such a good family that loves you and supports you for being you. Some people don't have the family or parents that support and love their children for who they are and what they wish to accomplish in their life. The people who do realize what they have they are grateful for what they have in life and those are the people who feel like they have more than enough in life. Those are the people who may seem like they don't have many treasures in life, but, they feel that they have the world in their hands," said Burgesis looking at me smiling.

"So *that* is what you noticed, Whiskers, that was the change in my daily routine that you noticed," I said as

Burgesis pointed his finger at me again.

"Exactly, exactly I had noticed Whiskers, had died, and therefore, I had noticed that a huge change in you had occurred. Not only because every morning you put him outside and for the past three days you didn't but, when you would go outside in the mornings, the light of happiness isn't as strong in you anymore. You know, now you don't even smile as much as you used to. When you didn't go outside for the past few days, I figured something was wrong, and that something may have happened to Whiskers," said Burgesis slowly.

"My poor Whiskers, he just wasn't doing well his last day, is this why you figured something bad had happened when you didn't notice him?" I asked sadly.

"Your cat, Whiskers, was a dear friend of mine, in another world, different from here. He helped me keep an eye on you growing up and his wife lives there, in that world. I have a gift and in truth, as it so happens, so do you," he said.

"What kind of gift?" I asked, "Can I fly? Do I grow wings? Can I control the weather on any given day?"

"No, no you misunderstand me…. When I mean gift, I do not mean superpowers," Burgesis said surprised at my excitement.

I was excited and nervous. I thought, this guy is mental or has gone mental. Gift? What does he mean gift? He's crazy!

He laughed suddenly.

"You think I have gone mental?" he asked incredulously.

"Wait, you can read my thoughts?" I asked quickly as I got up from the bench surprised.

"Only thoughts pertaining to me," he said as he got up off the bench as well and we walked on slowly. "People should not fear the unknown, only that they are capable of achieving what they need and want if they are positive and happy," he said trying to avoid my last question now.

"In life, sometimes our choices not only reflect us on who we are, and what we believe, but they also affect us in so many other ways. We then don't realize that other people may also be directly or indirectly impacted by our choices that we make. The love that you have shown for Whiskers, was noticed so strongly by us both. Whiskers showed me that in many ways that you are special, your heart shines light into our path ahead of us which represents your life," Burgesis said as he pointed ahead of us as we started down the path towards the light.

"But what if I make a bad choice or the wrong choice in the future? What happens if I make a choice that wasn't meant to be?" I asked worriedly.

"The fate of the world and your life at times reflects upon the good or poor choices that we make. Like I said before, it is up to you to decide what you do in your life. You oversee your own destiny, for example, what is in front of us right now?" asked Burgesis carefully.

"The path is now breaking into two, light is shining down both paths," I said as I thought it would be obvious which path to take if there wasn't any light down one of the paths.

"Correct. One must go through life making firm decisions having no regrets or as little as possible. It isn't very good to make decisions you are unsure of. Now I have a question I want to ask you before you decide which path we are going to take is, do you want to help me?" Burgesis asked slowly.
"Think about your answer first, because this question you are about to answer, could change your life if you let it. Your decision that you make, may even possibly require you to risk even your own life. We are talking about the possibly experiencing a world not very different from our own. A world that is full of evil as well and it has only glimpses of hope to restore peace to both our worlds."
"What are you talking about? Aren't you of 'this world'?" I asked unsure of his statement.
"Yes, I am of *'this world'* as you see fit, but I am more, and you are too if you wish to experience it. If not, I will only come back one more time in your life to give you this choice," Burgesis said looking at me.
"You need to put your life into perspective. I know I seem to be asking much of you right now, and maybe you are too young, I don't know. You must understand everything that is happening here. This *'help'* that I am asking from you, it's not just for me or you, but for the betterment of both of our

worlds, here and there," Burgesis said carefully looking at me. "Now I will be waiting for you at the end of each path you choose, whichever one that is. The left path takes you directly to your room and you will not remember my conversations with you or remember that I came to talk to you at your house. The right path takes you with me to the World of the Unknown, and there you can help me and help us all," Burgesis said.

"I am not too young, I can't be! But I need time to think…. Can you give me a few moments… will I be gone forever?" I asked slowly concerned.

"If and when you make the _choice_ to go with me, your parents will think you don't exist, _if and when_ you come back, no matter how many seasons have changed in the World of the Unknown, (which is the world we are going to) you can still come back and it will still be as if no time will have changed at all. It is like A Wrinkle in Time, do you understand?" asked Burgesis pausing a moment.

"Yes, I understand," I said standing between the two paths of light. "How does one get to this World of the Unknown?"

"You will see, should you decide to come along with me, on the path you choose to travel you will see the light tunnel before your eyes, however, this transition through time can only happen after a specific poem is said,"

Burgesis explained.

"What happens if I die in the World of the Unknown?" I asked looking back at the path behind us which was dark.

"Then you will cease to exist and never would have existed in the World of the Unknown, that is why the path you choose in life is so important. There are few times in life that we get to have second chances," Burgesis said sadly as he then disappeared into the night air.

I didn't know what to do, I had learned a lot from Burgesis, but going to this "World of the Unknown" with someone whom I barely knew, didn't feel right to me. I then considered the fact that, I haven't even seen the world yet. I stood there stunned trying to decide whether to take the left or the right path. Would it be best to take a path to a place where I would never have been? Or would it be better to take a path back home to be with my parents in a place I was comfortable? I was not sure what this World of the Unknown was, nor did I know Burgesis well. I looked behind me again and all I saw was the darkness still. I just wanted to live my life with purpose, to prove myself better than what was going on in the world. I knew that Burgesis needed my help. I wanted to improve life on Earth and make a difference, but then again, if I go home, tomorrow morning when I wake up I could

see my parents. So, I took a moment and remembered what my dad said to me earlier that day... "life on Earth is so unpredictable and we never know how long we are going to live. For all we know, your mom and I could die tomorrow."
I thought, what if my parents did die, what would I do? Who would I turn to? Losing Whiskers was hard to comprehend and to deal with. But to even imagine losing a family member seemed unbearable to think about. Then I continued to think if I wanted to enjoy life to the fullest, and what is life without a little risk? So, deciding and having made my decision firmly, I walked ahead and took the path that led to the right without regret, and without looking back....

Chapter 4
A Path Less Traveled

I walked down the dimly lit path ahead feeling excited at the expectation of going on this adventure, I wanted a taste of change in my life. As I got to the end of the stone path, I saw Burgesis standing there smiling at me. The source of light that was lighting the path ahead of us the whole time was floating in midair at my chest height. It was a floating orb which was a spectacular sight. Looking at the orb, I noticed that it was made of a globe of water. It had sun rays of light coming out of it reminding me of a water fountain with the lights coming from the middle of the orb and hitting the edges of the orb like fireworks.

"It is good to see you again, so you thought about what I said and still you decided to help me?" he asked looking at me with his eyebrows raised as I continued to look at the orb of light.

"Yes," I said firmly while nodding my head.

"I can tell from your personality that there are strong positive vibes of goodness and pure values in you," Burgesis said as he observed me.

I looked at him and noticed that he had a twinkle in his eyes as I smiled at him.

"Are you ready? Once we move on from this point forward, there is no turning back," he asked slowly.

"Yes, I am ready," I said firmly looking at him as he nodded.

"This orb of light is lit by all that is pure and good in you since it's your first time I decided this way of travel is only fitting," he said.

"How did you know I would help you?" I asked looking at the orb as I touched it.

"I have sensed a lot of determination in you, which is consistent with what Whiskers had reported to me. You feel the need to prove yourself to others around you. I don't think it's wise to feel like this all the time because then others will try to use this against you in your times of weakness. It is best to trust your instincts from this point forth," he instructed as I nodded in understanding. "This world that we are traveling to is like how the Earth is, in that it has four seasons. But the equator goes from Northeast to Southwest instead of from east to the west so it's different and the equator in the World of the Unknown can be cold and hot in different parts of it," he continued.

I reached out and touched the orb after he nodded for me to do so after he did. He then whispered quietly:

"There is a quiet place in my heart, like the one who rests from days of pain. A dream of places unimagined, of places unknown for the benefit of others of this world, to restore the peace and goodness of these world's today, in which we live. For in these worlds the life of "the one" who can help these two separated worlds which evil exists can and will put them together as one again in goodness and in peace forever. The powers and graces of our worlds that may reign forever, and if this is upheld, by the power of goodness and hope through faith may it overcome evil. Until death calls us..."

I couldn't hear the rest of it because whispering was heard around us, and the winds had picked up and suddenly there was complete darkness and then a blinding light from the orb. I then felt a push and a pull at that moment. I saw that we were going into a vortex of an endless tunnel of light turning and twisting around us as I looked around, I saw the wooded area disappear and we seemed to be in a tornado. I looked at Burgesis worriedly. He seemed to understand what I was thinking and feeling.

"Don't worry we will be gently put down above the World of the Unknown so I can explain everything that has happened to the best of my abilities," Burgesis said loudly over the rustling wind.

I was unsure of the meaning of the quote that he was saying, but I knew better than to ask now.

As we neared the end of the tunnel my short hair didn't seem to be blowing around much and I could

see dark clouds ahead that we were heading towards slowly. As the winds dissipated, we were slowly coming out of the tunnel of winds and light and we saw colors in the sky above and around us. I had wondered if we were in space. The orb of water had hit me suddenly as Burgesis then grabbed my hand. I felt motivated suddenly and I had felt an intense sense of power within me.
"No," said Burgesis aloud apparently reading my thoughts. "We are not in space Mark as you may understand it, but we are practically above the World of the Unknown." He said as he pointed towards the darkened clouds as we seemed to be floating. "Like I said before Mark, the orb was lit by the good and pure qualities that you hold in yourself, and with these qualities that you have within you, it can take you to unimaginable places!" Burgesis then pulled me, as he sat on this dark cloud and crossed his legs sitting on top of it. I followed suit next to him as he pointed down below us. All I could see was grey and black dark clouds moving around.

"You see, as you look below you, you see the current state of the World of the Unknown," said Burgesis sadly. "I know it looks bad, but it wasn't always this way."

I looked down and all I continued to see was grey darkness.

Burgesis whispered a few words and using his hand, made a waving movement in front him and the grey and black darkened clouds above the World of the Unknown moved temporarily out of the way as he looked down thoughtfully.

"What happened here?" I asked sadly as I felt cold air coming at us in a breeze from the World of the Unknown. "I can only see a part of this World of the Unknown below us."

"Describe what you _can_ see right now Mark," Burgesis said sadly as he pointed to a specific area below us and I looked down.

"Do I have to?" I asked sadly seeing the most horrific and awful sight that I had ever seen.

"You must, so that others can feel the pain and the distress that you feel right now looking at the world below us," Burgesis said sadly.

"What do you mean others?" I asked curiously.

"There are those of us who believe that there is always
someone there listening to what is going on in our lives spiritually. Someone who, when our time comes, will judge us by what we felt, what we said, what we thought, what we chose to act on, and how we chose to live our lives," said Burgesis wisely, nodding me on to describe the horror I was witnessing below.

"Below us, on the left, I see a city enclosed with a cement wall and it is guarded. Outside Metromark, there is wilderness for miles but there are some small villages in between. Directly below us, in the lower part of this World of the Unknown, I see a guy and two kids walking along this path. There are two soldiers who just stopped them from walking towards them and now the soldiers, are arguing with the family. Those poor kids are shouting for help to a nearby group of people who are just watching the scene," I said hesitantly as I then clasped my hands to my mouth in shock.

"Go on," said Burgesis who was looking down at the scene below with me.

"I... I.... just now saw, the guy, he was just slain brutally with a sword by one of the soldiers, and the kids are crying. The soldiers are just standing there, laughing at what they just did and what happened. Now the soldiers are walking away, leaving the girl and boy crying at the man's side. Was that the father of those two poor children who was slain?" I asked putting my hand in my mouth in horror. Burgesis motioned for me to continue to explain the events occurring below. "The children are leaving the man's body lying there on the path, running away, going the opposite direction the soldiers were going. Why aren't they doing anything to help their father or the family?" I pointed angrily at the nearby figures who had watched the scene and started to walk away. "Why did this happen? Why didn't anyone answer their cries for help?"

"Ah, you see, the girl and the boy belong to The Giant's Clan. Their father was an informant for Nerogroben, who had lied about information he knew, in order, to protect his family. Nerogroben's men killed their informant for reporting bad information, which is considered treason. No one from the satellite Elven Clan nearby who saw this occur is going to help them. The reason is that Giants and Trolls are the lowest in the hierarchy in the World of the Unknown," explained Burgesis in disgust as he moved the Grey Matter to cover the area below them again.

"That's horrible," I said thinking to myself, I turned to look at Burgesis and asked, "What's going on in the World of the Unknown that you need _my_ help for? Who is Nerogroben?"

Burgesis raised his eyebrows and looked at me surprised. "Did you not just see and explain to me what you saw going on down there?"

"Yes, I know, but how can I do anything about that?" I asked moving my hand towards the clouds that were covering the area where we had seen the family.

"You see below us is the World of the Unknown, it is a mysterious place, with many secrets,"

explained Burgesis as he shook his head. "Nerogroben...I will get to him. This is the World of the Unknown. Right now, we are sitting on top of "Grey Matter," which is a substance of sorts like a grey fog on top of this world. It is probably best if we don't stay here too long. Our negative energy that our bodies have, won't react to the Grey Matter right away. The reason is that everyone on Earth, in some form or another, has negativity in them, which we are naturally attracted to.
If we are in this area too long, or we talk about certain things, this cloud will start irritating and burn our skin. If it gets too uncomfortable, we will both have to go down," he said as I nodded and stayed silent. "I chose this spot to explain everything that you have seen here so far. The World of the Unknown is alike and different in many ways compared to Earth. This is one of the only other planets in the universe that you can breathe oxygen normally. Like Earth, it is similar in that it has a cold, the hot, the dryness, and the weather is pretty much the same as well. We just don't see sunlight anymore or feel its heat as hot as you and I are used to. Something that is different between both these worlds is that in _your_ world, you deal with pollution, which is something that we don't have to deal with. _Your_ world is now without water in many places and where there _is_

water now, like in the oceans for example on Earth, they are dirty and full of trash," said Burgesis who seemed to read my mind as he smiled at me.

I wondered, why he had said "_your_" world... as I looked at him and asked him this question.

"I say "_your_" world because, on Earth, I have to say it's my world as well, in order, to blend in. But when we go down to the World of the Unknown, you are going to change. I am telling you this now, so you won't be scared," said Burgesis as I nodded wondering what he was talking about and what I was going to change into.

Burgesis moved the clouds of Grey Matter again revealing more of what the World of the Unknown looks like. The surrounding land around the city was huge and it had enormous mountain ranges that could be seen along with proportionately large bodies of water. The wilderness didn't seem to have any homes directly outside of the city. Soldiers still seemed to be guarding the gates of the city which seemed dark and gloomy and it seemed like they were ready to be under attack. I wondered why this was so.

"Let me answer that thought on your mind," said Burgesis sadly as he moved more Grey Matter. "Almost an Earth's lifetime ago, this World of the Unknown was filled with all manner of Magical Creatures and Magical Human Elves alike. There was a common knowledge of elemental magic between them. It has changed so much since the Dark War, and it has never been the same since" he said carefully looking at me.

I was excited about the idea of this elemental magic, but I let him continue after his brief pause. "The World of the Unknown, before the Dark War, was a peaceful world, there was no hierarchy, no evil, hatred, or even a hint of Grey Matter. Before the Dark War started, villages were only a day travel apart, everyone got along quite well. This was how the World of the Unknown was, until that day. The day when one rather evil and disturbingly dark Troll was born. The troll's name is Nerogroben, and he one day decided that the world shouldn't be so. It's been believed by many that Nerogroben thought he owned the world, and everyone owed something to him. He had felt that all Magical Creatures must bow down to a supreme leader, not just any leader but a dominant leader. A leader that no one would question to be wrong. He thought that the World of the Unknown needed to have this superior leader, who was above all the other clans. A leader who was knowledgeable about everything and everyone, and who wouldn't quiver in fear, if they were tested or pushed to new limits. Nerogroben's personality is so dark and volatile that it had infected his followers around him. They all committed horrific and evil acts, destroying villages, killing, and torturing those who were rebellious against him in the name of future prosperity. This all, was an everyday occurrence, as he gradually grew extremely insecure. It has gotten worse over the years, to the point where he started wars against those who oppose him, many innocent and good lives have been lost so far," Burgesis explained as I sat in complete shock and disgust.

I looked at the World of the Unknown which was below us still as the Grey Matter moved like the clouds on Earth.

"During the Dark War, Nerogroben and his army killed all those who believed in goodness, love, and happiness. Especially those who were against him, and times grew dark. The Grey Matter that had started forming was extremely toxic. Make no mistake his powers are powerful, so powerful that if not under control, he can wipe out several people at once. Many of his followers started doing evil deeds like stealing, killing, lying, and were turning violent by the day. The Magical Human Elves didn't feel comfortable having the Magical Creatures learn any more elemental magic and secrets of the ancient magic from them, out of fear of the possible connected ties to Nerogroben himself. Over time it became that the inevitable happened,

Magical Humans and Magical Creatures grew scared of each other. This occurred because they didn't know whom they could trust or whom they could turn to. Their own friends within the clans were turning their back on them, out of sheer desperation of survival. There was just so much evil in the hearts, minds, and souls of the Magical Creatures, that the Magical Human Elves grew untrustworthy of any of them. Many of the good Magical Creatures and Magical Humans fled the area, hoping to seek refuge in hiding from Nerogroben. Magical Human Elves started kicking out Magical Creatures out of their homes in Metromark because they learned to not trust any of the Magical Creatures. Mark, _you_ have the power to fix this," said Burgesis finally looking at me worriedly.

"Me?" I asked. "How can I fix this? How do you expect me to be able to make that much of a difference in a world that is torn into two or more pieces?" I continued worriedly as I started thinking to myself.... I was just a kid, how was I supposed to make a difference? There are full adult Magical Creatures and Magical Human Elves down in this world who may not even want to listen to me. Then I thought and then said, "Wait are they Magical Humans or Magical Human Elves?"

"Oh, those are two separate clans; the Magical Humans are humanly sized elves with purple eyes who live in the city of Metromark. The Magical Elves are in the Woodland Elms, they are slightly smaller in size, but they aren't human," continued Burgesis looking at me as he smiled. "You really think that low of yourself that you may not be able to make that much of a difference? I told you I need your help because, in you, you possess many of the last pure qualities known to mankind on Earth. There were the sign Whiskers was supposed to make between us both when he found "the one." You have within you, the ability to lead us all by example, you possess the abilities to have magimarks which are the source of elemental magic. With your help and others like me on your side, we just might be able to change both our worlds as we know it."

I was just shocked, and I had started to be more afraid. I am just a 15-year-old kid, I don't have the powers to be able to defeat an evil magical Troll and his army I thought.

"Not yet you don't," said Burgesis smiling.

"What do you mean by magimarks," I asked carefully.

"Ah, in our world, magimarks are what you call tattoos on Earth, except these tattoos aren't regular ones. These magimarks are a source of our ancient magic. You get them based on your conscious. What I am trying to say is that you're the last child on Earth that has morals and values, and who is, in nature, naturally good, and full of peace and love. You proved that by loving and giving a nurturing hand to Whiskers when no one else would. Evil is so strong out in both of our worlds and we think that you are our last hope in this world," he explained.

"We, who is we?" I asked.

"Yes, BOTH OF US, need to help the World of the Unknown, this is prophecy!" he replied as he stood up grabbed by hand and the Grey Matter started to turn black and it started to cause my skin to irritate and burn me.

"Ouch!" I said rubbing the rash forming on my hand.

"Don't be alarmed. It only affects you because you don't have experience with it as much as others so eventually your body will get used to being on the Grey Matter and its effects. As we begin our descent down from here, we are both going to go through some physical changes, to a form that you truly are here in the World of the Unknown. The Grey Matter had turned black right now because we started to talk about your qualities that make you pure. You and I are Magical Human Elves, we look like the elves except we are taller and smarter, don't tell anyone I said that (especially the elves).

We have longer ears then them, but they help us to listen to things going on. We have great memory retention, that's what makes us so important because we learn the English-Latin spells faster and pretty much have a human genius type of mind. We can remember anything and any conversation that we have ever had. We also have high IQs in similarity to human Earthly intelligence. However, everyone may fear you because you haven't earned magimarks right away, at least, I don't know if you will. You earn them by your choices, thoughts, and actions that you have, and make in your life. By the time we land you could earn your first powerful one because of your determination to help others without selfishness and because you are willing to risk your life just being here. But just like you can earn them for good, you can also earn them for evil actions, thoughts, and emotions. Magimarks are like that orb, they will burn with that same amount of light on your skin," he said.
"How many do you think I will get?" I asked worriedly. I was not excited to feel burning sensations on my skin as we slowly started to descend on this newly formed white cloud that Burgesis had made with his fingers. He whispered quickly and quietly as it had appeared, and I had just followed him and stepped on it when I was talking.

"It is *very* rare that you get more than one at a time, only extremely powerful magical beings get more than one at a time. If it turns white, then they are good, if it turns red, then you got it for doing or thinking something bad or evil. Usually, your conscience guides the magimarks as they appear on you. It's been foretold that even you "the one" can destroy evil and bad magimarks off people because too much evil and fear are bad. The only way you get the bad magimarks off is if you do something good with the same amount of strength or energy to replace it or otherwise unless it is cursed off you, you are stuck with it being evil or good. The Ancients believe in the power of light and forgiveness to heal but only very few powerful magimarks men have this ability. In fact, they are said to be extinct. Controlling your emotions is essential to the magimarks. We are going to see what happens, for now, let's focus on getting down to the ground. Depending on how you feel, you might feel strengthened by the magimarks or weakened by them, and you might feel horrible pain, normally the first ones hurt though. We are going to land in the middle of the two cities Creaton and Metromark below. The first night we will make camp in the middle of the cities underground and out of sight at the Burgeons. They are magical Beavers, they live right by Beaver

Valley," he said as we slowly go close to the ground, and he jumped off the cloud and started walking.

"I thought we were Magical Humans, why are we staying with Magical Creatures? You said Beavers can talk here? Will I be, ok? Will I bleed?" I asked him worriedly.

"Yes, they talk and are extremely nice. Yes, you will be okay. No, you will not bleed, but you will feel burning on you just for your first magimarks. We are staying with Magical Creatures because of two reasons. First, I am having issues with the city now and my relationship with them is strained and things are extremely complicated with them now. Second, we are the first Magical Human Elves to start this rebellion with the Magical Creatures and they are trustworthy," he said carefully.

Burgesis had stopped walking and closed his eyes calmly as I saw Burgesis's skin start to change color to an orange and his hair turned to a red color and grew longer and in a ponytail. His beard disappeared, and his skin became smoother and less wrinkled. His clothes changed into a ripped jean jacket and shorts. Suddenly, his bald eagle tattoo turned into a real Bald Eagle and flew high in the air and made a screech. Then Burgesis put out his glove covered hand and the eagle dived and landed on it and he told the bird to keep quiet and make sure no one is around. Then the bird nodded to me and took off. As we walked on a few steps further I noticed Burgesis's skin started to glow and suddenly a few magimarks appeared white and there was a red one. His face looked much younger now, he looked now like a teenager from Earth with long ears and his magimarks started to extend to every visible area on him not covered by clothes. He had someone his face, neck, arms, and part of his legs and they were strange symbols I noticed and then suddenly, my body grew hot and then cold and then hot again as I doubled over in pain. Burgesis didn't notice at first as he kept walking as if nothing was happening and I had stopped walking. Suddenly, I fell over as I started to change. All over my body pain seared me as I started to scream in fear and terror as I started to cringe. I shouted in agony on my skin, and hair turned blue and grew longer and my skin started to glow. "Mark!" said Burgesis opening his eyes running to my side as he had run to my side looking at me worriedly. His voice wasn't gruff anymore but light in tone. "It's okay Mark, just relax, let the changes occur, just relax and take deep breaths, it is going to be over soon."

Suddenly, as I laid out flat on the warm ground, a warmth came over me for a few moments as I started to feel okay again, and I stood up. Then suddenly I doubled over in pain again, as I saw my skin grow brighter and started to feel warm and grew hotter. Four magimarks seared my soft delicate skin on my forearms, chest, and one formed on my back. I then fell over and blacked out in shock as I felt myself being dragged away on the ground into the darkness....

"What's going on?" said a gruff voice.

"It's just me," said Burgesis calmly who had picked me up and carried me on his shoulders. "We have only just arrived."

"Bring him inside," said the gruff voice again.

Chapter 5
A New Magical Being

I had woken up dizzy, weak, and my body was aching all over. I didn't open my eyes at first because I thought that everything that had happened, was a dream. I thought that I would wake up in my bed at my parent's house and had envisioned being able to see my mom and dad downstairs making eggs and pancakes for all of us. But then I had then realized that the bed I was laying in didn't feel the same and it smelled like dirt and mud around me. I didn't have any problems hearing anything going on around me. Silently I kept my eyes closed and listened as I had then heard voices of people whispering.

"How could you bring him here now?" said one voice.

"Whiskers had given me his sign Barty," said Burgesis's voice.

"Let the boy stay Barty, I think we should be honored that this child is here right now, under the circumstances," said another quiet voice timidly.

"Let us hope that he is indeed "the one," Jana! You know what will become of him if he isn't. What makes you think he will want to help us all anyway?" said Barty's voice gruffly.

There was a silence, as I had then wondered who these people were, and why they are saying they hope I'm "the one"? I thought quietly to myself. "Well, he will, and he is "the one," you will see, and now, he is up! See for yourself!" said Burgesis confidently, as I heard footsteps scurrying on the ground towards where I was. I opened my eyes after hearing the footsteps and Burgesis looked down at me and smiled. I saw a small amount of light escape into the dark room from the hallway outside. I had completely forgotten that he could hear my thoughts.

"Right, you are Mark, I can hear your thoughts, but it's good to see you are finally awake and made it through that ordeal alive! You are safe and you are in good hands," said Burgesis excitedly looking from. "This is Jana and Barty Burgeons, they have been so hospitable to us Mark!"

"Thank you for your kindness to me, and my friend Burgesis here and for your hospitality. I will always be grateful," I said smiling weakly looking at my blue gloved hands nervously.

I then thought to myself "How long was I out?"

"You were only out for a few days," said Burgesis aloud looking at Jana.

"You are absolutely welcome dear; we are honored to have you here!" said Jana whom I had noticed was a beaver and had completely forgotten that Burgesis said they were talking Beavers.

"Such kind manners," she whispered to her husband Barty from behind Burgesis who stood taller than the Beavers and Barty just grunted it off.

"You should always know that this here, is like my second home. I visit and stay here occasionally, in case you're wondering because of my things here in this room," Burgesis said pointing at the second bed and several shelves and cases in the corner. The room didn't have any windows but its walls were covered in dirt which had smelled.

"Oh, okay Burgesis," I said as I put my blue hands on my forehead as it started to hurt even though I was lying down.

"Now Mark just close your eyes, and rest for a while before you get up, ok?" said Burgesis calmly. Then he said something and waved his hand and a silvery mist had come from his hand as I nodded and breathed it in and fell into a deep sleep. They then had left the room and closed the door. Then an hour later, I woke up and got out of bed and snuck a peek through the keyhole outside the door and saw Barty, Jana, and Burgesis huddled around a table deep in conversation.

"Did you see the magimarks on him?" asked Jana eagerly surprised.

"He grew four on his first day and to be honest, I am surprised that they were so strong that he blacked out," stated Barty nodding at Jana.

"Yes, I know, that's why I knew that this is the right boy. Whiskers had seen him grow up and how he was with his peers in his school. He doesn't like evil, he is full of unwavering loyal potential. He has the rightful distaste for rudeness, not to mention that he is also attracted to positivism as per, Whiskers' report," said Burgesis smiling at Jana.

"How can you be sure that he is the right child?" asked Barty seemingly skeptical to Burgesis. "I mean, he doesn't even have any training yet."

"Exactly, exactly, but the light coming from his magimarks was a bright white, meaning he is pure in heart, not even a mark of red in the darkness. He is "the one," I trust him, and he is the last child who lives in the light on Earth. It was horrible trying to sift through the Grey Matter on Earth, but finally, we were able to find him," said Burgesis. "You know Grey Matter doesn't actually take a physical form on Earth, it's the human heart and mind. It is like a disease that could be very difficult to cure."

"Really? That sounds interesting! I would love to see if he is powerful enough to beat Nerogroben! He has got to be the most powerful Magical Human Elf in all our world!" said Jana smiling and looking at Burgesis excitedly.

"Now look, don't get ahead of yourself Jana," Barty said putting his paw up to her for her to settle down as he then looked from Burgesis and then towards my door, "Do you really believe in him?"

"Now Barty, I have already told you, we must trust him, somewhere along the line in your logical mind, you need to remember to have a little faith in others," said Jana carefully putting her hand on Barty's which was on the table as Barty then turned back towards his wife Jana.

"Yeah, but in a way Jana, Barty is right. Mark needs to be trained. Once he can learn the simple magic taught by us, he will then get into the more powerful magic taught by the professors at the school hopefully. This could take months or years, depending on how earnest, anxious, and fast of a learner he is," said Burgesis carefully.

"What if he doesn't want to be trained?" asked Barty cautiously.

"I am sure he will want to be trained, especially once he realizes what we are up against," said Burgesis.

"Give him a chance," said Jana to Barty.

"Imagine how he will be, once he is trained up by us, and then the others! We just need a lot of patience, and then he could be so powerful! So, we start tomorrow.... I should have him show me his magimarks, so we can see what we are dealing with. But for now... Do you mind if we stay undercover here at your home?" asked Burgesis carefully.

"Honestly Burgesis, do you really have to ask? It would be an honor for you to stay here," said Jana looking at Barty who pointed at her.

"As long as we or our clan isn't put into harm's way, then it is okay with me," said Barty cautiously looking over at Jana who nodded.

"Nerogroben's men have been hanging around outside in the area during the day and you are more apt to see them then. But you might not have as many problems at night covered by the nightly shadows," continued Barty.

I cautiously went back to bed and thought about what was said. Five minutes later, I sat up and walked towards the mirror in the room as I examined myself. On my right and left arms were dark blue X's, and then located within the X's, were dark blue dots. I lifted my shirt taking off revealing my chest and I could not tell what magimark it was. As I gazed into the mirror next to my bed, I saw my blue face. My blue eyes were now gazing at my now lengthened pointed ears and my hair stuck up like a wave in the front which was kind of cool. I felt taller by several inches. A Magimark formed on my right cheek past my jawline down part of my neck to my chest. I felt the outline and shape of the magimarks and pressed them. As I did, the Magimarks each grew bright and warmth had suddenly come over me. Then I had put my half glove covered hands off the magimark and the magimarks all went back to normal skin color. The gloves didn't cover the first part of my fingers, just my hand and I loved the blue. I smiled and admired them.

Because I had gotten so caught up with myself and my changes in appearance, I didn't hear the door open as I looked up from looking at my hands in front of me. Burgesis was standing there in the doorway smiling at me.

"So, I see that you approve of and are enjoying the changes," he said smiling as I smiled back in agreement. "That's awesome! Those gloves that you have are elemental magic proof, no matter what happens they cannot be destroyed, which are unique to your changes that were made. Now let me also show you something cool," Burgesis said with an odd smile.

I had not noticed but next to my bedside was a white candle, that was not lit up and Burgesis pointed to it with his index finger and whispered, "Flame, light the candle with the flame, Flamma, Illuminábit lucernam flamma."

It was then that a small flame appeared out of his fingertip and his eyes and his magimarks were glowing as the flame placed itself neatly on the wick and Burgesis put his finger and his hand down to his side again. Burgesis looked like a 19-year-old roughly in Earthly years, and he didn't have glasses which made him look cooler in my opinion.

"Thanks for that thought Mark but now you see how it works?" he said pointing to the candle as I nodded. "Now look, this is a small breeze," he continued as he then put his palm up to towards the direction of the candle and whispered, "Parva aura," and then a small breeze came out of his palms and blew the candle out.

"Is there more?" I asked interested and excited at the same time and thought to myself, "How does this happen? How does it work?"

I was then suddenly embarrassed that he was reading my thoughts and was awed at the same time.

"The magimarks are a source of power through your conscience. Remember, you earn them and sometimes it can be put on you by a skilled magimarksmen who are very rare. The words are Latin. People on Earth think that the Latin Language is dead, but here, here it is a way of life, and it is very much alive! The way in which you use the Latin words explains how strong or weak you want to the spell to be. For example, if you say the Latin words loud and strong and firm, so will the magic be. If you say the Latin words weaker or in a faint whisper, the magic won't be as strong. Magimarks, when you receive them they are very difficult to have, at times. The usage of the Latin words can be so strong, that when used, they then can physically and mentally break you down. If you have evil Red Magimarks your magic is uncontrolled and chaotic. You have pure white magimarks, which are all earned through goodness based off your conscience and using these will strengthen you and your control of the magic. We will start to train you tomorrow," said Burgesis seemingly observing how I am taking all this in.

I laid down on my bed wishing to start already, but at the same time I still felt weak, so I told Burgesis, I would rest some more, as he nodded and left me to sleep.

The next morning, everyone was barely starting to wake up as I did, except I had noticed that Burgesis was already up, observing me from the bed across the room. To be honest I don't think he slept. It seemed like, he already wanted to get me ready for training and was just as anxious as I was for me to start.

Jana and Barty had already made breakfast and had called me and Burgesis to join them at their table to eat. I was surprised that they made toast and eggs for us as they made fish and toast.

Just out of curiosity I asked, "Do you guys have bacon here?" Burgesis who hadn't eaten yet and had started eating rather fast abruptly stopped eating and put his fork down in surprise.

"No, they don't have bacon here in the World of the Unknown," said Burgesis carefully looking at me firmly seeing the direction of where the conversation was going.

"What's bacon?" asked Jana.

"It's a meat," I said looking at Jana

"They don't have livestock here in the World of the Unknown, Mark," said Burgesis.

"You mean they don't have chickens or cows or pigs?" I asked.

"What are those?" asked Barty curiously.

"That is right Mark," said Burgesis. "They really don't make foods from livestock here, they think it's unnatural."

At that point, I was surprised and asked: "Where is this egg from then?"

Jana had suddenly become offended, put her utensils down and said: "Why don't you just eat, I am sure that eating this food isn't going to kill you since it hasn't killed Burgesis yet!"

"Oh, I'm sorry, I just am trying to understand what is here in this World of the Unknown," I said quietly to Jana.

"That's quite alright, just eat and enjoy your meal," said Jana as Burgesis just smiled awkwardly and started eating his food again.

I looked at Barty and Jana who had already finished half their meals already. I was surprised at how quickly everyone ate here because I had barely eaten half of my food as the others were practically done eating.

Barty looked at me surprised "What? You don't like the food?"

"No, I love the food, it tastes great!" I said rather embarrassed. "I just don't normally eat fast on Earth."

"I forgot to mention some of the niceties here in the World of the Unknown, eating fast and burping shows the host that you loved the food and it was wonderful. I know on Earth it's rude, but they have always been backward," said Burgesis looking at me.

"Really, what about farting?" I asked surprised as I started to eat my toast and eggs again.

Burgesis looked at Jana and Barty who stopped eating and put their forks down and looked up "No Mark, that is still rude here, in fact, it's an insult to the host, and it means that you don't appreciate their hospitality," said Burgesis quietly.

"People are clean here, we have soap here too. I bring suitcases of supplies from the Earth here, to help them out and we don't have a pollution problem because I take the empty containers home, wash them, and refill them at my home on Earth. I am the only Magical Human who can transport goods like eggs for example and go between Metromark and Creaton and this world and Earth."

I was surprised that everyday things on Earth like forks, spoons, knives, and plates were used to eat with but then again, I think that was just normal for this world to have Earthly materials still. I finished my food and gave my plate fork and knife to Jana who had already finished washing half of the breakfast stuff.

"It is time Mark," said Burgesis. "Let's start your training outside.

Whenever you're ready let me know."

"Are you kidding? I have been ready," I said smiling looking at Burgesis.

"Wait here guys," said Barty. "I will set everything up

first before you leave here."

So, I sat in the living room anxiously waiting for Barty to come back, Jana and Burgesis sat across from me on the couch, and I just picked the corner love seat that had a candle next to it to sit at. There was a little noise outside and then down the hall to my right Barty came in through the front door about twenty minutes later with what looked like a light stick and looked at Burgesis saying "Burgesis, come outside really quick, I need your help."

"Ok," said Burgesis looking at me he stood up and followed Barty outside and after I watched them both walked out the front door. I looked at Jana who had been staring at me.

"What do you like about the World of the Unknown so far?" she asked me.

"To be honest I don't know much about what it looks like out there. I just want to learn about things as much and as fast as possible," I said looking at her serious face.

"I think you are going to be great," she said smiling finally.

Burgesis came in, "Jana the outside is set up, so we should be ok, I set up chairs for you both as well while I start to train him on these basics first, and you both can come outside now Mark," Burgesis said smiling.

We walked outside to see an open field next to the lake and there was a globed dome all around us. Burgesis seemed to be along the same lines of thinking as I was because he said "This is a security dome, we cast this with magic to protect us while we practice and train you to keep you safe from people being able to see us. If someone hits it or comes close to it, they won't even notice that they can't go that direction they will just go around the dome without realizing they are doing that," We then walked into the dome through an opening and then Barty sealed the dome behind Jana as she was the last one to come into a fully covered dome.

Chapter 6
The Basic Elements

One by one we entered this fully dome covered field. It looked like a unique looking football field with bleacher seating. Jana had taken a seat there on the bleachers as she watched Barty, Burgesis, and I walk towards the center of the field.
"The first thing you need to understand about the magic here is that it is based entirely off your conscience and personality," explained Burgesis looking at me as I nodded.
"How so?" I asked curiously looking at Barty
"Well let me outline it for you to the way we believe it goes," explained Barty looking at Burgesis carefully who avoided looking at him.
"First is water, water is an element that we believe goes with these specific qualities that you may or may not possess. Calm, relaxed, laid back, you may have a go with the flow attitude about life and you are wise to know to be adaptive to your surroundings. The next is air, you may be spontaneous, wild, free spirited if you will and this also makes you also adaptive to your surroundings. Next there is fire. You may be more aggressive, too fast and firm in your decision making without further thoughts of discernment about life decisions or decisions in general and you may feel the need

to prove yourself to others and may have a low self-esteem to think so low of yourself. Next is Earth, if you could have this naturally that means that you are naturally Grounded, everything is what it is the way it is, you feel that you are secure where you are, and you have a little to a lot of humility and you are not insecure. There are two more which I won't get into too much. These you are eventually going to learn but they are Electricity and Spirits. It is rare to behold all six of these elemental powers, but it is said that "the one" can wield them all without contest.

"Are you sure about this Burgesis?" asked Barty carefully. "Once we start these processes in teaching, there is no going back."

Burgesis paused for a few moments and nodded his head in understanding.

"It is time and up to both of us to show him what we know. Otherwise, if we don't and Nerogroben finds him, he won't know how to even defend himself. He must be shown. Otherwise, we would leave this poor child; naïve, sheltered, and defenseless," explained Burgesis slowly looking at Barty who nodded in agreement.

"Let me see what kind of magimarks he has to see what type of magic should be natural to him," Barty said slowly.

I walked up to Barty slowly and took off my gloves and rolled up my sleeves to show him the marks.
"I see," said Barty, "Curious, very interesting."
"What do you mean Barty?" asked Burgesis slowly.
"I don't know what these markings mean or are, but this child is very special, and very unique," said Barty slowly tracing his finger on the markings. "These are not markings that I am familiar with that attend to even one elemental magic."
Barty looked at Burgesis confused as Burgesis looked at him wide eyed and then to me silently.
"So, what does that mean for me? I can't learn magic?" I asked slowly looking at them both.
"It means that you are the first to be here and have these types of markings child," said Jana from behind me. "I'm sorry, but you guys were taking long, and I wanted to see what the commotion was about."
"It's okay Jana," said Burgesis smiling at her, "Barty was just saying that Mark is an alien here."
"So, what are you boys going to do?" asked Jana.
"We are going to see what happens," explained Barty shakily looking at Burgesis who's face turned serious.
"Now Barty, it would be very irresponsible of us to just "give it a go" and see how he handles it, I mean what if he says the words too loud or too crazily?" Burgesis said firmly.

"We ought to be perfectly well protected from being seen and as long as we eh, do a good job explaining everything first before he "gives it a go" and he makes a good aim for it, it should be okay," explained Barty.

"What do you guys mean if I say things too loudly? I thought we couldn't be overheard here?" I said not understanding the problem.

"Well see," explained Burgesis aloud reading my line of thinking, "The way elemental magic here works is, the louder you say it or the more quietly you say the Latin words, the more powerful or weak your magic is. The more magic you use depends on how loud you say it, and it drains you of your energy as well."

Burgesis then looked at Barty who nodded.

"The basic words go like this, I am just going to say them and not use them yet ok," Burgesis said as I nodded and continued to listen as Burgesis then explained. "Earth ground– terra /terram, water – aqua, fire – ignis, and finally air or wind aura /ventus."

Burgesis said as he looked at Barty knowing that he had something that he wanted to add.

"These can play a huge impact on you and the enemy if you don't play your cards right. Being forceful or too aggressive can be extremely risky, so be patient with yourself, especially during your fights, you must pay constant attention to your opponents and what's going on around you specifically your surroundings," said Barty said gruffly looking at me carefully.

"One thing you should know about Nerogroben's men is that they are mostly and usually are VERY aggressive and rash in their fighting tactics. Which is an advantage, because most Magical Creatures only can use two of the elements at a time, once you figure out what you're dealing with, as far as your enemies go, you will be ok. For example, the fairies know wind/air and then they have healing powers. We Beavers only use water and Earth or ground elements, and so forth. Nerogroben is almost aware of all the elements, except spirits and one other element I can't remember, but anyway he rarely uses them all," said Barty starting to side hug Jana who had walked over to the three of us unnoticed.

"Now the first element Burgesis will cover with you be fire, now the fire is known to be extremely helpful as you saw with the candle in the room yesterday. But it can be extremely dangerous, it is very important that you wait to use this element until it is an extremely desperate time to use it. I am saying this because of it being so destructive," said Barty observing me while talking to me and looking for reactions which I was careful not to show my excitement as he started to describe the power of these elements.

"Right now, the fastest way to lose control of the fight is if you use your full hand or fist to fight, because if you don't aim right sometimes you lose more and sometimes things happen that you can't take back or do anything about," said Barty quietly looking at Burgesis sternly as Burgesis looked over at him fast and quietly put his head down in sadness.

Burgesis then said "Will you excuse me? I got to prepare for more of his training." I nodded silently as he walked away slowly with his hands in his pockets looking down at the ground.

"You shouldn't have said that Barty," said Jana. "He is still not over it yet, it's too fresh, and that was very blunt!"

"What happened?" I asked looking at Barty who put his head down to shame and I looked at Jana. "Why is he so sad?"

"You don't realize how everyone is here do you?" Jana said quietly.

"No, I don't," I said truthfully looking at Jana.

"Well you see I have Barty," Jana said quietly grabbing his hand and Barty looked at Jana smiling weakly. "Everyone is mostly a couple in the World of the Unknown, there are very few, who don't have anyone to be with," said Jana carefully.

"Are you telling me that Burgesis lost his partner or wife?" I said

"He lost his fiancé when he first started learning the fire spells, years ago. When Burgesis was your age he lost control of his temper and he got impatient and aggressive in his learning. One night during a battle he got angry because someone had gotten his fiancé in electric chains and started shocking her. Burgesis lost control after hearing his fiancé screaming in a tortured pain. He shot a firestorm all around the area where we were fighting, and he lost control of it. It burned his fiancé and some of Nerogroben's men to death. Once this happened there was no undoing the fires and there was no way he could turn back time to adjust how he handled the situation. This was the reason Burgesis left Nerogroben's Army, this is actually his first time back in years to the World of the Unknown," Jana explained feeling bad for Burgesis

"What was his fiancé like? What happens after you kill someone you love?" I asked looking at Jana and Barty shuddered.

"She was very nice and a very beautiful Magical Human, when you kill or break up with someone you love, you have to carry that person around with you. The Eagle that Burgesis has, formed that night that same day before accidentally killing her. It's a constant reminder of her and he takes care of the eagle and on top of that, he has a broken heart magimark. Once you get a broken heart magimark, your powers are never as strong as they once were before. They then never really have a chance to fully recover because of the darkness that surrounds us," said Barty looking at me.

"Keep this in mind when you use these powers because they are strong, and accidents do happen especially if you lose your cool," said Jana as Burgesis walked back towards them.

"Practice for a little while and the word "prohibere" is the word you want to use to stop anything, so you say "prohibere" before the name of the spell you last used if you want to stop the spell from completely working.

If you lose focus on the power coming from you, it will also stop on it is own because your body will be able to communicate with the magimarks. Then it will be able to read your mind to know what you want to do. Now you keep practicing for a while. Meanwhile, I have to talk to these guys in the room back there," Jana said looking at Barty and Burgesis as he said "aqua target" and a target that looked like one of the ones that archers on Earth would use to practice on appeared out of Barty's fist that was made of water and then the three of them walked to the secondary globe and started to watch me as I snapped my fingers said "Flamma" and a flame appeared on my finger, it was warm but it didn't burn my hands, or my glove and then I said "Prohibere Flamma" and the flame disappeared...

Chapter 7
Fire and Air/Wind

Meanwhile in a secondary room with see through walls within the dome, while I was practicing my elemental magic Barty, Burgesis, and Jana talked privately...

"I'm sorry Burgesis," Barty said carefully as he walked into the dome and turned around looking at Burgesis who had his head looking down to the ground.

"It's ok, Mark needed to know, and I am happy that it was you guys who had told him instead of someone else," said Burgesis slowly looking up. "I should've realized coming back was also going to reopen up old wounds. But you know the Eagle tattoo was from both councils not because of her..."

"Well, you know we wanted to make a point, I mean did you not see him and his reactions to the elemental magic when he saw it? Did you see not his face when you showed him, especially the power of fire?" asked Barty to Burgesis and Jana as they watched me from behind the clear soundproof wall.

"He did seem fascinated by it, but I don't think we have to worry too much about that. I mean, now that we have explained the dangers that can

happen with the fire element, or when you are too aggressive in general with the magic," said Jana cautiously aware that Burgesis was looking at her. "Yes, but I mean, you should expect that no one from Earth has ever seen this kind of power like what we have here in the World of the Unknown, at least give him a chance," said Burgesis looking at the other two who nodded carefully.
Barty looked at Jana concerned and said, "We are going to have to be careful about how we train him."
"He will be fine," said Burgesis following Barty and Jana as they left the secondary room.

      They returned to see me as I had said, "Flamma Balls." It was then that several fireballs came out from my fist and all my magimarks lit up as a slow warmth came over me. I threw them at the target that was made of water. The flames shot across from me and as they did, I saw Burgesis shudder at my smiling face looking at him and the fireball just disappeared in the water target.
"Prohibere Flamma Balls," I said. Then the fire flames disappeared from my fists.
"Ok so I see you figured out how to handle the fireballs," said Burgesis acting surprised looking at Jana, "So, you can use them of course as fireballs but you can also do other things as well, move out of the way so you can just observe me," as I

moved behind Burgesis as he stepped ahead of us and pointed his palms in front of him.

"Ignis tempests," said Burgesis as his magimarks lit up, a wave of fire came from his palms and he guided the fire ahead of him as it burned the grass in what looked like an actual firestorm. "This is a fire blaze, "incendia" you can even make a tornado with the fire, "flamma tornado." Just as Burgesis said that a tornado formed in front of us burning the field more in front of us. It was at that point that I understood what the three of them meant as I saw the fire as it passed through, and it started to scare me.

Burgesis said, "Prohibere flamma tornado" and the tornado went away in midair. "It's good you're realizing how destructive fire is," said Burgesis noticing my thinking and how I observed the burnt grass after the fire tornado disappeared.

"I thought you could only use Latin for these spells," I asked curiously.

"Sometimes it just depends, you can use some English words like a tornado if you're unsure about the Latin. Remember, the elements are within you, it knows you, and what your body is comfortable with. You just need to listen to its ancient voice within you, and you can use the other elements as well or instead of just fire all the time in battles," Burgesis explained.

"Let's get to the next lesson, Burgesis," said Barty looking at Burgesis calmly who nodded in agreement.

"Time for your next element," said Burgesis. "Wind or air is very powerful, so powerful it can be used to spread water, spread fire, like in fire you have to use your fingers, your fists, and your palms, and the tone of your voice to control the strength of the wind that you would like. The word "Venta" is the word you use to describe wind but whether you want a slight wind Ventulus, or a violent windstorm "subito ventus turbo."

Each time Burgesis said each of these words, Barty used the exact elements as wind gusts came from the beaver's fists and his eyes turned a light white and he could stand his ground. Then he raised his hands in the air and said "Prohibere" and all was calm again.

"Wind or air is the only one you can stop with your hand
in the air like this. Then you say "Prohibere," and everything in the air will calm, and will slowly go back to normal," said Jana.

"Water is very important to us all in any world especially this world. It's not only the element for purity but the basic element for life. Barty and I will teach you what we know about water since it is one of our strong suits. We don't really use fire ourselves in fights because it is what we are used to naturally," said Jana. "So, if you know that your opponent knows water, then you know that they don't know fire or electricity."

"Electricity?" I asked looking at Burgesis. Barty nudged Jana as she covered her mouth.

"Don't worry about that for now," said Burgesis carefully looking at Jana. "Let's move on to the next lesson."

"It's ok, I will only use it when it's necessary because I see what you mean about it being destructive," I said shuddering to look at the burnt grasses in front of us. It gave me chills when I used fire, it almost made me feel angry when I used it for no apparent reason.

Burgesis just smiled and sighed in relief, looking, and nodding quietly at Barty, noticing he had read my mind.

Chapter 8
Water and Earth

"Water can be controlled by two things: wind, and by the Earth. What I mean by the Earth is that you can use Earth to deter water from an area or towards an area of your choosing whether it be through a canal, a river, or using it as a shield or you can make levies to block the water from other people. We can control where the water goes, or you can use wind forces to push it. You must understand that with any of these elements, the use of any one of them can change the ecosystem or the world in which we live. The moment you use an element to make weather, for instance, it can become destructible. Not everyone here in this world can use magic at all. Here, it is a gift that is given to you in your teenage years. Kids younger than ten cannot use its powers and only those who are transitioning into teens start to have the powers and they are not to be misused in any way or form," said Jana firmly looking to the land ahead of them.

"It is when creatures and humans alike become of age when they get to attend the School of the Unknown to study and learn control," Barty explained so let's continue Jana.

"The word "aqua," can be used to describe words like; rain, lake, river, sea, stream, or just water. The words "free aquam," can be used to mean bring water to, the words "dare aqua ad bibendum," means to give water to drink. To obtain water use the words "ad adaquo." To supply with water, "usum aquarum". The word "aqua fluente" can be used to describe flowing water. To destroy with water, use the word "perdere aqua." To surround with water, use the word "circumdare aqua." For Hot water use the word "aqua calida." For ice, cold water uses the word "glaciem frigidam." With water, you can do a lot of things, most living organisms can't function without it. It also can be used to heal as well when bones are broken etc.," said Jana as she showed me how to use water as a flow of energy when using each of the spells.
"Moving fluidly helps the water to move more in an organized way and not like a super soaker," said Barty quietly.
"Water is the hardest to use without concentration because lack of it doesn't make you a pro. It takes a lot of patience and practice to improve on this set of spells more so than the others. These spells can take a lot out of you," said Jana calmly.
"Let me show him the next set of spells," said Burgesis.
"Ok," said Barty.

"The word "tellus" or "terra" can be used to describe Earth," said Burgesis as he moved his hands like he was moving Earth around them "circumdamus et terram" is to surround with Earth. He then made a grab in midair and he started shaking and said: "concussionem terra" is shaking of the Earth, "insidiatur in terra" is trapped in the Earth. Huge Rock is "saxum ingēns" and a huge rock appeared above them and Burgesis then said, "Prohibere saxum ingēns" and the rock disappeared in mid-air.

"Earth spells, they are neutral, because they are grounded," said Jana.

"The other good thing about not wearing shoes is because if you feel correct you can tell where your opponents are and how you can maneuver a response to their attacks," said Burgesis looking at my feet.

"No I am not taking my shoes off," I thought to myself shaking my head thinking about how I loved these shoes.

Burgesis just smiled shaking his head at me.

"Oh yeah, he can read my mind," I thought to myself.

Burgesis looked at me and said, "Yeah that's right Mark," smiling.

"Now these were the four original elements now the others are really advanced and not as easy to explain. In the last four years, have barely been discovered by everyone, we have been fortunate to know at least a little about these elements. Magical Humans have known about the Ancient Magic for years, but it is all very heavily guarded now," Burgesis said carefully.

"Burgesis will show you them as well if you progress with these four really well," said Jana looking at me carefully.

"I think I am ready for the other elements," I said confidently.

"Not until we have seen you progress past these four first," said Burgesis.

"No, I think I already know them well enough to move on," I said confidently looking at Barty.

"Really? We shall see," said Barty looking at Burgesis smiling.

"Let's get some rest and we will challenge you later this afternoon, after lunch," said Burgesis.

"Ok, cool," I said looking at them both excitedly. Just then Jana said looking at Barty and Burgesis, "Ok boys, let's go get some lunch in us ok? That's enough for now."

We all got back inside Barty and Jana's house and sat at the table to see the meal that Jana had already prepared, bread and pasta were set up nicely on plates on the table, and we all sat and ate silently quickly, I was gratefully filled afterward.

As soon as I was done, I went to my room thinking about the challenge and rested for a little while. Then about two hours later I walked outside, and everything was still set up, but this time it was for the challenge and I was ready for whatever they would throw at me.

Chapter 9
The Challenge

"Flamma," I said as I had snapped my fingers and a flame appeared and then I said "Prohibere Flamma and the flame disappeared, as I walked outside. The challenge was me against Barty and Burgesis. Burgesis threw a water ball at me, and I used a boulder to block it. I then threw a wind gust at Barty with my other hand at the same time before he could have a chance to through a fireball at me. I then made a water globe with my hands and placed both Burgesis and Barty in it and it started spinning them in a sphere around me above my head and I then placed them in Earth mounds above the ground in which they were stuck for about five minutes. It was then that Jana said that I had won. After taking them both out of the Earth mounds, they both congratulated me impressed with my abilities to use two different elements at once. After using all those spells, I started to feel tired, so I told Burgesis and Barty that I wanted to rest. So, I went back into the house to rest in the bed in Burgesis's room and fell fast asleep.
Meanwhile, outside Jana and Barty started talking excitedly to each other.

"I can't believe how fast he soaks up these spells and how well he is handling the magic," said Jana quietly.

"He is learning almost too quickly," said Barty wisely seemingly slightly concerned at this thought, "Do you think we are doing the right thing, teaching him this quickly?"

"Guys we are doing great! I don't think we have much to worry about and we still have the rebels, and on top of that we have "the one." Nerogroben's army won't stand a chance against Mark," said Burgesis excitedly.

"His reaction time is really good, and he does pay attention to what's going on around him," said Jana satisfied with Burgesis's excitement looking at Barty who shook his head.

"We don't have the rebels and the clans yet, remember they are not getting along with each other among even just the basic higher, middle, and lower classes. To top that off Mark must gain the loyalty from those clan leaders to prove to the leaders that he is worthy to follow," said Barty dusting off some dirt that was in his fur on his shoulders.

"Still? After all these years?" asked Burgesis as Barty nodded silently with his head down.

"What about the council?" asked Burgesis carefully.

"What council?" asked Barty looking at Burgesis frowning.

"You know the one that I started," Burgesis said

"What about it?" asked Jana carefully. "We haven't met since before you left."

"So, you leaders of the clans aren't even getting along?" Burgesis said astounded.

"Burgesis it was the leaders who thought that those were only temporary meetings, we didn't see the need to continue meeting after what happened to the previous "the one." Everyone just dispersed and didn't keep in touch because they didn't believe in the cause, or even you."

"So, Mark has to do what now?" asked Burgesis carefully.

"The only way we have any hope like I said is maybe getting the leaders together again so that we can form an alliance of some sort with the rebels that we do have," said Jana thoughtfully.

"I hope your right," said Barty worriedly looking at Jana and then to Burgesis.

"He is much better than *the others*, haven't you seen how pure his heart is?" asked Jana looking at Barty.

"He will need to convince the leaders and prove himself worthy now to them before they will even try to attempt to go to their clans and talk to them with him," said Burgesis.

How is he going to do it though, we can't even get along ourselves with others, I mean he is literally our last hope," said Barty worriedly as they all turned silent.

"I think we should continue his training," said Burgesis carefully.

"I thought we were going to take him to the School of the Unknown?" Barty said cautiously.

"I thought so too," said Jana curiously looking at Burgesis.

"I think we should at least show him the other elements. At least so he is at least aware of the other elements out there," said Burgesis carefully looking at the others.

"We shall talk about this in the morning more," said Jana as she looked at Barty and he nodded.

"Alright, in the morning then," said Burgesis nodding in agreement. "Good night Jana and Barty."

"Good night Burgesis," they both said.

Chapter 10
The Others

I woke up the next morning feeling refreshed and went out to the dining room and saw Barty, Jana, and Burgesis huddled up.

"What's going on?" I asked curiously looking at Burgesis.

"We are debating whether to tell you the other elements or let the others teach you," said Burgesis. Barty shot his wife a worried face.

"Others?" I asked blankly at Barty and Jana and then to Burgesis who ignored my question.

"I think I have decided what I want to do," said Burgesis as Jana looked worriedly at him. "I want you to be aware of the elements out there. I will not tell you what the exact spell names are, but I want you to promise me that you will only use those basic spells for now. At least until we can find you the proper teachers," He continued looking at Barty for support.

"Agreed, we want to make sure you are aware that there are good people as well out there. But you should also be aware that, there are also those who will do anything and everything to make themselves stronger and more powerful, this is not the way. I would rather you know of these other elements in case you come across people who are just as evil as Nerogroben himself," said Barty looking at Burgesis.

"It would not do you any justice to just have taught you the basics without knowing of the other elements. It would also be wrong of us not to tell you, that not everyone outside of these walls will be ok with you being around," said Burgesis as I nodded and agreed.

"The fifth element is Electricity it is powerful and can be used to shock people, put them in a coma, or kill them.

Very few of us understand it, in fact I am the only one here who knows how to use it out of the three of us and it is very advanced magic. You must be accomplished in it with a magimark and it is only given by only the Electro-men. It is a rare gift to get that magimark on your own," said Burgesis looking at me as he said a few words under his breath and an orb of electricity appeared around his fist.

"The only elements that work against them are water and Earth. So, going back to the four elements it is best if you use the opposite power of the one, they are using so you know how to beat them in battle. Fighting evil fires with fire will never help you win the battles. In the end, that will just cause death and destruction. You must use what you know and what's true to you at the time of the battle and opposites work, most of the time. Burgesis being the only exception, if they know electricity, they don't know water or ground," said Jana softly sitting on my left at the table holding Barty's hand from across the table.

"Killing the enemy with elements is easier, it's one less loyalist to have to worry about later, during the Great Battle," said Barty looking at me.

"But you said that sometimes doing a bad thing can destroy your magimark or give you a bad magimark. How does one decide what kill of the enemy is good or bad?" I said, "How does killing another, make it right to kill at all? Does it make us any better than them? Is there a shield for the killing spells?"

"You have a really good point, and it's up to you in the end in how you handle the situation, the magimarks are formed based off your conscience. But you must remember that your opponent might try to kill you and might not go as easy on you as you might think. These people and creatures that are in Nerogroben's army have lost their conscience. They kill because they feel like this is what they must do to keep themselves from being killed by Nerogroben. They don't feel that killing is wrong because they lack the good judgment like they used to have because of the effects of the Grey Matter," said Burgesis. It was at that very moment that I quietly decided that I didn't want to ever use the elements or anything to kill anyone if I could help it.

"We should try to call the council of yours. The Smithertons, the Fortesques, the Pillowdrums, the Figwiggins, the Ersals, the Eubinks, and the Chunnings, over to help to," said Barty thoughtfully looking at Burgesis who nodded.

"I will send messages out," said Burgesis urgently as he stood up.

"No," said Jana sternly as she motioned for him to sit.

"Why not?" asked Burgesis who sat back down and looked at Jana quizzically.

"Because messages have been intercepted by Nerogroben's men as of late," said Jana. "We have heard bad talk amongst the trees."

"What's the best way of communication without being seen or caught now?" Burgesis asked Barty darkly.

"The only way now is to go to these families and ask in person," Barty said. "Jana and I can help with that."

"Tonight..." Burgesis started to say as he saw me looking at him through the doorway.

"You and I are going to need to go out too then and help," Burgesis said to me from across the hallway in the living-room.

"No!" said Barty and Jana together. "The boy will be too risky! He stays here. We don't want to call for war too early for him."

"Yes, I understand that, but I will be with him," said Burgesis. "I doubt we will have trouble."

"NO!" said Barty and his wife sternly. "We don't want anything happening to Mark, we will bring the families here. Besides yes, he is good at fighting, but he hasn't had nearly enough practice to make sure nothing will happen to him."

"I really don't know if killing or destroying an army is what I am cut out to do," I said aloud as the three had jumped at the same time surprised to remember that I was still there.

"You just have to figure out your own moral system that's all," said Burgesis thoughtfully.

"Maybe this is good that he isn't going," said Barty looking at me carefully.

"Yeah," said Jana agreeing. "It seems like you two have to talk about a few things. For now, maybe it's best for you to let us get the word to the Fortesque's house tonight and have them spread the word to the specific families we mentioned before. Don't worry Barty and I will be fine," said Jana looking at Burgesis's worried face as he turned a stern look at me.

"But you said yourself that the council hasn't met in years," said Burgesis

"Yes, this much is true," said Barty.

"I doubt it will be the same since the leaders have moved around back and forth on sides since you left," said Jana.

"The council?" I asked Burgesis who looked at Barty.

"Like I said before, I doubt they will all get along," said Barty shaking his head sadly.

"There is only one way to find out," said Burgesis smiling at Jana and Barty who nodded seriously. "Good Luck to you both then!"

Chapter 11
Morals and Virtues

In less than ten minutes both Beavers left their home from their underground burrow as they disappeared into the tranquil night air. It was after they left when Burgesis looked me in deep severity from across the table. I knew that Burgesis wasn't happy with me, but this was the first time that he had disagreed with me. I had felt very strongly about this issue.

"Burgesis," I started. "I don't think that I want to destroy an army. Yes, I understand that they have done some terrible things in the name of Nerogroben himself. I just feel that it doesn't mean that they are in fact evil beings. Killing at all, in general, and in my opinion, is something hard for me to comprehend a need for, or even to consider and think about. To me, it feels like we would stoop down to their level, the level of brutes, in order, for us to get our own way and "win this war." But what would we have done at that point? "Won the war"? Or did we do what Nerogroben was trying to do "create a bigger one"? To accomplish the same thing, take over and rule? I feel that there must be other ways to handle these situations first to try to exhaust. Someone who killed another being on Earth gets punished for it. Sometimes it is the victim's family or friends, that try to exact revenge for the dead, but there doesn't seem to be any purpose for this. I mean it doesn't bring back that dead person from the dead. Why not follow with rehabilitation to help that killer change or improve themselves? Maybe there is a way to not make him kill anymore, or we can forgive them for what they have done? It also helps for people to be merciful to them and forgive themselves afterwards for having those thoughts and prejudices in the first place. I mean these are beings who are mentally sick," I explained calmly looking down and then I looked up at Burgesis who had turned a completely dark red in anger. "Because that doesn't work, just saying, "here is some rehab," or "I forgive you" won't stop people from doing what they are doing again. On Earth, in America, they lock up murderers, thieves, rapists, and killers of all sorts or they do the lethal injection, they aren't going to just slap the person on the hands and say bad boy or bad girl for killing someone. Justice takes its course as it ought to, here in this World of the Unknown!" Burgesis said shouting loudly pointing outside. "What did you think that defense of the elements was for? Lighting campfires, giving you water glasses, and a nice breeze and shade on a warm sunny day?" asked Burgesis angrily.

"What did you all have here before Nerogroben then?" I asked

"We didn't. Before Nerogroben, there wasn't any need to have any sort of justice system in place because there was no Grey Matter, no evil, I **TOLD YOU!**" said Burgesis angrily.

"Your wrong about how to handle this situation Burgesis. I don't believe I should go against my own integrity, values, and what I believe to "win the war." It will work by reconciliation, those were great powerful spells, but does it make it right to kill a few thousand people for the sake of a million or billion Magical Humans and Magical Creatures? Killing, in general, has always been wrong to me, I don't see how you can make something so horrible seem socially acceptable, regarding the magimarks," I responded shaking my head calmly to Burgesis from across the table.

"It's because they are just trolls and evil beings in the end! You can't train an old dog new trick! They all hate each other now," said Burgesis. "It doesn't matter!"

"You may not be able to teach an old dog new tricks, but there is certainly hope for those dogs that are younger and less corrupted than Nerogroben himself!" I said insistently as he shook his head stubbornly.

"I can understand what you are saying, and in this one case, does it does make sense to kill a few thousand to save a million or billion? It does make any sense, but I urge you to view things from a different perspective if you win the war without violence, or a lot of casualties then you will surprise me. The evil out there will always seem to have the upper hand," said Burgesis starting to calm down as he put up his right hand and put his finger gradually on each of the tops of his fingers as he said, "The magimarks have five standards they base themselves on. Number one, your conscious, number two, your physical strength, number three, your emotional strength in which you say the words with, number four, your morals and values, number five lastly, your virtues. If you teach yourself, that when killing these people, who are not only trying to kill you, but everything that you stand for, you train your conscious that it is okay, and then you will not get red magimarks. By doing so, you earn good magimarks, now if you accomplish something that you feel proud of, or that you stand for, strive for, or even something that represents who you are, then you will earn good magimarks. The moment you doubt yourself, become depressed, angry, or anything of the sort like this, you will get bad magimarks. That is why there is constantly changing in yourself because you change every day between your experiences, attitudes, knowledge, and the wisdom that you receive. In fact, I won't be surprised if tomorrow you wake up in pain, or strengthened because of what you have accomplished today," Burgesis said looking at me.

"Would you say that if the army was to change it is the focus, it would become a good army?" I asked.

"I suppose so, it's a huge stretch. I believe that it's possible," said Burgesis. "I suppose, but keep in mind there are thousands in his army and some of them would do anything to become just as powerful and just as strong as Nerogroben."

"I suppose then it will be okay to kill Nerogroben or his army in the end if there is an absolute need in the end when the time comes. I think I would prefer to try to use the elements first," I explained looking at Burgesis who seemed to calm down more. "Good night Burgesis," I said as I yawned. I thought about our conversation and still, in my heart, I knew that even this didn't sit right with me as I walked back to my room. I closed the door, laid in bed, and closed my eyes and went to sleep.

The next morning, I was awakened with a start, as Burgesis shook me awake. "Wake up Mark, Barty and Jana haven't come back yet! I think something bad has happened to them," said Burgesis worriedly.

"The enemy doesn't know that I am here, do they?" I asked cautiously as I was wide awake now and sat bolt straight up.

"I don't know. It's possible, I mean, all it would have taken is someone to have watched this burrow, and kept an eye on it, and capture Barty and Jana as they left," said Burgesis as he frantically looked around at my room trying to think.

"Isn't it possible that maybe they just stayed overnight at the Fortesques? Things could have gotten rather difficult to leave if his men were all over the place around their home. I think we should wait until tomorrow night to worry if they are coming back home yet or not. They would need time to travel to the Fortesque's house depending on how far away they are," I suggested calmly as Burgesis nodded. "Anyway, it wouldn't do us any good. They were right, I haven't practiced enough yet to be able to leave this place safely," I told Burgesis as he pulled a book off a shelf that he had been looking at for a while.

"Your right, okay, we will give them until tomorrow night," said Burgesis distractedly. "Here take this." He continued as he threw me an English-Latin Dictionary that was in his hands. "All the words in this book are guaranteed to help you eventually anyway," said Burgesis slowly with purpose.

As I caught the dictionary in the air, I had decided that he was right, so I started at the beginning of the alphabet. As I read the words, I thought of ways in which it would be helpful to use them in combination, with other words. I seemed to already know how to utilize the different objects and materials in the dictionary with magic as I read them with complete interest. Burgesis seemed to have left the room quietly because I didn't notice after a while that he was gone, as I was lost in the book.

I started to take notes and wrote down the English words and their Latin translations making my own portable English to Latin Dictionary and started to feel proud of it. By feeling this way, almost immediately, I started to feel the power within as I took a deep breath and warmth came over me. As I looked, I had noticed that I gained a magimark. It was shining bright, lighting up the dark room as I looked at it with awe.

Burgesis slowly walked in and saw the light burning my skin as he smiled, "I remember when I got my first magimarks and felt proud of myself. Oh, the good old days," he shook his head smiling as he walked out of the room and sat in the family room. I began to read the book as fast as I could. While reading, I wrote down these words frantically as if one of them could help me at any moment starting from A - Abduct/kidnap – Abripio to D- Destroy – abolefacio.

"Hey ready for lunch?" called Burgesis from the kitchen.

"Yeah, be there in a minute," I called out in reply. I closed my book, laid it on my bed and walked out to the kitchen.

"No word from Barty and Jana yet?" I asked Burgesis who was cutting a freshly made sandwich on a plate that was sitting on the counter in front of him in the kitchen where he was standing.

"No, not yet" he replied handing me a sandwich on a
plate.

"Don't worry they will be back," I said reassuringly. "Burgesis, just how long and how well do you know Barty and Jana? Do you trust them? How did you meet them?"

"I have known them for years since before I was in Nerogroben's army, they are good people. I know they aren't trying to get Nerogroben's men here, they would die first. Out of everyone I know, here in the World of the Unknown, I trust them the most. They have been there for me in times when they have been the most difficult, and they are very understanding. They will do anything to help you, Mark. I am going to be adding a second layer of protection on this place from outside, so I need you to preoccupy yourself for a few hours. If I take more than five hours by adding more protection, you best stay inside until the secondary security force comes," Burgesis said.

"What do you mean by secondary security force?" I asked.

"The secondary security force is a high security transfer for rebels in emergencies. You only need to say help in Latin and point to the sky and they come to assist you. To be honest, I don't think I will be longer than two hours adding the protective enchantments on the house," explained Burgesis.

"Don't worry, I can preoccupy myself especially with that book you gave me," I said looking at Burgesis.

"I wouldn't tell anyone else about that book I gave you because technically it is unlawful to have one and there
are many secrets in it," Burgesis said slowly to me as I nodded.

"Ok," I said curiously as I finished my sandwich.

I walked into my room and Burgesis looked at me.

"Be careful when I am gone, don't open the front door or unlock your room door no matter who they claim they are. The secondary force and I are the only ones who know that the safe key code for any doors to be opened is "depraesentiarum," which means, "here and now." Now I must go before we

are on our own any longer," said Burgesis as he opened and locked the front door behind him.
I locked my room door and continued writing down words from my Latin dictionary onto a notebook that was originally on my bedside table. I turned on the lamp on the bedside table and opened the book to where I left off and got comfortable on my bed and continued to write down various words between Detect – olefacto to Dove- Columba. Then I stumbled on the word "Dragon- anquis" "I wonder," I said aloud to myself, but then decided not to use it right now. I continued writing, Eagle – Aquila, Eavesdrop – subausculto. Then I saw the word "Electrica" for Electric and remembered what Barty, Jana, and Burgesis had said about it being a questionable element. They also had stated that only the most powerful use it. I decided to try to wait for the right time and moment to use it responsibly. Then for the next hour and a half, I continued to pick various words from the dictionary between Flashlight- Lucis afflatus to Fog – nebula and then stumbled on the word Knife- and in Latin is Culter.
I had finished writing down some of the more important words to know in my opinion, now it was only a question of applying them. I had noticed things were very quiet outside. After waiting another fifteen minutes there was a set of three

knocks at the door and the word "depraesentiarum," was said, so I opened the door to find Burgesis, Barty, and Jana.
"I added the extra protection, but I am afraid it won't last," said Burgesis looking at me.
"Nerogroben's men have been around here too much for my comfort," said Barty looking at Jana.
"I think we should move you both, tonight before things get too difficult," said Jana as I placed the Latin dictionary in my jacket pocket.
"There has been a rumor that "the one" is here," said Barty to Burgesis in a whisper which I could hear well considering my big ears.
Burgesis ran into the room where I had been sleeping and had pointed to several cases as they had opened on their own and several things went into them off the shelves above. These items were then self-packing themselves into a neat little duffle bag which when full had shrunk in size and was in the form of a pill box. Burgesis had shoved into his pocket smiling looking at my face of amazement and said, "I travel light."
Then Jana and Barty had followed suit packing items and moving things around as I watched in amazement. Burgesis put on a sheet over my body, which covered me from head to foot. Then he had whispered, "Occaeco," after placing his hand on my head and I became invisible. Within a few minutes,

we were outside the hut. I then took a deep breath and breathed in the cool night air through the sheet.

"Follow us this way," said Barty to Burgesis and me as we nodded. Jana then closed and locked the door behind us. Barty and Jana started running ahead of us as we then ran and followed them into the darkness. We could see the lights from the hut disappear in between the trees in the distance as we began our adventure.

Chapter 12
On the Run

We had run for what seemed like hours and thank goodness it was still dark. Nerogroben's men could be heard from their various campsites between the trees in the woods as we passed them. We had stopped every so often for a few breaths of air and then we would run some more as if our lives depended on it. Finally, we found a clearing in which it was decided that we would make camp. We set up tents and a protection around our campsite preventing people from passing through the clearing.

Then the next morning when we awoke, Jana had made some sandwiches for us all before we had left the house the night before. She had taken them from Barty's pack. After we had finished eating, we packed up and started to prepare to travel again. Burgesis made sure that I was completely covered with an invisibility sheet. During this travel, I had noticed that every chance Jana, Barty, and Burgesis could get away from me, they were deep in whispering conversations in which I was prevented from either physically or magically from listening in or participating in. It was a fortnight that I finally had become thoroughly annoyed by this.

I had started to feel frustrated thinking, where were we going? What were we going to do? I just wanted to go home; I didn't want to run from anything anymore. Burgesis seemed to be in tune to what I was thinking and feeling about things.

"We are almost there," said Burgesis.

"Where are we running to?" I asked frustrated looking at Burgesis who nodded at Barty silently.

"Do you remember when we told you about Nerogroben's army?" asked Barty after slowly looking at Burgesis and then to Jana and then to me.

"Yeah," I said impatiently.

"Well, there are those of us who are loyal to Nerogroben and his army," said Burgesis carefully.

"Okay," I said still wondering what the big deal was.

"Well, we, Barty and I," said Jana. "We called up the rebels you can say, that is why we took so long. We were sending messages to, um..." as she stopped nervously looking at Barty and Burgesis for help.

I couldn't understand why there were nervous but seemingly excited. In several conversations, over the past few days, when they thought I was sleeping, they had forgotten to add the magical enchantments to deter me from overhearing them. I was able to hear them in their tents with tidbits of information about a gathering of some sort.

Burgesis noticed what I was thinking and how upset I was to be talked about behind my back.

"I know your frustrated with us, so I will tell you what's going on," said Burgesis. "We are all extremely nervous because we don't know how you will handle what we are about to tell you," he continued looking at Jana and Barty.

"I can handle it," I said looking at Burgesis reassuringly. "Jana was about to say something about the rebels?" I continued looking at Jana who looked at Burgesis and then to Barty for help. Then she nudged Barty as I continued to look at her.

"Um, yes, well, look... ok, here is goes... you have to understand that both Magical Human and Magical Creatures have alliances towards Nerogroben and his army or to..." said Barty trying to explain but then looked to Burgesis.

"You, because you are, "the one," said Burgesis looking at me carefully for a reaction as I didn't show any and was sure to make sure not to think anything about it right away. "They believe in the prophecy that was foretold of your coming."

"I thought they don't get along?" I said.

"They don't but these are beings who are willing to lay down their lives, willing to be killed for this cause. They just want peace, for all our futures, both for the Earth and for the World of the Unknown. They would rather be killed, then allow

Nerogroben and his army to cause a disaster in the future for the children of both our worlds. They are on your side for you, they believe in you and what you represent," said Burgesis.
"But why me? Why not you Burgesis?" I asked. "Why are beings here willing to lay down their lives for me? They don't even know me!" I started to say as Burgesis put up his hand to dispute.
"They know the prophecy, and they know what you can do potentially, and the powers you have inside yourself!" said Burgesis smiling.
"We all have such great power within ourselves, and we all are capable of doing such great things. People should follow you because you know more about magimarks than me," I insisted.
"Um, that's not a good idea," said Barty. "If are "the one" now, this was meant for you, and then that means that this was supposed to be your destiny. You just don't understand," Barty continued looking at Burgesis.
"What do you mean IF? Why not you Burgesis? What don't I understand?" I asked confused.
"You need to know more about me, so that you will see why it has to be this way, excuse us for a minute," Burgesis said looking at me.
For a few minutes Jana, Barty, and Burgesis left me in my tent and Burgesis came back.

"Let's go for a walk," Burgesis said carefully to me as I nodded, stood up, and followed Burgesis and Barty.

We left the large tent on the cover of my sheet into the darkness. Burgesis, Barty, and I walked together outside of the camp. Jana stayed behind to keep an eye on the camp.

"You must understand how things are right now for us, everything we do is scrutinized, and judged by others. Every time you have a conversation with someone you must make sure that you can trust them, otherwise you never know what will happen tomorrow. Beings here always have to be concerned if whether the person that they are talking to is of Nerogroben's army or worse one of his beloved informants," said Barty roughly to me.

After walking in silence for a few minutes, we came upon a stick in the ground with a sign on it in a weird language as I looked at it with curiosity.

"That is the marker, of where the first attack before the Dark War occurred. When the news of Nerogroben taking over the World of the Unknown was spreading, there were a growing number of beings that were in support of his power. He convinced everyone that all the clan leaders were corrupt and all they wanted was money and power and that they weren't concerned about their clans. This caused a huge uproar and, in some cases, unfortunately. he was right. This was the house where my mom, brother, and sister, who were in allegiance to Nerogroben at the time had died," said Burgesis pointing to a burnt down house. It was a dark day in my life for me. I had already pledged myself loyal to Nerogroben and was a part of his army at first and had gone through with the training. His idea was to attack my village, which was one of the closest to Metromark, to show force and to persuade others not to be disloyal to him. I didn't know until we were on our way and started to charge and attack. My family didn't have a chance to get out before his surprise attack," continued Burgesis tearing up and started to cry as he nodded to Barty to continue.

"Burgesis's father survived, he was deep in the forest in the back of the house cutting logs for the fireplace in the house. His father hasn't been able to see Burgesis for years. We think his father is not aware of his son's existence," said Barty carefully.

"Where is your dad now Burgesis?" I asked slowly looking at the remains of the old hut as we passed the remains of Petal Village, it was desolate, and no one remained.

"My father lives in Metromark," Burgesis said slowly, "According to Brendan Alicea, Chancellor Rain's assistant. The Chancellor wanted me to prove myself and my disloyalty to Nerogroben, before allowing me to be able to see my father again. I was the original, "the one," but I failed. I joined Nerogroben and was tricked and was cheated. Yes, I was a part of his army, not one of my proudest moments in my life. That is why I can't lead the rebellion against him. The fact is though that, I was trained by them, so I know how they fight and how to help you. The people who lived in this village were a mixture of Magical Humans, and Magical Creatures, such beautiful and loving people. They were innocent, and should not have died," Burgesis continued as he started to cry again.

"As Nerogroben grew powerful his continued thoughts became his beliefs that Magical Humans and Magical Creatures shouldn't be mixed. It caused panic and distrust, also it spread dark hatred amongst the clans causing segregation. The Magical Humans made the guarded and impenetrable city of Metromark. Some say it was protection against the evils of Nerogroben and his army. In my opinion, it isn't protection, they to this day use it as an explanation of cowardice."

"Why and how am I "the chosen one"? Why do you think I am the right person if others were thinking that you were "the one"?" I asked nervously looking at Burgesis who had a smile on his face.

"Whiskers thought you were "the one," he continued looking at me with a twinkle in his eyes. "Also, let me just say, Whiskers did not see me as "the one" that was prophesized about."

"Really?' I asked incredulously looking at Burgesis. "Wait, What? How does Mark know Whiskers?" Barty asked curiously.

"For Whiskers and me to look for "the one," we needed a way to not just blend in, but for us to search without it looking like we were in search of someone," Burgesis started to explain as Barty nodded.

I was wondering how they selected me as well because there were thousands of kids on Earth who probably could have been good picks. Burgesis nodded as he understood what I was thinking.

"Your right Mark, for years, Whiskers and I went through a lot of families and kids hoping and praying that we would find the right child in time through our observations," Burgesis explained.

"In time?" I asked frowning.

"You see, we aren't the only ones on Earth looking for "the one," Burgesis pushed on. "The governments are trying to find people with particular qualities to find the person who is supposed to help their world as well, it's the same child that they are after."

"Is that why you were worried I would be killed?" I asked worriedly. "Who is it that is after me?"
"But that's the thing, we don't know for sure yet about you. Only through our own rigorous tests that Whiskers would give kids did he eventually feel he found the right child, you Mark," explained Burgesis as he continued. "The second night after you fed him, he had read your compassionate heart, and through observing you he knew increasingly that you were pure in heart. We both agreed that upon his death on Earth, I would know that this was his sign to me that he found "the one," the one pure child. The final test I was to give you, was to see how well you handled grief, pain, struggle, and loss of your life. You pushed yourself to go to school, and you met with me and left your room to come downstairs to me at the door, which was another sign for me that you were trying to accept what had happened. But that part of things was my job to confirm. If you failed, we would have just moved on. You responded to the situation, and you didn't emotionally react completely to everything. Yes, your emotions were on over drive, but you kept your composure around me in your living room," explained Burgesis seriously as I kept quiet taking it all in and trying to process it all.
"You have lived in your home on Earth for how long?" asked Barty looking at me.

"All my life," I replied.

"You see?" Burgesis said.

"See what?" I asked confused.

"You see, you have not traveled the world as we have," said Burgesis.

"Sure, I have seen you grow up a little across the street from me, but you see, while you have done so, you have not experienced how people are around the world. You only see how people act around "your world" and all you see is their goodness in them. We have seen that in your heart, you don't see others as evil, untrustworthy, lazy, or arrogant. But if I might add, you are not impressed with how the world as it is," he continued seemingly reading my mind as he nodded at me.

"Everything that *you* do from now on will be looked at as the right way to handle the situations we are about to put ourselves in. You are our new conscious, our new moral compass. You will be able to morally guide this army of loyal rebel supporters, magical people, and creatures alike, and show them a pure, and the unselfish world and how to live properly amongst friends," Barty added.

"But what if I make a fool of myself? Who is going to listen to me? I am just a kid, who doesn't know what he doesn't know," I explained, "I am not special or smart or disciplined enough to be able to guide people, I can barely guide my current life."

"You are a very humble and special, what happened to your positivity?" Burgesis asked looking at me with a frown.

"I want to be positive here, but I don't know what I am up against.

How many supporters do I have? How many are in Nerogroben's army?" I asked worriedly.

"You will have better faith when you see how much faith people have in you, and how loyal they will be to you as we get closer. The word is slowly getting out to the rest of the families, and then they will be meeting with people who will change and will be excited," Barty explained looking at Burgesis who smiled and nodded in agreement.

"But people haven't even met me!" I said wearily feeling pressure.

"Here, however, is something you need to keep in mind Mark. We are all capable of doing great things in difficult situations. People will follow you because of what you do for them, and what you do for others. They will also follow you because of not only what you believe in, but also what you represent," explained Burgesis.

"Oh yeah, and what do I represent?" I asked unconvinced.

"Hope, Mark, hope! You are our leader and people will look up to you even just because of that!" said Burgesis smiling through tears as I nodded.

We continued to follow the path back to the campsite as Jana had already had dinner ready for us which we ate in silence. I then went to sleep feeling a little better now that I understood at least a little more of what was going on. I just felt bad for Burgesis and what had happened to his family. I wanted nothing more than for him to get back to see his father. It was at that point that I decided that the only way for this to happen was for Chancellor Rain to see that Burgesis was on our side and that he was completely and totally against Nerogroben.

Chapter 13
The River of Peace

The next morning, I woke up early on my own, I wanted to have some time to think of a plan which, I could begin to apply the magic I had taught myself.

Silently with as clear of a mind as I could, I left the security of our encampment. As I slowly walked along the clearing, I found that there was a river. It was early in the morning and not a soul was in sight as I had double checked the area.

I raised my hands in front of me as I took in a deep breath and closed my eyes. I felt at peace.

As I waved my hands around, I found moving the water along the river to be very relaxing while being able to allow it to flow through me. It pushed itself around and against the current, all the while making water waves.

After doing so for a few moments I stopped suddenly as there was something moving in the water around my water currents, I was making upstream.

"Barty?? Jana?? If that is you, stop playing games!" I said feeling nervous, but there was no response coming from the brown fur of the being that was headed towards my way. So, I used the currents stronger to push against this creature/being that was heading towards me down stream.

"Why and how are you throwing that water Mr.," asked the creature who perked his head up.

"Sorry," I said carefully still having my hands up defensively.

"It's okay, I was just noticing how it wasn't easy to swim here and I saw that you were moving the current the opposite direction that the rest of the river was going. Who are you?" asked the creature.

"My name is Mark," I said carefully noticing that the creature was a beaver as it stood on its hind legs.

"Nice to meet you, Mark. What Clan are you from?" asked the beaver.

"I am from the..." I started and then jumped as the beaver had his hands up defensively against me.

"Mark, what are you doing down here? You were supposed to stay with us! Who are you talking to?" asked Barty from behind the bushes as Jana came up behind him both putting their hands up defensively as they approached me. "What the Dickens!" said Jana quickly looking at Barty nervously.

"Oh, it's only you, Dickens," said Barty as he and Jana relaxed quickly.

"What do you mean only me?" said Dickens looking at me frowning. "What are you guys doing so far away from Beaver Valley and with him?"

"We thought you were one of Nerogroben's," said Jana worriedly carefully looking at Barty.
"Around these parts?" asked Dickens smiling mischievously. "Let them try to come near me and this river! Is Mark with you?"
"Yeah, he is with us," said Barty carefully looking at Jana. "We are escorting him back home."
"Yeah, he got lost when the currents pushed him away from the school, and so we are trying to get him back to the school of the Unknown," said Jana nodding.
"That's odd," said Dickens as he walked closer to me in the water suspiciously. "A moment ago, he was pushing the water quite well."
"Are you on your own Dickens?" asked Barty interrupting.
"Yes, of course, I am on my own," said Dickens. "The rest of our clan is in Beaver Valley as you very well know!"
"So, we see that you have met our young Mark Trogmyer," said Burgesis smiling from behind me as I jumped and looked at him.
"Ah, at last, Burgesis, your return has been greatly anticipated!" said Dickens smiling as he came to the water's edge closer to me and hugged Burgesis as they laughed.
"So, none of you have answered why your stories don't match, who is Mark? Why all this secrecy?"

asked Dickens carefully and still suspiciously looking at me and then to Barty, Jana, and Burgesis. They all looked at me.

Then Barty and Jana and Dickens looked at Burgesis who just continued to look at me as if trying to read my mind. I thought Burgesis, only if you can guarantee that Dickens can be trusted then reveal me. I will trust your judgement, for now, to ensure that my presence will not be revealed to the wrong people until you feel I am ready. Burgesis nodded in understanding.

"Mark is a trusted friend of mine; I go back to childhood with him. He is a runaway from the school, he felt it was very corrupt there. His parents don't know that he has run away yet please keep this information to yourself for now," Burgesis said as Dickens thought about the information for a minute and then nodded his head. "You got that right, those wizards there have been trying to raise an army there to defend their school from being overridden. There is a lot of corruption and evil within those walls," said Dickens understandingly. "Well good luck with your future endeavors Mark, may you stay in the light. Commanders, I will be at the clan houses if you need me." Dickens finished as he nodded respectfully to Jana and Barty and swam away downstream.

"This is the last remaining thing that has been left untouched by Nerogroben's army. This is the River of Peace, it's extremely powerful and precious to us, isn't it beautiful?" Burgesis said looking at the river waters moving downstream as I nodded in agreement. It was very peaceful by this large river; it was surrounded by several trees, bushes, and shrubbery.

"Whew, that was close," said Barty.

"Commanders?" I asked thinking of what Dickens had said. Burgesis nodded.

"All the leaders are their own Commanders of their own clans," explained Burgesis. "It's a sign of respect."

"Oh okay, I am assuming, Dickens isn't trustworthy?" I asked Burgesis.

"He is, but the thing is, since we are this early in the game, the few people know about you, for now, the better."

I nodded. Burgesis had a great point. The more people that knew about me in the World of the Unknown, the more chances of my life being in danger before I even have a chance to fight against Nerogroben. We walked back to the secured encampment and ate breakfast and packed our things quickly. The sheet was placed over me before we moved on in the cover of the trees. We followed parallel to the river that was near the campsite.

Up ahead I just saw rows of shrubs and bushes and tall trees that seemed to give us plenty of cover and protection from being discovered. We stopped to rest, freshen up, and eat lunch. It was after lunch that Barty, Jana, and Burgesis wanted to catch their breath. I stood by the river which downstream further I could see it partially flow into a lake. I had felt free enough to be able to practice. Slowly I raised my hands up with palms up and said "Hydra," as I softly spoke and lifted my fingers gently. A fountain of water sprouted up from the body of water and as I waved my hands around, so did a small amount of water.

I moved my hands in a circular motion focusing on the energy of the water as if it was flowing through me. I had stood with my feet apart, as I started to move my hands as if I was shaping putty into a ball, raising my hands. I looked at the water in front of me, there was a water globe circulating in midair above the water. Barty and Jana had been talking in the background about how far the rebels were away, but they suddenly stopped talking when they noticed my element magic.

"You are getting stronger Mark," said Burgesis from behind me as I jumped with a start and froze the water and threw the daggers at him and he put his

hand up and the icicles stopped mid-air and he changed it back to free-
flowing water again as it fell to the ground like rain drops.

"Wow, sorry about that," said Burgesis laughing. "I should have known you would have been on high alert. I was thinking about how you should be learning the elements and remember how I told you if you adjust the words, you can make the element stronger or weaker?"

"Yeah," I replied blushing as I was remembering the earlier conversation.

"The only thing that you have to keep in mind is that the louder you say the word, the more powerful in strength it is. The quieter you say the word, the weaker and the less powerful in strength it has," Burgesis reexplained as he walked next to me beside the riverbank as I nodded.

"Why is it that the others don't get to go to Earth, and you have the only ability to?" I asked carefully.

"I am the only one authorized by your world to go there, hence the Eagle tattoo. My fiancé was very supportive of me and wanted me to be successful and was happy that I was selected to be able to travel to find "the one." If and when I die, the Eagle then chooses its next representative on it is own, based off that persons/creatures' principles of morality and traditional beliefs. If they are the same as the ones held on Earth at the time, the eagle lays itself peacefully on that person, but the eagle never dies. It's a symbol of my representation for Earth here and I bring supplies here from there like soap, some foods, etc. That is why I had said, "I will come back to you later, had you said "no" to me this past time to come to the World of the Unknown," Burgesis said.

"Oh ok," I answered as we followed the path for about ten minutes.

"Trust me," Burgesis said reading my thoughts. "The life around here is very aware of what could be and is to come. When you become able to understand the language of nature, you will see what I mean when I say they are afraid, *very afraid*, believe me..." he finished as his voice trailed off and he stood up and started adding protection enchantments to help prevent us from being seen.

"Well, what is the language of..." I started to ask looking at Burgesis who started shushing me.

"Shhh, keep your voice down!" said Burgesis as Jana and Barty ran towards me with fear in their eyes. "The reason is that we can't trust plant life around here. Every tree, bush, and blade of grass has a voice and is either for or against "the chosen one," or for and against Nerogroben. We never know who is on whose side and it is best to keep things quiet, we do not need certain people to find out specific information," said Barty cautiously looking around as I nodded in understanding.

Just then Barty and Jana jumped as several ducks and seagulls took off from the ground hard, further down the path. We could see two of Nerogroben's men coming up along the path up ahead. I could tell this was what Burgesis saw coming up ahead, we just hadn't been noticed yet by them.

"It seems like we have company up ahead," said Barty nodding quietly towards up the path ahead.

"I know," said Burgesis whispering "I saw them up ahead, but I didn't want to worry you guys, so we have some added protection near us, so we can't be spotted immediately. I am just trying to come up with a plan."

"Quick, hide in these bushes," said Jana nervously as they had all followed her direction and quick thinking.

Nerogroben's trolls walked a just a little passed the group of us and were deep in conversation standing about two hundred feet away and I could hear them talking.

"I can't believe the boss wants us to do this, this is going to cause a full uprising against him, and both Magical Humans and Magical Creatures alike live off this water. It is like he doesn't care what happens to people who are loyal to him," said one of the trolls who were rather skinny wearing armor.

"That's because he doesn't care," said the other rather fat Troll indifferently. "Just begin. We must do as we are told otherwise it's the end of the line for us."

The skinny Troll nodded, and he put his hands on the edge of the water whispering deeply, the other Troll was closely keeping watch.

The Troll started whispering and slowly a dark dye appeared to be trickling down his arms and into the river right before our eyes. We noticed immediately the water creatures come up to the surface nearby gasping for air as we began to see the last remaining body of water that was suitable for drinking being poisoned. As the water turned black, the birds nearby began to ferociously attack the two guards. The guards then responded with fire and strong wind attacks.

Then the plant life tried to come to the rescue but to no end. The Lake of Peace was poisoned and for a while, Barty and Jana looked at each other with scared eyes. In the next moment, the lake was pitch dark as the soldier took his arms from the water.

I jumped out of hiding suddenly and shouted and pointed to the elves and said "STOP!" to the fat Troll.

"You can't make us," said the fat Troll as he shot fire balls at me. Burgesis blocked them.

Jana said, "No Mark, don't do anything!"
Barty shouted, "Leave them alone and we can go safely."
"No wait, let him handle this, let's see what he's got," said Burgesis, suddenly, holding back Jana and Barty curiously.
I felt myself get angry, as a magimark burned and had appeared to me in the shape of a lightning bolt. It was at that point that I realized that I had the elemental magic within me, as I looked up at the already now darkening sky. I felt myself going into a weird state, my eyes rolled back but I could still see. I then put my hands up in the air, clouds formed dark above me.
They started covering the sky above and the area around the lake, and getting darker with rain, the second little Troll guard started poisoning the area around the lake faster, so I then shouted "Lightningum Forte!" and bolts of lightning came out across the sky. I pointed my fingers to the Troll guards directly and I then began striking them with lightning bolts, until the smaller guard stopped. Then the fat guard stopped trying to shoot fire balls at me.
Within in two minutes, the trolls were stunned. I then raised both the guards in the air with powerful winds and bound them up with stone and hardened Earth against a nearby random brick wall that was

randomly by the river. It was then that I decided to place a huge stone tablet near them and with lightning, on the stone, I wrote:

> "LEAVE THIS NEWLY NAMED RIVER OF PEACE AND LAKE OF PROMISE ALONE, THIS IS A WARNING TO ALL BY "THE ONE." SHOULD THIS RIVER OR LAKE OR ANY CREATURES AROUND THIS RIVER OR LAKE BE HARMED OR DAMAGED AT ALL... THIS IS WHAT WILL HAPPEN TO THOSE RESPONSIBLE."

After a few minutes, the trolls reawakened stunned to find themselves pinned against the wall as they read the sign in fear. I was completely angry with them for being so cruel as I shouted at them.
"NO ONE will try to destroy this sacred river again," I then whispered some enchantments that suddenly came to me weirdly and added a curse to harm those who try to harm the lake or anyone around or in the lake.
As I waved my hands a silvery mist came from them. I then whispered an incantation and the river and connected lake started to clean itself. It

started to flow into the nearby river again and it was not black anymore.

I slowly walked back to the now shocked looking, Jana, Barty, and Burgesis. They had stood there observing and couldn't help but smile and clap in complete astonishment.

"You know, I told you lightning was not an option for elemental magic usage, and you said, "No killing huh?" said Burgesis concerned looking at the two trolls who were still squirming trying to get away.

"Well, I decided to try it because for some reason it automatically came to me. Whoever hurts this world in front of me will pay twice the pain and yes, the guards are still alive, I didn't kill them, I would just say I just left them there shocked," I said "ad sanandum" and a light came from within, and I felt strength come to me as I have never felt before.

"This type of magic is not controlled easily down here. To have used this for your first time, and to be this successful at the first shot, is honestly saying how remarkably powerful you are getting. There are only two other people I know who have used lightning, you, me, and Nerogroben. Nerogroben doesn't have direct control of it, as you seem to have," Burgesis continued as we walked back to the campsite.

"Get some rest, for now, Mark," said Barty looking at me.

I walked closer to the fire and set my sleeping bag down by it and laid down looking at the fire and started thinking about what had happened today. It was interesting to have met Dickens, I hoped to meet him again in more honest circumstances in the future. Burgesis had been right, I wasn't impressed with how our worlds were. I mean there is a lot of evils, in both worlds that are vamped up by so much fear, anger, frustration, greed, and jealousy. I mean, beings don't act the same way with courtesy and respect anymore as they used to. Overall, everyone can be selfish, and rude to each other without a care in the world of it is the effect on the other person's feelings or self-esteem. I wanted to try to change that, I made the promise to myself that if I wanted to make the difference in the lives of those around me, I needed to care more and try to set a better example.

"Is everything ok?" Jana asked looking curiously at me as she had just sat at my feet by the fire. Barty and Burgesis had already gone to sleep in the sleeping bags across from the fire.

"Yeah, I am just concerned that I may disappoint those who are loyal to me, I don't feel worthy to lead such an army, especially since I am not trained fully in all the elements yet," I said looking at Jana.

"I know you don't feel that you will do a good job now and you are not showing any self-confidence about this, but you have to understand that you can make a difference in our lives, and you will Mark!" said Jana

"But how? How can I make a difference in the lives of others around me?" I asked worriedly.

"Your so unsure of yourself that you don't realize that you have already made a difference for Barty and me," explained Jana. "Barty never used to be so worried about others and trusting so easily. You have boosted our confidence in your and therefore really do believe in you and the difference that you can make in our lives here in the World of the Unknown, you will do wonderfully Mark," said Jana who was smiling. "You have to remember that, to know how to use the elemental magic is different from knowing when to use it."

"How do I train more?" I asked. "I really didn't know what I was going to do, it just came to me. I just knew a bunch of Latin words and put them together. I realize that if I don't learn the elemental magic, as this whole world seems to depend on me to do, things could fall apart. I just feel so overwhelmed. I have a lot to learn still, and a long way to go before I could even begin to live up to everyone's expectations."

"You have to learn to control your emotions and be confident," said Burgesis suddenly from across the way.

"Sorry, but when you get worried, I can hear your thoughts. I can hear them so much louder than I normally can when you aren't stressed. I had fallen asleep, but you had woken me up, that is not cool," said Burgesis bitterly. "There are people out there who like me can read people's minds. You need to learn how to control your emotions, and block others out of your mind…"

"Who else can read minds?" I asked curiously.

"I know of only one other person, Brendan Alicea, the Chancellor's assistant," explained Burgesis. "Relax, you are going to be meeting some, pretty cool beings' tomorrow, who will see if you are the one if you pass their tests, and hopefully maybe they can help you train some more. You can sleep in peace since our perimeter is secure tonight Mark," said Jana happily. "Good night!"

The next morning, I was the last one to wake as everyone was getting ready to leave. They had almost finished packing up.

"We are heading out, it's only just a little way further to walk," said Barty.

Almost an hour later, we had been walking in silence still.

Burgesis turned to me and said, "It is close, ouch; you just stepped on my foot, Mark."

"I'm sorry Burgesis," I asked.

"The Rebels," Jana said as she pursed her lips nervously looking around at the trees. "Keep your voice down, we are almost at the house."

"The rebels?" I asked whisperingly as we had been on this path surrounded by this open field.

"Yes, some of the leaders of the clans of the people who might support you. We are in the Field of Dreams right now, and we are almost at the house," whispered Barty walking ahead of me as I saw bubbles floating in midair.

"Might support me?" I asked loudly.

"Shhh," said Jana as we carefully walked further. Two minutes later we came to a house, and it was dark inside, Burgesis said a phrase and waved his hand, the lights came on in the inside and I was ushered inside by Barty.

"It's strange that no one is here, I guess they will be here eventually," said Burgesis shrugging it off. I was surprised at how big the house was and we all were tired from all the walking. Burgesis took a guard first while we all started to get some rest in the living room. I had been sleeping in the living room with Barty and Jana, while Burgesis stood guard for maybe two hours before there was a loud crack and a boom. I opened my eyes, and I saw *at least* six figures in the darkness coming at us, and all that could be seen was bright lights hitting our protective shield from them.

Chapter 14
The Rebels

As they approached closer Burgesis yelled, "The Rebels!" and he removed the protective shield and turned a candle on. There were twenty-six beings/creatures in the room in total.

"Mark, I would like you to meet the leaders of the Rebellion Army (second in command after you if you are proven to be "the one") they represent each of the fourteen communities in the World of the Unknown," explained Burgesis smiling at them hugging and shaking their hands and replacing the protective shield around the house. Everyone gradually started walking into the huge room next to the living room.

"So let me explain the different communities and their protective magical guardians," Burgesis started. "First, of course, you already know Barty and Jana. They are both *Representatives of the Beaver Clan* as they continued to nod once being recognized. Everyone gradually then started to sit at this long table, that had appeared almost out of nowhere.

Burgesis looked at Barty and Jana as they sat down, and he pulled out one of the chairs for a couple of very beautiful, but small kid sized elves. Reading my thoughts, Burgesis said "Um, this is

Andrea and Mike Smitherton, of the Woodland Elms, that they guard and protect," Mike nodded at me as he had sat down next to Andrea. Everyone remained silent glaring at each other uncomfortably as they observed me closely. It felt awkward and I could feel the harsh discomfort in the room that everyone had with each other, and it made it difficult to breathe.

"This is *Alice and Jack Pillowdrum*, they are phoenixes who are very great travelers, and they have immortality," said Jana looking at Burgesis.

"We are *Chris and Elizabeth Ersal*, as you probably just heard we are recently engaged, we are fairies of the west at your service," said Elizabeth looking at me in awe and proceeded to sit at the table in an orderly fashion with everyone else.

"This is *Angie Cunnings*, and my name is *Martin Cunnings*," said Martin helping Angie into her seat. They both looked like foxes with orange hair and I turned to look at Burgesis to see how he turned away almost in disapproval as they sat down next to him who had sat at one end of the table.

"My name is *George*, and this is my wife, *Donna Eubinks*. We are trolls, and we humbly ask for your forgiveness. We are sorry to have caused such an upheaval in the realm of the World of the Unknown," he said looking around for comfort from the other leaders then to his wife who just looked down trying to avoid eye contact.

"You have failed us all, as a leader of the Trolls! You have made a critical error in judgment in the way in which you feel that your title makes you a leader in our community! You have failed in the way in which you handled the destruction of your clan. The trolls lack loyalty and respect to its leaders in your clan. They are weak because they are easily corruptible and greedy. You have lost loyalty from your subjects and it's irresponsible and disgraceful! We Magical Human Elves would never have allowed that to happen within our ranks! My name is *John Popper,* and this is my wife *Terry Popper,*" said John looking at George and Donna with disgust before looking at me. I could tell they were *Magical Human Elves* and not just elves. It was not only just because they are taller than the elves, but their eyes were naturally a purple color as Burgesis had previously explained as he smiled at me.

"They should be stripped of their leadership representation of this council," said George abruptly and everyone stood up and started yelling and shouting at one another for two minutes.

I sat observing everyone, and I stood up suddenly and shouted "SIIIILLLLENNNCE!!!! EVERYONE PLEASE!!!"

Almost as abruptly as everyone started shouting and arguing with one another they stopped and looked at Burgesis who said, "He is our new leader, let him speak because his word is final as he is indeed "the one."

"We shall see about that in time," said John Popper calmly as everyone muttered and then silenced. Everyone then turned their heads toward me in silence looking at me. As I sat down, and they all did the same seating themselves around the table.

"Thank you, I am so happy to be here, as I want to help things here in the World of the Unknown with good intent. I couldn't help but notice that it seems like you all don't get along. I need you to understand that without unity there can be no success. Without success, Nerogroben will thrive and he will become completely the ruler of the World of the Unknown as your world darkens. Which is why I am asking that if you are a leader in your clans, under loyalty to me, you will all learn to respect each other better. You will also end up being in complete peace. My name is Mark Trogmyer, and you all can call me Mark. Secondly, I need to be completely honest when I say that I can only help guide you all and can only help those who ask for it. Now back to my first issue, I want you to understand that more things can be accomplished without anger, judgement, distrust, and miscommunication. I know there are many disdainful feelings towards each other within our leadership and good leadership needs good direction otherwise, how can you hope to accomplish anything. You can't, it's not possible, you need trust, unity, and a shared common communication. Certainly, we can all agree on many things. First, what is going on in the World of the Unknown is unacceptable," I said looking around. Many looked to be persuaded to change their attitudes towards each other in the room as they nodded and agreed with me thus far. "Those who are causing the problems within this world need to be stopped. But how can we do this if we don't get along amongst ourselves? I must insist, what is of the past is now the past, it cannot be changed, it can only be learned from. It is my opinion, that George and Donna should stay on as our representative leaders from the trolls. I am sure that they are the only ones aware of only the trolls who may still be on our side, and they know who is against us. It is easy for us to shift blame towards a certain group of beings or creatures, but is this right? Good leaders provide trust unity, and shared common communication. But above all, love, peace, and forgiveness, can be the push that we all need with each other and within our own clans to push us forward. The fact remains that any one of you, could have stopped this chaos a long time ago had you all formed this leadership, got along, and communicated better with each other. How can we all move forward from these prejudices that we seem to have with one another? Those are the basics between all relationships in life that we need. I will not have my leaders quarreling with each other and criticizing each other's leadership roles. That is my duty, and to ensure, that there is; loyalty, trust, and respect through good leadership practices of myself, to you," I said looking around and everyone was nodding in agreement with my words. "I can only sympathize minimally for you George and Donna. While I respect that you came forward to me with humility and respect and are being responsible for taking the blame for this error in judgement, because that takes a lot of courage, and you should be proud of yourselves for that. However, now that I am here, I will be wanting to keep a closer eye on everyone's leadership ability. The reason being is, because in this world, you can turn up a rock or stone, and you never know what evil may be under it," I said looking at George and Donna who nodded as I started looking around the table at everyone who had their head down in shame for a while. As I looked around at everyone there I noticed that there were a few who hadn't introduced themselves yet looking towards the end of the table. "and who do we have left here?"

"My name is *Pine*, and this is my wife *Rose Plantoligong*," said Pine a small hummingbird at the end of the table who had sat next to the Ersals. "We oversee, the plants, the trees, and the bugs," I nodded in acknowledgement.

My name is *Danny*, and this is my wife *Jamie Fortescue*, we oversee the Giants in the east," said Danny the Giant smiling.

"Wonderful! Welcome!" I said happily smiling at Danny.

"My name is *Brittany* and my husbands' name is *James* we are the *Figwiggins*. We oversee the donkeys, the mules, and the horses, we are ancient creatures of old, we are wise, and we are..." said Brittany was taken aback.

"Unicorns," I said in awe standing up and walking towards them. "Sorry for interrupting you but in my world on Earth, one can only read of a unicorn's existence and not see one in person," I continued standing up and walking towards them as they walked up to the table. "You both are beautiful," I said as I touched them.

"Thank you," they both said together smiling.

"You still have three more couples to meet Mark," said Burgesis pointing at them standing by the wall.

"Oh right, yeah," I said retreating to my seat at the end of the table.

"We are Tom and Jerry, we are Ravens in charge of birds except for Eagles and Hummingbirds, we don't help them out," said Tom looking at me.

"As from this moment on all my leaders are going to be helping each other out no matter what community clan

they are from," I said looking around to everyone.

"That will be difficult since we have our own clans and communities and they at times, rival each other," said James looking around awkwardly.

"Ok well, this must be adjusted immediately. I want more frequent meetings like this so that we can all be on the same page and work on getting along better to start focusing on uniting everyone. Uniting everyone for the same cause, which is fortunately found in our hearts. We need peace for us all, and the only way this is going to work is if we actually try our best to work together and unite," I proclaimed. Lastly, there were two couples left in the campsite to sit down at this large table.

"Finally, this is Eggbert and Jenny Kromopolis, Eggbert is a warlock, and he has a higher class of Magic, and is extremely powerful," said Burgesis looking at Eggbert who had been smoking his pipe.

"It's a pleasure to meet you, Mark," said Eggbert

thoughtfully looking at me while he was smoking his pipe.

"This is his wife Jenny, she is not just a witch, but the Head Witch, of her clan. Last, but not least, Shirley and Matt Lookings, they are flying above us over our meeting. They have good hearing, and they are Eagles and who are keeping a sharp lookout for us all as per usual," continued Burgesis.

"Great! Thank you, Matt and Shirley, I appreciate it," I said aloud looking up in the sky at them. "So, what are you all doing here?" I asked expectantly.

"We are here for our meeting and to see if the rumors of

your arrival was true or not," said James looking at me.

"Well, here I am," I said looking around at everyone.

"Well for a little while longer you're going to be my protégé since you are not aware of what needs to be discussed now but definitely voice your opinion," said Burgesis as I nodded.

Chapter 15
The Protégé

After a few seconds of complete awkward silence, there came a loud booming voice.

Burgesis had stood up and said, "I call this meeting to order to let all the unknown, be known, in our world today, this day November 18, 3176. I, Mr. Burgesis, presiding speaker, along with Mark Trogmyer, "the one" of the seven, Supreme Chief Clan Leader of the Fourteen clans, guardian, and keeper of all that is known and unknown in the World of the Unknown. Accompanied today by twenty-six council member representatives of the realm and various clans. Mr. Barty Burgeons you have the floor to inform the council of your concerns without judgement or immediate opinion from others present," said Burgesis looking at Barty who nodded.

"Right well, thank you Mr. Speaker," said Barty looking at Burgesis seriously. "Item One, what are your plans for continuing the training for Mark?"

"Training?" I said Incredulously. "Training? I have been studying from this Latin book for what seems like weeks!" I complained looking at Barty and then I looked at Burgesis, slamming the book down in front of me as a few leaders around the table jumped in surprise as they looked at the book and then to Barty with raised eyebrows. Burgesis then put his hand up for me to calm down as he motioned for me to put the book away. "Do I honestly need more training? I have learned the elements of Earth, fire, wind, and water, you said yourself that I need to just learn the basics." I continued hotly.

"I am actually entrusting the rest of Mark's training to Eggbert Kromopolis at the School of the Unknown, where it will be safe from the likes of Nerogroben."

"It would be an honor," said Eggbert looking up from the table smiling as he raised a glass of water towards Burgesis as he took a swig of it and placed it down in front of him.

"This means that all future meetings will be at the School of the Unknown seeing that Mark wants more meetings and more frequently we will have them once a month instead of once every six months," continued Burgesis looking around for disapproval.

"That sounds good," said Barty looking confidently at Eggbert and then to his wife Jana, who was sitting next to him as she stood up.

"Item two, where and when is this war going to start and break out?" Jana asked nervously looking around at everyone and then she looked at me.

"This war is not going to be an easy one, it's going to be different from the last time," said Burgesis heavily. "As far as where and when this war is going to take place will be extremely dependent on Mark's strategy, his training, and his trainers of course. It's also going to be dependent on how fast he learns our clan lessons," said Burgesis looking around.

"Here, here!" said many of them.

"Clan lessons?" I asked confused. "What do you mean clan lessons? I am "the one," I thought that we were going right into war once I learned the basics of the elements?"

"What do you mean, you're "the one"? asked Eggbert as he frowned.

"You know "the one" who is prophesized about," I said impatiently.

"What lesson have you proved that you are worthy of our clans to be followed?" asked Danny the Giant.

"I am from Earth, I am the last known pure human child," I explained.

"I don't know that, we don't know that, how do I know that you are not a liar sitting there?" said Jamie Fortesque who agreed with her husband Danny who was sitting next to her.

"You see," explained Eggbert looking at Burgesis, Barty, and Jana and then looked straight at me seriously. "You may have been told that you are "the one." In many ways, they think you are "the one," but you must prove this to us, that you are even worthy of that title, to be followed with loyalty to fight Nerogroben and his loyalists."

"Why wouldn't I be?" I asked Eggbert seriously as he had smoked from his pipe thoughtfully.

"Each of our clans has a lesson that you need to pass to prove that you know and understand their lesson. Then it is at that point when we go to our clan councils and our clans and tell them about you. We tell them what happened during the test we gave you and why we think that you deserve our loyalty," explained Eggbert as he then smoked his pipe again. Danny and Jamie Fortesque nodded in agreement.

"So far," explained Danny in front of everyone as my ears turned red. "Let it be known that Mark has failed our clan lesson thus far, he lacks humility."

I started to tear in sadness, as Eggbert was eying me the whole time while smoking his pipe after explaining.

"You see Mark, you may have been selected by Whiskers on Earth, but you have a lot to prove to them," explained Burgesis "They all have to go back to their clans and tell them to join our cause. The issue is, without proper cause, we cannot hope to gain full support. That is why it's crucial that

Eggbert and the Wizards and teachers at the School of the Unknown teach you."

"Fair warning, your grace, I am not an easy trainer. Now that you are supposedly finished the basics, you might find it easy, or difficult to continue. It is all depending on your skills and how well you were taught the basics," said Eggbert looking at Burgesis while smoking his pipe. Eggbert then looked up turning away looking at the others and asked.

"What's the status report Matt and Shirley?"

"We have sightings and reports that Nerogroben, has been reacting out of fear, after hearing from others that "the one," has returned, or is going to return. We have learned that he has doubled his guard and his patrols. His spies are anxious to find out about any information on his whereabouts, etc. of where "the one" is," said Matt swooping down on an empty chair at the table.

"What if we are followed? We have also heard some other reports that there is a weapon that he is furnishing in his castle to use against "the one." The knowledge of what it is and what it does has been well hidden, deep within his castle, Valfador, in Creaton," said Shirley looking at Burgesis worriedly after she had swooped down sitting on the edge of the chair where Matt was.

"We could set off a false trail leading away from us as we travel," suggested Danny.

"Do we have any proof or knowledge of what this weapon is, or what we may be up against, Eggbert?" Burgesis asked curiously.

"Unfortunately, our powers in the magical realm are not allowing us to foresee anything within Valfador, it has protections that are so strong and dark they are almost unspeakable!" said Eggbert shuddering to look at his wife Jenny who was afraid.

"This is intriguing, and none of you have heard anything about this "secret weapon" of Nerogroben's?" asked Barty astounded looking around the table.

"Our spies say that it can lock itself on the good in the hearts of others and shoots automatically a stronger from of Grey Matter and it has a very good success rate," said Martin smugly.

"*You are a fox*; how can you know?" said Barty frustrated looking at Martin.

"We are sly and have the abilities to play both sides of the coin where needed," said Angie confidently.

"Wait, how is it that you don't know anything about the secret weapon Burgesis?" I thought, he looked at me and said aloud "I wasn't there when that was started, Mark."

"Enough! Can we move on, please? I don't want us to be caught here for too long with our pants down with "the one" here before he is even fully trained. We have a wedding to plan! What is the next item on the list?" said Chris the fairy looking at his wife Elizabeth impatiently, who nodded in agreement. There was a muttering of agreement around the table and then Jack the Phoenix said, "Item 3: What are we doing about the protection of "the one," while he is training and in training?"

"Are you seriously doubting the protections and enchantments that are at my school?" asked Eggbert looking around at Jack with his eyebrows raised indignantly.

"We are," said Alice looking at Burgesis for backup slowly "Time and time again, we can see how so much evil can soak through the walls of that school. We are concerned about the protection of the School of the Unknown, and of course, our children that are there."

"What do you suggest?" asked Jana looking around.

"We are suggesting that each of the representatives of the realm add additional security and security sweeps, protections, and take shifts guarding the school and protecting "the one," while he is in training," said Jack looking at the others who seemed to mutter amongst themselves. Everyone then looked at Eggbert who was flabbergasted and had turned a dark red.

"We all need to agree about this, this means everyone," said Burgesis looking at Eggbert slowly. "I have never been so offended in my life! For the realm to feel as if the school isn't perfectly well protected, in the first place," said Eggbert incredulously.

"We are, after all, wanting to carefully hold concern over the protection of "the one," at least, while he is in training. It is also a matter of the security for the futures of us here of the World of the Unknown," said Alice looking at Eggbert and his wife Jenny.

Jenny finally nodded and looked at Eggbert and put her hand on her husbands in comfort.

"They are right, we need as much help and protection from the rebels against Nerogroben's Army as possible," said Jenny. "This would make the school impenetrable and would add more protection for NOT just "the one," but our students this year as well."

Eggbert put his finger up and holding his pipe in the other hand as he leaned forward and said: "Oh alright, but this cannot interfere with the daily activities of the school."

"On record please take note that Eggbert Headmaster of the School of the Unknown, and his wife Jenny, both agree to the added protection to their school. This will occur during the time of

Mark's training. This will only be there at the school until such time when Mark is finished with his training, as of this day. Protections will be added upon the arrival of Mark to the School of the Unknown," said Burgesis.

"How is he traveling to the school without detection?" asked Jana looking at Barty curiously.

"That is next item of this list," said Barty looking at the parchment list in front of him and then to Burgesis.

"Before we move on to that next item on the list, I was going to ask this council first to vote in unanimous agreement that we all add protective charms and magic native to our own clans and do security sweeps and patrols at the school upon his arrival to the school. Can we all say "yes," in agreement before moving on to the next and final part of this itemized list?" asked Burgesis looking around at everyone.

Everyone in the room said "Yes," this time except Angie and Martin, the foxes, and everyone looked at them in expectation.

"We agree but only to do security sweeps daily during the time "the one," is there training, we are not adding our magical clan powers to the school as they are not only instinctual to us, but they are also sacred," said Martin slowly as Angie nodded her head in agreement with her husband.

"Then it is settled then, let the record be known that all the leaders in the realm agreed to add protection in the School of the Unknown during Mark's training," Burgesis said.

"The next item on this list I want to discuss is the temporary displacement of the eleven clans," said Mike Smitherton the small elf carefully. "I want to apologize to everyone, but this is the most unfortunate thing that I have had to decide to do since our clan is ever growing."

Everyone mumbled.

"I know that as elves, we are not on the highest of the hierarchy here, but we request an expansion of our clan," said Andrea carefully.

"You sit here at this table and put us here in this position in front of "the one," to try to inherit more of our lands! You're a growing disgust to the rest of us with your teachings of very extremist views and pushing it on us all in our own clans! Its propaganda from your clan that has influenced our world as well!" said Tom angrily looking at Jerry. "Our clan has gotten bigger, but you don't see us requesting more land!"

"But in all fairness, you all have the skies and various trees etc. Our clan is very sophisticated and has their homes traditionally built a certain way," explained Mike slowly looking at me.

"What is going on?" I asked trying to understand what the big deal was.

"Well to get more land, we must submit a request with the leaders so that we can spread ourselves out further," said Andrea looking at me. "Our clan can't prosper in such tight quarters."

Andrea finished looking at Tom and Jerry frustrated.

"Why aren't we attempting to try to get along with everyone better and being more tolerant of each other?" I asked looking around the table as there was silence again.

"What do you mean by spreading propaganda?" I asked Tom carefully.

"Their extremist views within their clan have changed the very fabric of our society," said Jerry.

"What do you mean extremist views?" I asked.

"Some of their teachings have been that there shouldn't be any separation of the clans. That we all should be living together, communal living of some sort," said Tom.

"Why wouldn't that be a good idea?" I asked carefully as the rest of the table was in shock and had their mouths opened.

"We have always stayed within our own clans, and we know our own ways in which we do things," said Barty abruptly as he was the first to recover.

"You know, the way in which things were explained to me by Burgesis was that Magical Creatures and Magical Human Elves used to live together, and now they don't. How is that different from how things could be out here?" I asked carefully. "I mean who's to say that an elf cannot sleep next to a unicorn on a cold night?"

"We would never!" said Brittany in disgust. "Our kind is pure, and we don't "hang out" with the likes *them*! They want us to have each other protect each other from Nerogroben risking our own lives for someone beneath us. They want us to trust everyone and turn a blind eye to those who are prejudice against us and have been more welcoming to others. How can we do that if we are all different?"

"Well, things are going to change," I said. "We need to be more tolerant of each other, otherwise how do you think we are going to overcome this Grey Matter? If my leaders can't get along, then what do you think is going to happen when our rebels get together?"

"But the rebels are already together," said Jana carefully.

"Oh, so they get along, and they are okay sleeping in the same quarters and there is open communication with everyone?" I asked.

"No, there isn't open communication, and they certainly don't sleep in the same rooms, but they do get along without fighting with one another," said Burgesis.

"We need unity, we need to get along better," I insisted looking around shaking my head.

"What is the next item on the list?" I asked Burgesis.

"Finally, the last item on the list for today, the moving of Mark. Due to the security behind this detail, only eleven of us will know exactly what is going on and what will happen. As for the rest of us, the meeting is adjourned. Mark will be picking his security detail of those whom he feels he can trust," said Burgesis looking down at the table and avoiding eye contact with me and everyone else stared looking at me.

Chapter 16
The Guard

"First, I am honored to be able to pick my own security detail. Being that this whole journey has started with you three," I said looking at Barty, Jana, and then Burgesis. "I am first going to be picking, and by right, you ought to be at my side on top of the Security detail, *Burgesis*, I am also picking *Jana*, and *Barty Burgeons*. Obviously, since it is Eggbert's and Jenny's School I would like *Eggbert* to come along as part of the protection detail. I was also hoping he would give me a tour of the school upon arrival as well," I continued as the Eggbert smiled and nodded. "Since it was *Alice* and *Jack Pillowdrum* who brought up the need for my protecting, I would like them both to be a part of my security detail. I would also like *Matt Lookings* the eagle and *Chris Ersal* the Fairy. I would also like *John of the Magical Humans, Brittany of the Unicorns*, and *Tom of the Ravens* to join the security detail," I said as each of the specific members nodded and smiled and said words of thanks for the honor of being selected as part of my security detail.

"Let it be known that the eleven of us are a part of the security detail for "the one," said Burgesis looking around to the others. "Now I am closing this meeting for today and those of you who were chosen as part of this security detail, please stay behind."

So, I stood up from the table and I waited by the door to gradually say goodbyes to the remaining people, Andrea and Mike Smitherton of the elves, Elizabeth from the fairies as she also hugged and kissed her husband goodbye. Next to leave was James and Donna of the Trolls who respectfully nodded before they left. Terry from the Magical Humans as she also said goodbye to her husband. Pine and Rose of the Hummingbirds were the next to leave.

Danny and Jamie of the Giants were next to leave as they shook my hand but before leaving Jamie said to me "Remember the word humility, and be humble," I nodded as I hugged her goodbye.

Next to leave was James from the Unicorns whom also said goodbye to his wife Brittany. Jerry of the Ravens left shortly after as he said goodbye to his partner Tom. Shirley from the eagles left the room and was the last to leave, as she said goodbye to her husband Matt.

Burgesis closed the door of the house and added a few more protective charms in the room. I sat down and just those whom I had selected for The Guard, had stayed in their seats.

"I *must* impress upon each of you that no one is supposed to speak of this to anyone I added a few protective charms on the door so as you leave you will be silenced on all matters regarding today's meeting and regarding the matters of the security detail of Mark, who we believe is "the one." Do you all agree to uphold the secrecy of this meeting until death do you part?" said Burgesis carefully looking at everyone.

"Yes, we all agree to uphold the secrecy of this meeting even until death," Eggbert said as everyone nodded without flaw and then there was a flash of blue light that encircled us for a few minutes at the table and then orange flickering lights came out of it and it disappeared.

"Now that this was settled, what *IS* the plan?" asked Barty looking around at the rest of the newly elected guard for answers or ideas.

"The problem first that we need to figure out is, which route we should take and how we should safely get the boy to the school without being seen or noticed. If he just has basic training who knows how he would do against Nerogroben's men right now," said Matt Lookings the Eagle who had been flying above the meeting earlier but had perched himself on the top end of the chair and had seated himself comfortably looking around concerned as he had finished talking.

"You're right," said Alice the phoenix agreement, "Then we can figure out the safest way to move around him as his guard."

"We are right now in the middle of the Field of Dreams, why don't we go south first through the cover of the barren desert then through the Mountains of Perseverance and through the Red Valley of Skulls?" asked Eggbert looking around.

"No, not through the Red Valley of Skulls or *those* mountains, it is not safe and that Valley stinks of blood and has flies everywhere still from the last Dark War," said Burgesis carefully as he pulled out a map thoughtfully from his jacket. I wondered why it was called the Red Valley of Skulls but thought it was better not to ask now.

"I think the best route is through the Greens of Middle Kingdom, through then through Beaver Valley down to the River Ritz and then through the River of Desperation where there is a secret entrance to Metromark. Then we can go to the School of the Unknown from Metromark if we can get some assistance from our friends John carefully. With the right permissions, this may be possible," continued Burgesis looking at Barty and then at John.

John was looking blankly and then sat up straighter in his chair noticing he was being talked to and said, "Oh, um, yes, maybe I can get the right clearance, if not, we may get caught and it might get us into trouble, if by the wrong people. Give me some time to get clearance on my end, otherwise I may have another way we can get to the school," said John confidently as everyone was looking at him with great interest.

"I will first send a message to Chancellor Rain and see if I can get permission and clearance for us to go to the school through the protection of Metromark," said John looking at me and then grabbed a paper and pen and wrote out a letter. As soon as he finished writing the letter he folded it up, wrapped it around his finger, and said "Praemittere." Then Burgesis whispered in my ear, "it means "send forward" in Latin," as I had wondered what "Praemittere" meant. Then blue flames appeared from his fingers and surrounded the letter and then the letter disappeared.

"I should find out rather quickly," said John looking around at everyone amused.

Three minutes later, after much silence, there was a green flame that appeared over John's hand and in it was a piece of paper floating. John grabbed the piece of paper slowly that was floating in front of him over his hand and he opened the paper. He nodded his head as he read the paper aloud.

"You have permission for The Guard to enter the School of the Unknown through the Guarded City of

Metromark. Under the condition that it isn't in an act of war against the city. Nor can you stay there in our city for too long within its walls, out in the open," said John smiling.

"Is this the only safest way?" I asked Burgesis unsurely

"We are kind of safe, doesn't this break the accords that we have with Metromark?" Barty interrupted looking at John and then to Burgesis. Burgesis reading my mind said "The accords that Barty is speaking of, the one he fears that we are breaking, are the ones made between Metromark and Valfador. Which is, of course, Nerogroben's Castle within Creaton, and his army, and loyalists. When Nerogroben had started to come to power, the negotiation that was approved between him for the Magical Creatures and Chancellor Rain for the Magical Humans with the hope that they could co-exist, if no acts of war were brought onto each other. This also meant that no one could enter Metromark without approval and consent of both Metromark and the city of Creaton and the castle of Valfador."

"Which means, that if we aren't caught sneaking in, we will be ok," said John.

"This all seems kind of risky," said Barty whose voice sounded distrusting as he pointed a finger at John who shook his head and looked seriously at me.

"Wait, how are you able to get here and leave Metromark then?" I interrupted and asked raising my eyebrows surprised.

"Through the same way, through the school," said John calmly smiling.

"It's been foretold of "the one's" arrival, Chancellor Rain of the Guarded City Metromark, also asked me and my wife to represent the city, secretly, of course," said John looking at me.

"Oh, so that's how you can get away with it," I said aloud looking at John.

"We wouldn't say get away with it because we aren't here to start trouble," said John assuredly.

"But you are willing to be the cause of the start of the trouble here, aren't you?" said Brittany indignantly.

"We just hope to be on the winning side of things you could say, your powers are legend that you have within you. It is our hope that we can help you in that way so that you can use them properly with the best training," said John looking at Eggbert.

"If we don't get caught going to the school, I can assume that this is the safest route for us," Burgesis said confidently to me.

"What do you mean if? Call me crazy here or paranoid for that matter, but I just want to make sure that this route that we take, is not for granted. Are you sure that this is more than secure, Burgesis?" asked Barty incredulously.

"What happens if we are caught by the wrong person?" I asked Burgesis curiously looking at him next to me at the table.

"Then this war starts sooner than everyone anticipated,"

said Burgesis grimly as he slowly looked at me and then to the now silent guard.

"Chancellor Rain wanted me to apologize to you personally that he couldn't be here to meet you. Politics just forbade this. Just him leaving Metromark would be an act of war," said John carefully as I nodded in understanding.

"So, we will attempt this route as planned, meeting adjourned..." said Burgesis as everyone started to slowly gather their things and stand up.

"No, we are not done with this meeting yet!" I interrupted, and everyone quickly sat down with their eyes wide open looking at Burgesis and then to me.

"I'm sorry but we need to figure out when and how this will happen," I said looking at everyone.

"Oh, that's right, I am sorry," said Burgesis looking at everyone flustered

"I need two days' time to clear the travel with Metromark," said John looking at Burgesis carefully.

"This needs to be played under the radar from most people of his arrival because he isn't fully trained yet."

"Clearly," said Eggbert looking at me smiling. "No one knows this more than I, but as far as how we are traveling there I have been contemplating that very same issue," Eggbert said looking around.

"We need to do this *very* quickly and under *good* cover and without notice," said Barty sternly looking at Eggbert.

"Obviously, and someone as narrow minded as a beaver could not have come up with any more of a cleverer idea than I have," said Eggbert sounding slightly annoyed as he looked up at me and winked, "Who likes traveling in pea soup?" He asked calmly. Everyone sat rather quietly and confused.

Chapter 17
Harmony Meadow

Meanwhile, during The Guard meeting, not far away in Harmony Meadow there is a Nerogroben scout camp house. In this house lives a loyal Elven family to Nerogroben's Army. They have lived there for a long time, they have a 15-year-old boy, Eladius. "Son, someday you will understand what's involved with supporting this family. You will then know what Nerogroben, and his men are like. Someday you will learn that you, just have to suck it up, and pledge allegiance to that king, no matter the circumstances of his decisions, that you may or may not fully agree with. Still, it is what it is, for this is a burden of loyalty," said Andrew to his son Eladius in their living-room who was sitting down. "Dad, you have complained to me in the past, that ever since the Dark Wars of Nerogroben, things have been difficult for us. You have always said that the pay to give information to Nerogroben isn't much to survive on. Why don't we do something else about it, instead of trying to be comfortable with where we are and struggling all of the time?" asked Eladius looking down on the floor.
 "Your mom and I pledged our loyalty to the king when

we were of age. It is our credit to him that we have food in our home, a bed to sleep on every night, and a home," said Andrew his elven father gratefully.

"But he is an evil king, who kills people, and tortures them within his castle walls, how could you support that?" said Eladius surprised at his own words.

"I know son, but we don't have a choice. This is all we know, and we can't get out of this situation. How would we survive? Who would help us?" said Andrew looking at his son, worriedly.

"Mary at the camp scout house on the bridge says, there is another King who has just arrived, who is going to change things," said Eladius looking at his father in desperation, who then had looked at his wife, Pam.

"Why can't we side with him, if he is a good and fair king?" Eladius asked his parents.

"Do Mary's parents know this information?" asked Pam curiously.

"I don't know, but I am tired of staying here all the time!" said Eladius anxiously as he sat up on the couch, "I want to see what's out there! I wanna see what our world has in store for us! I wanna go on an adventure and see other clans! Aren't you curious to see what's out there? Haven't you know that there is more than this meadow out there? Aren't you curious as to where those waters lead? What places we could go just by following the waters currently, I mean maybe they would lead us to this other king, I heard about!"

"Stop talking nonsense, go play in the meadow with Mary before it is time for bed. Also, you had better tell Mary, not to speak of that information to anyone," snapped Andrew's wife Pam in an almost inaudible whisper while looking at Eladius and then to her husband. Eladius started to go outside and out of frustration he said, "When I turn 18, I am not giving my allegiance to that murderous King Nerogroben!" and he stormed out the door.

"I don't know, but if he isn't careful and keeps talking like that to the wrong person, he could be killed, or they could question us for treason!" said Pam worriedly.

"The only people who we know, who would know if this information is true is Andrea and Mike Smitherton," said Andrew carefully. "I should contact them, or take a trip there if I can't reach them, and talk to them,"

"But that is all the way in the Elven lands of Goldor by the Woodland Elms," said Pam.

"Then I will talk to them through our fire and add antitracking powder to it," said Andrew looking at his wife desperately.

"Are you sure that's wise?" asked Pam.

"Yeah it's worth the risk," said Andrew looking at the fireplace and starting to prepare it. He pulled out a brick in the fire place and revealed it is hollow inside with a plastic over the back of it. Andrew pulled the plastic piece off the back of the brick revealing blue and red powder in it, which he added a few pinches of it to the flames, which turned green. Then he replaced the brick in the fireplace wall and stepped into the fire and said, "Mike Smitherton" and he turned around to face the inside of the fireplace and saw that Mike Smitherton was sitting at a desk in his office.
"Hey Mike, is it safe to talk?" asked Andrew through the flames.
"Yes, it is safe to talk, it is only you and I here," said Mike to the flames from his desk not looking up.
"Um, we heard some news that "the one" has arrived, can you confirm this information?" asked Andrew to Mike, who didn't react to the news.
"If you are reporting this, I am sure that I don't know what you mean. One hears many whispers and rumors among the wilderness, you shouldn't trust such gusts of wind," said Mike who didn't react to being questioned.
"It's alright Mike, I am not here to officially report anything," said Andrew carefully.
"Unfortunately, I am sorry, on or off the record I

cannot confirm or deny this bit of information," said Mike continuing to look at papers on his desk and not looking at Andrew.

"Would it be possible for me to see you in person to discuss this?" asked Andrew carefully.

"Yes, in a few weeks, you can come by and meet me at our usual place away from the clan, goodbye," said Mike still not even looking at Andrew.

Andrew stepped away from the flames and they changed back to their normal color. Andrew stepped further away from adding water from a bucket that was full next to the fireplace at the flames and started to remake the fire confused and unsure what to make of what just happened.

"That was interesting Pam, usually I can rely on Mike for information," said Andrew curiously looking at his wife after a small flame had started to crackle at the freshly made fire, now made with fresh dry wood. Andrew had recounted what had happened to his wife.

"Well then it must be true if this is a heavily guarded rumor and you know he wouldn't make you travel that far if there wasn't any truth in that matter," said Pam slowly.

"No, you're right, and I think Eladius is coming on to something..." said Andrew carefully looking at his wife.

"Why? What do you mean not say anything? Do you realize that we could get precious gold and treasures if we report this?" asked Pam incredulously. "If we don't report this, we could be killed or worse tortured?"

"No, my loyalty is to my family first then to the ruler, and I don't believe Nerogroben is our answer to a happy future for any of us like I used to believe. Pam, you say this all the time, "we will get a lot of gold," but in the end, we only end up with a few pieces of silver, and that's it," said Andrew "then for what? So Nerogroben's Army can go and kill people or torture them? How does this make it right? What are we trying to teach our son? To be evil or to be good?"

"Oh no, you don't! No! Don't you turn that one on me! So now, after all these years, 15 years, you are saying that your allegiance to King Nerogroben is nullified now? After all those nights of us crying ourselves to sleep. After all those days, and nights of hearing those screams from our neighbors, now, your denouncing him?" asked

Pam with eyebrows raised and she was now shouting.

"Have you heard what has been foretold about "the one"?" asked Andrew to his wife who was sitting at the kitchen table across from him with her arms crossed.

"Yeah, yes, I have heard, but that isn't said to happen in our lifetime! He "supposedly" has the power to change people's hearts and get rid of all the Grey Matter. Also, we wouldn't have to live around fire camp lights as much anymore. That we will then start to feel and see natural heat and light around us instead of the clouds of the Grey Matter covering the sun," said Pam sarcastically.

"I think we should become double agents for this new king!" said Andrew smiling at the idea and at Pam.

Pam looked at her husband shuddering, and said "Are you out of your mind? Do you realize what you are saying, double agents? We could be killed if we are caught or worse treated as spies. What will everyone at the other scout camps say and do?"

"Who cares!" said Andrew excitedly. "Who cares what others think and say! We both know that right now that we are still struggling and stressed that we may not have enough information to report to Nerogroben's men to keep us open. We are barely getting by, and we are already spies! I can't expect change if I don't change what I am already doing! You must understand that what we have been doing, what we are doing, it isn't and hasn't made things easier. In fact, over the years' things have gotten worse for us. I think this could be the open door that we needed!" said Andrew continuing on surprised at his own words as he was smiling.

"Why are you so happy suddenly, Andrew? I think you should talk to Mike first about this whole rumor because he *was* our leader and we don't want to report it if it is false," said Pam worriedly looking at Andrew who was still smiling at the table.

Pam stood up and called out their door "Eladius! It's time to come inside for bed!" She then came back into the kitchen to her husband who was still sitting at the table smiling at her. "Not a word of this to Eladius, Andrew!"

Andrew kept quiet and nodded as he hid his smile. It was then that Eladius threw his last stone in his hand in the meadow as it skipped and then he turned to go inside.

Eladius headed into bed thinking about what it would be like to meet "the one." He fell asleep with his window open next to his bed. Andrew followed suit shortly afterwards and went to bed that night with a feeling of hope, smiling, something that since the Dark War, he had scarcely felt and done in years.

Chapter 18
The Guard Continued

Meanwhile, back at the meeting everyone still sat around the table rather quietly and confused...
"What do you mean, pea soup?" said Brittany looking at Eggbert
"Well, what I mean is, that in a few days' time, we can expect fog as thick as pea soup. You won't be able to see but a few inches in front of you. This would be the safest way to travel, other than maybe except for possibly night," said Eggbert still annoyed.
"This would provide good cover for Mark," said Burgesis thoughtfully.
"I agree," said Barty nodding his head looking around at the others in the guard.
"He can ride on me so that we can be sure to get going faster before anyone realizes what is going on," said Brittany looking at me.
I smiled back.
"Right and Barty and I will walk ahead of you to protect the front and the ground below," said Jana putting her head on Barty's shoulders.
"John and I will be on the front sides of you to make sure no one sneaks at us from around corners," said Burgesis.

"Alice and Jack can be in the air with me protecting the skies above making sure to warn you all of the people ahead of you, or behind you, so they don't attack," said Matt Lookings the eagle.

"The same goes for me too," said Tom the raven.

"Eggbert and I will be on guard in the rear then," said Chris the fairy.

"This all sounds like a good movement plan," said Burgesis.

"I like this idea," I said smiling. "Great work! The meeting is adjourned!"

Everyone stood up after I stood up, as they left they all kissed my hand in respect as they said their goodbyes and went into the night air of the Field of Dreams. The only people left were Barty, Jana, Burgesis, Eggbert, and myself.

I walked back into the house and Eggbert had sat in a love seat chair after he had changed the room into a more comfortable family room. He then pulled out his pipe from his robe and started to smoke it. I observed him silently for a while as he looked as if he was deep in thought. Suddenly, there was a wide smile on his face as he looked at me.

"So tell me, Mark, how far has your training gone? What are the basics that you know?" said Eggbert looking at him. "I couldn't help but notice you seemed like you had never seen a map of the

World of the Unknown, after Burgesis had taken it out," said Eggbert looking at me.

"Yeah that was the first time I saw the map of the World of the Unknown and I know the four basic elements," I said.

"Burgesis take out your map and show it to Mark. He ought to be taught that basic resource first," said Eggbert as he put the end of his pipe in between his teeth and sat up. Burgesis looked at the wizard and reluctantly pulled out the map and laid it on the coffee table in front of all of us. Eggbert helped Burgesis add weights to the corners of the map to keep it still. There was a small breeze coming from the window into the living-room, as I sat on the couch, and Eggbert sat across from us.

"You see this is the World of the Unknown," Eggbert explained showing me and then he used his left hand and waved it across the top of the map and with his pipe still in his mouth partially he said "Revelio." The map came to life and became three dimensional with a holographic look to it off the table.

"Woah!" I said surprised.

"You see this, is really, the World of the Unknown," said Eggbert and as you touched each part of the map the area would zoom in and it showed who was there in real time and what was going on.

"Show off," said Burgesis crossing his arms.

"Our magic is so powerful and so unlimited, that it is so much more than the elements!" said Eggbert looking at Burgesis.

"I want you to meet someone," said Eggbert he then touched above the area of Harmony Meadow which was like the rest of the World of the Unknown, beautiful. The map then zoomed in to an Elf whom was sleeping in his bed. "This is Eladius, he has already made changes that will affect our futures as of today," continued Eggbert looking at Barty and Jana.

"Harmony Meadow is a very beautiful place that has good and evils inside it," said Eggbert to Burgesis.

"I thought Harmony Meadow was being controlled by two scout camp houses," said Barty looking at Burgesis and Eggbert suspiciously.

"Not anymore! You see there is still goodness in us all. Earlier today, after our meeting, Mike Smitherton met with Eladius's Dad, Andrew, and no, he didn't share any information of your presence here Mark. But Eladius has given birth to new hope within his father, Andrew. This simple fact has attracted us wizards to this family. My brother wizards and I realized after today, that there is plenty of hope for us all. This hope was born within their family, and therefore spread to my brother wizards. The faith that we have for the World of the Unknown has been strengthen today. Eladius has started to help his parents to see that following Nerogroben isn't helping his family. Rather it's killing others, leads to their torture and distrust of others as well. This has brought hope into our world," explained Eggbert as everyone was watching Eladius and Andrew sleeping. "But you must realize the outcome of this," said Eggbert as he pulled out his hand again from his robe and said, "Futurero," and the map futuristically showed what would/could happen....

Chapter 19
Hope

"Mike Smitherton said, "That Andrew must go to see him in a few weeks, to know more about the existence of "the one," the problem is that this can split families too," said Eggbert to me.

"So, what, families are split all the time because of mixed loyalty," said Barty crossing his arms.

"What do you mean?" I asked Eggbert worriedly looking at the map.

"His mom, his wife," said Eggbert as the images changed from Pam to Eladius and to Andrew and then to Pam again, "Is extremely loyal to Nerogroben. I'm afraid that this is going to separate his family up because of her lack of loyalty to you," Eggbert stayed silent.

"What do we do to people who are loyal to Nerogroben that we catch?" I asked Burgesis who looked at me silently observing me and not responding.

"What do they do to us? We do the same, we imprison, torture, and kill them as well. They are treasonous people!" said Barty who snorted in smugness.

"Eggbert, please bring Eladius and his family to the school upon my arrival and ensure their safety. Have them stay at the school with me there," I asked looking at Eggbert who shook his head sadly before I even asked him.

"That will not be possible, I'm afraid my brothers would not agree to that," said Eggbert carefully.

"Then send word to Mike to invite them sooner to his place and instead of going to the school. First, we shall go to the Elven lands of Goldor," I said confidently.

"That would be most unwise Mark," said Jana looking at me.

"She will be a traitor, what's the point of wasting your time, and our time on this issue?" said Barty impatiently to Eggbert, almost sounding angry.

"Then I want you to bring them here Eggbert," I concluded stubbornly not paying attention to the impatient sounds coming from Barty and Jana.

"WHAT?!" said Jana, Barty, and Burgesis altogether.

"Here? To this house, this is a secret meeting house," said Barty wide eyed.

"All the safer and the more reason to keep them asleep for now while transporting them," I said.

"We have two extra rooms here I want them to be brought here while in their beds to those extra rooms upstairs and keep them in a deep sleep while doing so," I commanded Eggbert who looked at me.

"My child, why do you want them here and why right now?" Eggbert asked.

"Because I know what it is like to lose someone, and I don't want it to happen to Eladius," I said looking at Burgesis, who nodded in understanding. "After all, even you said, "With magic can do so much more," I repeated his words looking at Eggbert who had looked at me and was about to say something, but then bowed his head, and left the room. While watching the map, one by one, each of them, Eladius, Andrew, and Pam, disappeared and three bangs could be heard upstairs. Eggbert came down the stairs and out of the next room.

"You realize that they are going to be scared and worried at first when they wake up," said Eggbert sitting down again.

"They won't wake until I ask you to wake them, right?" I asked him.

"That is correct," said Eggbert. "But if you don't wake them up after seven hours the deep sleep can lead to a deep everlasting sleep until death."

"I want you to lock their doors," said Barty looking at Eggbert. "They are criminals, the enemy, I don't trust them!"

"You don't know them Barty, open your heart, forgive others for their bad choices and wrongdoing. Then forgive yourselves for judging and thinking ill of others around you," I said calmly looking at Barty and Jana who crossed their arms.

"Nor do you, you don't know them either! We know what they are capable of and that's enough for me!" said Jana next to me agreeing with Barty as she put her hand on his leg and he nodded stubbornly.

"We are all capable of great things both good, and bad. At least, listen to what I am saying, trust me, I am saying open your hearts," I told them as I got up and left the room. Burgesis who had been sitting next to me on the couch followed suit, as Jana and Barty sat open mouthed. Eggbert picked up his tea mug off the coffee table in front of them and smiled behind his mug and drank quietly.

"I hope you know what you are doing," said Burgesis to me quietly as we walked outside the house.

"I do," I said confidently as I sat on the bench outside the house looking out into the field.

"I have faith in you," Burgesis said, as he sat next to me on the bench outside. "Like they say on Earth: Are you trying to kill two birds with one stone? Like are you trying to help them to switch to our side by having them spy for us? Or are you trying to punish them for their crime of treason?" asked Burgesis looking at me as I was looking at the sky.

"You can do far more with a stone and two birds then just kill the two birds with "the one" stone," I

said confidently picking up a rock off the ground by my feet. *"You can throw the stone and miss to save them both from certain death,"* I said as I threw the rock and smiled at Burgesis who was already smiling, and I placed my hand on his shoulder before walking back inside slowly.

Everyone was where I had left them, and I said to Eggbert, "First I want you to bring Eladius outside to me and then wake him up while I am sitting next to him." Eggbert left the room. I then went back outside sitting on the long bench and Burgesis was still outside standing and looking around as I had come outside again.

"Eggbert is bringing Eladius outside, I need an extra shield of protection out here if possible," I said quietly to Burgesis who nodded and followed suit with his hand.

Within a minute, Eggbert placed Eladius on his back and put his head on my legs and put his hand on Eladius forehead and closed his eyes and whispered some words and slowly Eladius woke up. Eladius opened his eyes as I pushed his long hair back out of his eyes as he slowly opened them and looked at me.

"Where am I? Who are you?" Eladius said worriedly slowly getting up.

"My name is Mark Trogmyer, some have called me "the one," but I would prefer you to just call me

Mark. I would prefer you to see me as your equal, you are awake, and you are not dreaming. I have summoned you by the great Wizard, Eggbert, who brought you here to my secret home," I said to him calmly.

"Eladius, I need you to confirm with me something that has been brought to my attention. I have heard that you have faith in me, and that you wish you and your family were disbanded from the hands of Nerogroben and his army," I said looking at Eladius who was shocked and who stood up in front of me.

"This is true, and how do you know my name? What makes me so special that you know my name," he asked

me suddenly aware that he was addressing me and bowed and added. "I'm sorry, your highness, Mark."

"If this is true, then it is my duty to know all those who follow me by name. I want you to know you are safe and you are free to speak your mind. You don't have to bow your head Eladius or call me your highness," I said calmly.

"Where are my parents?" Eladius asked raising his head smiling at me.

"They will be out here momentarily, it has been my wish to speak to you and your family," I said and nodded to Eggbert and then he disappeared to go and bring Andrew and his wife, Pam out.

"Why do you want to talk to us?" Eladius said to me sounding scared.

"I want you to trust me and not be afraid of me like your family is of Nerogroben. I want you to know that you can trust me. I have had you brought here safely, and I have ensured your safety here," I said looking at Eladius who tried to grab my hand and kiss it.

"You don't need to pay homage to me my friend, and I am simply making sure that you know that you can trust me. You will be brought safely back home after I have chatted with you and your family if that is your will," I said. "How has life been for you back at the scout camp all these years?" I asked him cautiously.

"Life hasn't been easy, Mark. My dad and mom have been through so much trying to support our family. Just by simply doing that we have done so much evil that it started to hurt me inside. There have been times when because of the evil that was around us, we all would just feel so angry, all the time, and it has made life unbearable! They have tried to be good parents, and it's because we were surrounded by so much hatred and evil that we all had become victims to it. There have been nights we all would wake up because of the screams and cries from the people Nerogroben's army would torture and eventually killed. I have just felt like there is no point to living like this anymore. I don't know about my parent's opinion, but I trust you, and I would be honored to be able to follow your army and defeat Nerogroben. Maybe I can be of service to you, because I do know of Nerogroben and his army and how they operate," Eladius said carefully looking for any changes in my behavior which I was careful to act indifferent about.

"Well the Grey Matter hurts you because you still have a conscious in-tact still. I feel horrible that you have seen so much evil and horrors in your life so far. Thank you for your trust in me. What I am worried about is because you have seen so much evil, are you really capable of empathy?" I asked Eladius carefully.

"Empathy?" Eladius asked.

"Yes, it's the ability to identify with another's feelings," I said carefully.

"It's because of the guilt that I feel, that I even had mentioned to my parents yesterday that I wanted to switch sides. I am ashamed to have been a contributing part of Nerogroben's Army and to be living at his scout camp. It's against my own integrity. There are so many nights that I have cried myself to sleep, because of all the terrors I have seen and feel that I have caused. I feel that knowledge is not power like Nerogroben's regime says," said Eladius starting to tear and cry as I patted him on his back feeling reassured that his feelings and emotion were a true reflection of his character.

"It's okay, I have seen your heart, the only thing you must do is start to forgive yourself and hopefully we can help others start to forgive you. I am going to have a talk with your parents. Burgesis is going to escort you to Jana and Barty, who will talk to you hopefully as well," I said to Eladius who nodded as I walked to Burgesis.

"The forgiveness should start with them. Please tell them to put their differences aside by forgiving, and learn to love others," I whispered to Burgesis who nodded then walked up to Eladius and held Eladius shoulder and guided him to the house and towards the living-room.

Less than a minute later both Andrew and Pam were floating midair in front of Eggbert and they were slowly placed in front of me in chairs and Eggbert slowly awoke them both.

"What's going on, where are we?" asked Andrew confused, rubbing his eyes.

"Who are you? What are we doing here?" asked Pam also confused and seemingly embarrassed because she was in sleep attire.

"My name is Mark Trogmyer and some call me "the one," but you can call me Mark," I said looking at them both sternly and almost immediately they got up on their feet wide eyed and bowed to me.

"It is not necessary that you pay respect to me, please rise and take your seats. It was me who summoned you and who wanted you to meet me in this way," I said looking at them more calmly and softly.

"Where is our son?" asked Pam worriedly. "Is he still back home? Is the house locked?"

"Your son is with us in the house, I needed to talk to you both privately and away from your son. You have no choice but to trust me that he is safe inside, as I have ensured that you were safely brought here by the great wizard, Eggbert," I continued.

"I am sorry, I don't know if we are allowed, to ask one last question or not. Why have you summoned us?" asked Andrew calmly and quietly looking down.

"You are free to speak your opinions, comments, and concerns at your own will. You are also free to look up at me. I am not like the cruel hearted King Nerogroben who likes to shut people up in front of him. Nothing can be accomplished in this manner. The only thing I ask is that you listen with an open mind to what I say and that you do not interrupt me," I said slowly and wisely. "I have summoned you here today, because I fear for not just your futures, but also the future of your son. It is my belief, that this future of mine and yours, depends greatly upon your feelings, actions, and decisions that you make from this point forth," I continued looking at Andrew and Pam who were both surprised.

"I need to remind you that you are speaking to someone who can and will make a difference in the future. I have seen how you all live, and I have seen how you have questioned your own loyalty. I am here to offer you a fresh start, free of evils, pain, judgement, and full of positive goodness and virtues," I said slowly as Pam and Andrew looked at each other in silence.

Meanwhile, Eladius had a chance to meet with Barty and Jana who were still sitting quietly in the darkened living room as Eladius was guided into the room by Burgesis.

"He said that forgiveness starts today with you, and to put your differences and prejudices aside. He wants you both to forgive, and learn to love others, and in many ways, he is right, the revolution starts with us," said Burgesis looking sternly at Barty and Jana who nodded and looked at Eladius who was smiling.

"Are you guys' part of the rebellion?" asked Eladius curiously looking at Burgesis. "You beavers? Awesome!

"Yes we are a few of many. We follow Mark because we believe that he has the power to change the world to be a better place," said Burgesis who smiled silently.

"Yes, we think that he will defeat Nerogroben and the evil Grey Matter that he is trying to spread into our world. We want to have a better relationship with the Magical Humans again," said Barty gruffly looking at Eladius expecting retort.

"I hope so too," said Eladius looking at Barty and Jana smiling excitedly, "I am tired of all the evil and torture going on in our world because of Nerogroben and his army. I want them eradicated, I just want peace."

Stunned and surprised Barty and Jana ran up to Eladius and hugged him.

"Aww this is possible!" said Jana tearing up as she continued to hug Eladius.

"I forgive you, and your family, for all that you have done," said Barty tearing up and Eladius hugged them both in return and suddenly the room got brighter and lighter in feeling. Burgesis started laughing as they all hugged.

This was occurring back in the living-room. I still sat outside, and I looked at Andrew who was looking at his wife and said, "Before we answer, I would like to talk with my wife and son privately before we make any decisions."

"That will be fine, I will give you until this afternoon to decide. I want you to know that if you decide not to join us, you will be safely brought back home. You will not have to worry about your safety or your lives. I give you my word on that," I said looking at Pam intently. "If, however, you feel you may be rewarded better and will have a better way of life with me and our side, you will of course be given a new facility and living quarters in which to live. You will be given enough food for your fill, and a lot of love and support from us all. We all will need to learn to love our enemies, but take the first steps, and forgive others," I said looking at Andrew as he nodded.

"Thank you, can we go to see our son?" asked Andrew quietly.

"Yes of course, we will go see him inside immediately," I said and nodded to Eggbert who ushered us in. As soon as we walked in Burgesis was tearing up as he watched Barty, Jana, and Eladius hugging.

"Man is it me, or this room is a lot easier to breathe in?" I asked looking at Eggbert who was smiling and laughing through tears.

"What is our son doing?" asked Pam shocked looking at her husband and then to Eggbert in complete shock. "Beavers have never hugged elves, Elves and Beavers have never been on the same level of social status."

"I don't understand, we are in the same middle class," said Eladius.

"No, beavers have always been stuck up about being a level above those even within the same social class on the
Social Hierarchy Clan Chart," explained Pam slowly.

"Regardless of the past, we are going to change that with people like your son who has just learned how to take a major step for the future," said Eggbert smiling, and his eyes started tearing up.

"He has learned the power of forgiveness and love!"

"Eladius get over here!" said Andrew worriedly.

"It's okay mom and dad, I have learned my purpose," said
Eladius releasing the hug from the Beavers and walking to his parents.

"We need to talk about this," said Pam looking at me.

"You can have some privacy upstairs and it's the first door to your right," I said and nodded seriously.

Almost immediately, they both started up the stairs and started talking in the room quietly. As soon as they went upstairs I turned to Barty, Jana, and Burgesis, who were all still tearing and starting to laugh.

"I haven't heard you laugh since before the Dark War, Burgesis," said Eggbert who started tearing and laughing.

"You have done it, Mark!" said Burgesis as he ran up to me and hugged me. "I haven't seen Barty smiling in years!"

"Who knew that something so small could be so powerful!" said Barty tearing.

It was at that moment that Eggbert bowed to me... "Congratulations Mark, you have passed your first lesson from the Wizards Clan... how to handle situations rationally and responsibly." It was at that moment that I felt proud of myself, and I had felt a warmth come over me, it was a clan Magimark.

"To be honest this is just the beginning, this is just one small step, Burgesis can you come with me? The rest of you, would you excuse me?" I said as I left the room. "I am going to get Pam; can you wait for me outside? I want us to go sit outside but I don't want to get into unprotected trouble out there," I said to Burgesis who nodded and went out the door.

Chapter 20
Pam and the Family Decision

It was now, that I had decided that I had wanted to talk to Pam, I was seriously still worried about her and the decision that she could impact her family with. So, I went up the stairs and knocked on the door.

"I would like to see if I could talk to you alone Pam," I said to her who had looked mad and was sitting on the bed. Pam stepped up and followed me down the stairs and outside to the bench without saying a word. When we went outside, she continued to look at Burgesis with fear because he was a Magical Human Elf like me and she was just an Elf. I didn't understand why they didn't get along but figured things would eventually be explained to me over time.

"I have told you that I wanted you to speak freely, and I don't want you to be alarmed. Burgesis is just our guard out here," I said looking at Pam who nodded silently looking at Burgesis with some distrust.

"I want to know what is going through your mind right now, and I wanted to get your opinion on what I have offered you and your family," I explained to Pam.

"Why me?" she asked.

"Because a female has just as much impact on the family, politically, emotionally, and socially, just as much as males," I explained.

"But why would you ask me my opinion out of the three of us?" asked Pam. "Do you distrust me the most out of the three of us? I saw how you were staring at me intently when you were making your offer to us," she continued.

"I realize how scary this must be for you, most of all, a mother who just wants what is best for her son and her family. It's like my mom back on Earth would want of me," I said putting my hand on hers as she had flinched. "It's ok," I continued. "I am not going to hurt you or your family. I need you to ignore what is going on in the world in regard to this so called, "Social Hierarchy." You have been taught something that is so wrong, on so many levels. No matter where you come from, or who you are, you and your family matter to me. It is my understanding that your loyalty was to King Nerogroben and has been for years," I explained as I looked at her and she nodded and had tears in her eyes that I had wiped away.

"Since I had gotten married to Andrew, our loyalty was and always has been to Nerogroben. You want us to throw that away and join you just like that?" she asked looking up at me. I then looked up at the sky and saw the Grey Matter get lighter around us.

"As soon as Eladius woke up, I told him that I needed you all to trust me. I got you here safely and I have made sure Nerogroben's evil henchmen haven't found me with you. He was also surprised that I knew his name, I told him that I do care about all those who follow me. I meant what I said. I take the time to get to know, that your name is Pam, and that your husband's name is Andrew. I also know that he has had a glimpse of hope, which is something that he hasn't felt in years. Things will get better with me on your family's side. I love all my followers. I want to make sure that they have the proper housing, support, and provisions to be okay within the protection of all my followers. I am not casting you out or going to imprison you, torture you or others for information, or even judge you for supporting Nerogroben. I am not that type of leader or person," I said looking at Pam.
"I can tell you genuinely care about us but being there in Nerogroben's army is all we know," said Pam worriedly.
"That is okay, if your family chooses too, you can be scouts like you were for Nerogroben, that is an option," I said looking at Pam who seemed to not be receptive to that idea. So, I then suggested. "You know, I think that you and your family have seen more than your share of destruction, death, torture, and murders. I think I would love to see

you and your family in peace and just, be my supporters and be loyal to me, that is all I ask for. In fact, this is what I would want is for you and your family, to be in peace, and happy. You all have been through so much pain, and seen so much evil that, I don't want to see your family suffering anymore. If you need anything, anything at all, I want you to know that you can have it. I will support you all if you continue to support me and support others who support me. Most importantly, I need you to understand that I forgive you for what you have done to me and my followers through Nerogroben's army," I said to Pam calmly and sincerely looking at her.

At that moment, Pam started crying and she fell into my arms. A great feeling of relief had come over her and it was at that moment that I knew Eladius would be okay. I figured at that point that they would probably end up joining our rebellion against Nerogroben and his army at whatever capacity they chose. Pam released me from her hug as I looked at her and she nodded. I then looked at Burgesis.

"Burgesis, will you escort Pam back to Andrew and Eladius. This way they can talk some more and give me their final decision after dinner?" I asked Burgesis who nodded and helped Pam up off the bench.

"Thank you, Mark, I can tell that you have a kind and gentle heart," said Pam as she turned to look back at me through her tears.

"You are very welcome, and I want you to know that you can talk to me at any time, I am very easy to get a hold of," I said smiling looking back at her as she turned and walked back in the house.

A few minutes later, Burgesis came outside.

"You have already started to change people's hearts. I don't know how you do it!" said Burgesis sitting next to me amazed.

"I am doing the opposite of what Nerogroben has done, I am trying to undo what has been done restore trust, with understanding, love, respect, and compassion," I said looking at Burgesis seriously who nodded as we looked up at the sky," I slowly asked Burgesis. "Where are our rebellion prisoners kept?" who then turned away and looked at the field.

Meanwhile back in the room...

"Mom why are you crying?" asked Eladius looking at Pam worriedly who walked into the room.

"Did they hurt you?" asked Andrew worriedly.

"No sweetheart, not at all," said Pam looking at her husband who was shocked to see her crying.

"I would like to say I think I am ready for us to side with "the one" said Pam looking at them both,

"Mark will be happy," Eladius said to Pam smiling.

"Eladius, I don't think he said that you should call him by his name," said Andrew cautiously.

"He told us to," said Eladius "He wants us to call him Mark, he said that he isn't a king. I think he feels that we are all equal and on the same level."

"I don't know Eladius, it seems kind of disrespectful not to call him king," said Andrew looking at Pam

"I called him Mark," said Pam quietly sitting between her son and her husband.

"Why the change of heart?" asked Andrew concerned.

"I am okay Andrew, it's just that I have finally felt the power of forgiveness and love. For once, I can now say the words "I love you," a lot easier," said Pam looking at Andrew who was surprised because he hadn't heard his wife say that to him in years. He then stood up and kissed her and started to tear, cry, and laugh at the same time. Pam stood up and reached out to Eladius and they group hugged.

"This feeling here that I have been feeling is so nice. I feel so much lighter now," said Eladius looking at his mom "To be honest, I don't want us to be spies anymore mom."

"We have to go downstairs for dinner soon, and then we have to give them an answer," said Pam quietly looking at Andrew and then to Eladius through tears of happiness still smiling.

Meanwhile downstairs and outside on the porch...

"Where are our prisoners being kept?" I asked Burgesis again.

"I will bring you there after your training, so you can be prepared to face *those* people," said Burgesis sternly looking ahead in the Field of Dreams.

"What do you mean "*those* people"?" I asked Burgesis who was avoiding my eye contact.

"They are not like you and me, they are different, they are stealing our food, killing people who are like you and I, they are full of hatred, they think they are better or deserve more than we do! Mark, they just aren't good beings, they are worse than Pam and Andrew. They are now hardened people," said Burgesis looking at me. "You aren't ready to face them."

"I am ready! It has been working, you said it yourself!

You must understand that love and forgiveness is contagious! We must move forward and look past our differences if we hope to overcome this disunity! We must try to be better than ourselves in order, to save our clans," I said to Burgesis as I stood up.

"How can you say that? You don't know how these beings are! You don't understand that they don't easily forget or forgive or move forward without grudges! The Troll clan was the one that started

this disunity and they spread their hatred through Nerogroben's leadership, and they used him as the excuse of how things should be! They took him by what he said when he was coming to power, and using this fear, he spread it onto his followers."
I shook my head and said "That maybe the case, but we don't have to stoop down to Nerogroben's level to be better people! We can be better ourselves and spread love and forgiveness to others by leading by example! Where is your faith in me that you had?" I asked Burgesis angrily as his eyes started to fill with tears, I then turned and started to walk inside to help Jana and Barty with the set-up of dinner and went into the dining room. A red magimark formed on me as I felt regret for saying what I did in reaction through emotion to Burgesis without thinking about it first.
I saw that a smaller table, for the eight of us, was set up already. Barty told me that I was to sit at the head of the table, and the others would sit on the sides of the table.
"We are having dinner in a few minutes if you want to make sure the others are ready for dinner," said Jana looking at me.
I then left the dining-room and went upstairs and knocked on the door of Pam and Andrew's Room and opened the door to find the three of them hugging.

"Love is contagious," I said happily. "I am assuming this is good news, possibly? I am looking forward to hearing about your decision after dinner which will be ready in a few minutes. I just wanted to let you know that you can come down when you are ready."

"Thank you, Mark," said Eladius to me.

"No, I want to thank you, Eladius," I said as he smiled as I turned towards

the stairs and began to walk downstairs.

As I walked down everyone was standing at the table waiting for me and there were four empty seats left at the table and as I stood by my seat. A moment later, Eladius, Andrew, and Pam all stood by their seats. I sat down and then everyone else followed suit.

"First, I wish to give thanks for the meal that we have here today and give thanks for the friends we have gathered here," I said looking around at the table. I saw Burgesis at the other end of the table sitting next to Jana avoiding my eye contact, wiping away his tears still. "Second, I would like to apologize to Burgesis for my behavior, it was uncalled for and childish. I assume I will know what I was asking you about when you know and feel when I am ready," Burgesis nodded and looked at me and silently.

"Okay, let's eat," I said looking around at everyone and everyone started eating.

After a very silent meal of satisfaction and enjoyment, I stood up and said, "Could I ask everyone to step into the living-room and sit please?" Everyone got up and sat in the living-room and I stood up and walked to the living-room and stood in front of everyone who stared expectantly at me. "First, I want it to be known that I am not going to judge, criticize, banish, torture or kill anyone who chooses to support Nerogroben at first. I want it to be known that it is far more beneficial to support me. Also, my followers are never to punish anyone who isn't loyal to me. I only ask that those who aren't loyal at first to me, come to me with an open mind, and be willing to listen to what I have to say," I said looking at Burgesis who avoided my eye contact and then I looked at Eggbert who felt relieved as well. "Andrew, I am curious to know what you and your family have individually decided and as head of household it is your job to ensure that this is followed and not broken. I want you to also know that I am not going to do anything against you or your family if you decide to continue your loyalty to Nerogroben. I just will have Eggbert put you all to sleep and in your beds and you all will just go back to your rooms, and it will be as if nothing happened. *If,* however, you have decided that you wish to follow me and my rebellion against Nerogroben, I ask that you leave your belongings behind except for two bags worth of things. You would be escorted back to your home with Eggbert and have just enough time to fill your bags with things and then he will take you back here with us," I said looking at Andrew expectantly.

"Mark, you have shown us great love, respect, comfort, and have perhaps changed the very nature of our family. You have shown us compassion, love, and have given us peace, it would be our honor to follow you and be a part of your rebellion, against the cruel king. We all have individually decided to follow you, and this is all with our own accord. Thank you for what you have done for us," said Andrew tearing up and starting to cry.

I stood up and then everyone followed suit and hugged each other as I said "I love you all and will ensure your safety. You only have tonight to fill up two bags each of your belongings and then you will sleep here tonight, and tomorrow you will journey with us. Thank you so much for your support and thank you for making the best decision of your life," I said sincerely.

"Aww this is going to make me cry again," said Jana looking at us.

We all laughed.

With that Eggbert and the three of them disappeared after dinner and within the hour they came back. That night when I went to bed I woke up in so much pain that Burgesis had to heal me in the middle of the night because six more magimarks appeared, and my red magimark disappeared. All I could think of was, at least I would be able to ride on Brittany the unicorn, since they appeared on my legs, and one had appeared near my heart. I was grateful as well because they all burned white.

Chapter 21
The Transfer

The next morning Eggbert was right, there was a dense fog everywhere when the guard had arrived early that morning. It was around that time when gradually Eggbert could shrink everyone's bags that they brought. It enabled us all to travel easier and more discretely.

I was then able to introduce the Guard to the new family. At first The Guard was untrusting, and after a while, I convinced the Guard to forgive them for what they had done in Nerogroben's Army. Then they all had become changed as well. Eggbert smiled at what he had observed and then he walked fast up to me.

"I am very impressed with how fast you are making a difference in the lives of others," whispered Eggbert looking at me as we had started moving.

"Thank you, Eggbert," I said continuing to look back at Andrew, Eladius, and Pam who also decided to guard the rear as I then looked at Eggbert. "I am very surprised as well," I said quietly.

"Mark, we are going to fly lower. When we fly too high from you, we lose visibility of you and the guard, because of the fog. It's so dense that we cannot afford that," said Matt from the rear to the right of me in the sky.

"That is fine," I said looking up at Matt. "I would appreciate it if the guard could adjust as they see fit so that they can see me, during our journey." Everyone laughed and nodded in agreement.

As we left the edge of the Field of Dreams we started to head towards Jana and Barty's house through the Greens of the Middle Kingdom, as we were walking, I asked Eggbert quietly, "What made you tell me about Eladius?"

Eggbert looked at me and smiled.

"Oh, I'm afraid, I must admit. This all was a clan test of my brother wizards to you,"

"To me?" I asked looking at Eggbert

"Why did they want to test me?" I asked.

"It's true," Eggbert started to say quietly, "that it has been foretold that "the one" is supposed to have a great deal of immense power to change the hearts of many. You have proved that much so far. It has also been foretold, that "the one," is actually human, and is likely to err," explained Eggbert to me.

"You expected me to make a mistake?" I asked looking at him surprised.

"Oh, but you have already erred," said Eggbert smiling at me smugly looking at Burgesis. "That is why you apologized to Burgesis. You *may still have,* the ability, to pass the other clan tests even if you err, like you did with ours and the test of the Giants."

"Why am I being tested? What do you mean *"may have"*?" I asked frustrated. "Everyone has kept saying I have to prove myself. Why can't I just go and talk to these clans myself and deal with it just like that, it would be so much easier to talk and convince them instead of having to worry about clan tests."

"Ah, you see sometimes what is easier to do in life isn't the answer, you are being tested, and yes, it is one from each of the clans of our realm. This must be because in life, we all are tested, at different times of our lives. Your tests just happen to be one from each of the clan leaders. You have already passed our test for the Wizard clan. Just like the average person suffers through agonies in life, you must be tested by each of the clan leaders. They must ensure your heart, body, and soul, is like their clan's teachings. Once you pass their clan tests, those leaders can go back to their clans and tell them of your abilities. Then in the end, try to convince them to follow you," said Eggbert looking at Eladius.

"This seems fair," I said "When will I know I am being tested?"

"If I am not mistaken, it may be as simple as walking up to *some* of the leaders and find out what their test for you is. Otherwise, it will happen as we move along here. You should do well to remember that you need to always do what is right. Always follow what your heart is telling you to do. But be careful because you very well know that there is a difference between saying you can and will do something and keeping your word," said Eggbert quietly looking back at Andrew and Pam who were talking with Eladius.

"What are you saying? That I am dishonest? That I am untrustworthy, or that I am a liar? Or that I am a manipulator?" I asked Eggbert carefully.

"Well how can you promise not to raise a hand to your enemies and still win a war against Nerogroben?" said Eggbert carefully.

"I refuse to raise a hand against someone who hasn't personally done me any wrong or done any wrong in front of me," I said looking at Eggbert who raised his eyebrows.

"What about those who have done wrong to others?" asked Eggbert looking at me with his eyebrows raised surprised.

"I have reflected on these matters and have already decided that from the moment that I talked to Eladius forth, I will keep my word. It is true that I am human in another world, and in another time, but in that world, we have sayings that have meaning. They are for the most part, followed. One of them is, "Do onto others the way you want them to treat you," and another saying is "Love thine enemy," because as you love the enemy, they have, and they begin to have, no reason to hate or harm you," I said calmly.

"So, you don't see this as a war, full of weapons or artillery?" asked Eggbert incredulously as we passed Jana and Barty's house.

"No, in fact, this is just a war on virtues, values, and the differences of perspective or opinion. I have not seen this as that kind of war in my perspective," I explained. "It's all about perception. Yes, the enemy as you say may have bigger guns and fast artillery, planes, or whatever. But you can't fight and win a war with fire against fire; it's not going to go anywhere or at least very far. There will be too many deaths, pain, and suffering from that to where there will not be any more room for peace. There would be so much evil and fighting that there won't be much of a world left. It will be destroyed by the very acts and destruction of war," I said calmly we then turned a corner and headed into the Woodland Elms towards Beaver Valley. For a few moments Eggbert continued to walk in silence talking and thinking about what I said to himself.

"He is going to do what he sees fit to do," said Brittany rather coolly as Eggbert forgot she was there.

"Thank you, Brittany," I said smiling at her as she smiled back as I started petting her mane on the back of her neck.

"How can you plan to fight and win a war without the casualties and without death and weapons?" asked Eggbert.

"Don't worry my friend, have faith in me, as I have had faith in you," I said softly.

I knew Eggbert was right on both counts I knew that there was probably going to be some deaths. At the same time, though I also knew, that I needed to keep my word to Eladius and his family. I knew that I would eventually come up with the best plan to make everything work out better. We started to walk through the Woodland Elms and in it hidden, were many elves, they were peeking their heads out between the trees, to see "the one," better and more clearly out of curiosity. They were chatting and whispering amongst themselves within the trees, a few were smiling and waving, and I smiled and started slowly waving back, as we continued down the path. As we continued down the path the fog began to clear, and The Guard had become more alert. About five minutes into the walk down the path further up ahead stood Andrea and Mike Smitherton, with their arms, folded standing side by side in the middle of the path.

Chapter 22
The Family Connection

"Is this an attempted act of war on us, Burgesis?" asked Mike who was angrily looking at Burgesis.
"Oh no, by no means is this an act of war to you or your clan, my friend," said Burgesis looking around in a calm loud voice for all to hear.
"We are merely The Guard for "the one," in which we have staked our lives to protect him against the foul King Nerogroben and his army," said Burgesis looking around and then he bowed to Andrea and Mike Smitherton respectfully as the rest of The Guard and myself followed suit.
I got off Brittany the unicorn, Burgesis and John got up and held their palm out to guard in front of me as everyone slowly rose from their bowing positions.
"We wish to be sure from everyone that is here, that no harm comes to "the one," while we pass through," said John loudly.
Everyone looked amazed to see a Magical Human outside of Metromark protecting me, no one said a word at first.
"Nonsense, you have no enemies here in our realm to worry about, we especially have been tormented by King Nerogroben," said Andrea looking around.
"We are honored and happy to see you here,"

Everyone then came to a brief applause as Andrea and Mike unfolded their arms.

"Please come, stop by our home for tea before continuing on your journey," said Mike ushering them ahead on the path forward.

"Besides, you all must be hungry from traveling this far," said Andrea looking at me.

"Good idea, thank you, we will go with you to your home for tea," I said looking at my guard not realizing how tired they were looking. "I wonder maybe we could have permission to rest in the protection of your realm as well?"

"You may, Mark," Andrea said nicely as we walked deeper and deeper into the woods, we came to a clearing in which we saw many homes in the trees and one on the ground level. The guard relaxed and slowly followed Andrea inside their home it was a good size home made of wood and brick and thickly thatched grass roof, it looked like a wooded cabin in which only the back part was brick. As I walked in, I noticed that the ceilings were high, and the door opened to a hallway in which there were many doors ahead. To the left were the dining room and kitchen, and to the right was the family room where we were asked to be seated and Mike had put a protective charm over the room to not be heard and Barty closed the curtains, and Andrea started to passing tea and biscuits.

"Sorry Mark and Burgesis," said Mike looking at us. "No one knows or can know that we had met privately before this, so we had to put on a show."
"No, it's fine, I understand," I said looking at Mike smiling, behind my cup of tea, as I sipped it.
"As do I," said Burgesis smiling and taking a bite of his biscuit.
Mike and Andrea felt relieved.
"I assume you are all going to the school right now, is that correct?" asked Mike looking around at the others and squinted at Andrew who was sitting hidden behind Jana and Barty.
No one responded and kept still and sipping their tea.
"Oh right, not allowed to say anything," said Mike nervously.
Everyone smiled and there was an awkward silence as I continued to look at Andrew and he moved to get a better look at Andrew.
"Everyone is so glad the rumors are true after all," said Mike looking at Andrew curiously and scoffed.
"Oh it's you, I noticed you found out sooner about "the one," then I anticipated," said Mike getting up looking at Andrew who avoided his eye contact.
"Everything is fine now, yes, this was at Mark's request. You see, he has pledged his loyalty to our side now," Eggbert said looking from Andrew to

me, putting his hand on Mike's shoulders to calm him.

"We shall see about that," Mike said roughly. I placed myself in front of Andrew and in between Mike. Then the Guard was on my immediate defense in front of and in between Mike and I. Mike just started looking at me curiously as I stood up in front of him.

"Why did you immediately stand up for him? What makes his life worth more than yours?" asked Mike Smitherton as I kept quiet. "I am an Elf, so is he. I am at least an Elf who is trustworthy enough to be loyal to you!

Unlike the likes of him!"

I could tell there was immediate animosity between Mike Smitherton and Andrew. I couldn't tell what it was, all I knew is that whatever it was, there was an immediate dislike for each other. They were of the same clan, but it was just a strange situation between the two of them. They didn't even look at one another while in the same room until Mike noticed him at which point I had noticed it was Andrew whom avoided the eye contact and looked down to the ground.

"We need to learn to forgive," I said looking at Mike sternly putting my hand on Andrew who was avoiding Mike.

"Easy for you to say, you have never lost family or friends due to information passed through him and his family as they passed it on to Nerogroben himself!" said Mike angrily through tears, and he left the room.

"I will go talk to him," said Andrew finally looking at me and walking out of the room.

"I need you to apologize to him from me for touching a nerve, but also tell him why you and your family believe in me," I said to Andrew as he nodded his head and left the room in silence.

"I'm sorry about that Mark," said Andrea to me as I sipped my tea and she poured tea refills out to everyone around the room who sat in a silence.

"My husband has not been the same since his parents and his friend died. It's been years since his son, my step son, and wife left us he doesn't talk about them. I don't know if he would recognize them if he saw them, it has been many years," she continued as I looked at the flowery pattern on the teacup in her hand as I noticed that it matched the rest of the tea set.

"It's okay, I understand. Nerogroben has a lot to answer for and has made it hard for us all. Have you met your step son and his wife before?" I asked meaningfully as we all sat in silence enjoying the tea and biscuits.

"No, I mean, it's been years, so I probably would not recognize them myself at all if I saw them again. I am going to check on my husband and make sure he is okay," said Andrea looking at me as I nodded in understanding.

Meanwhile outside in the next room in the dining room, Andrew followed Mike and grabbed his shoulder.

"Wait," said Andrew looking at Mike who avoided eye contact.

"How can you play Mark like this?" said Mike clenching his fists and gritting his teeth looking around wildly still avoiding eye contact and pacing worriedly.

"What do you mean?" said Andrew confused.

"You pledged allegiance to Nerogroben and his Army and now you think that Mark is just going to believe you. You don't think he will not have some reservations in us, or trusting you? Why me? Why? Why me? Me of all people! Why does this happen to me? This is the whole reason you and your wife got kicked out of our clan, out of our realm! Are you a double agent now or something Andrew?" said Mike angrily pacing back and forth.

"NO DAD!" said Andrew as he grabbed Mike by his shoulders and placed him in front of him who stood there in place still avoiding eye contact.

"It's me, Dad, your son! Look at me! I. I...I want to come home, Dad, all of us, my wife, and my... my... my.... son too... we want to come home. We honestly have changed so much because of Mark. He has helped us, because of Eladius's change of heart which has spread to me and Pam. We are ready to try to be a family again. Eladius deserves to know who his grandparents are, and how they are exemplary parents!" said Andrew through tears as he started crying trying to hug his father who stood stunned. "I'm sorry Dad! I am so sorry for what I have done. I shouldn't have run out on you. I should have fixed my beliefs. I should have talked to you better! I, I should have been more open to you and open minded in general. I should not have run out on the clan, life has been so miserable that we, fell victim to Grey Matter, me and my wife, and our son," said Andrew in tears crying in Mike's shoulders still standing in front of him.

"Am I to understand that you named your son after me?" asked Mike quietly padding his son's shoulders shocked, still trying to grasp what Andrew was talking about as it seemed to take a while for it to register.

"Yes. Eladius Michael Smitherton," said Andrew now hugging his father who was stunned.

"He has my middle name as his first name and my first name as his middle name and then our last name?" asked Mike trying to put his grandson's name together.

"Yes, I could never hate you dad I could never forget you, or what you have done for me. Worse of all, I couldn't ever forget what I did to my own father," said Andrew tearing.

"You really have changed! Oh, my goodness, I can't believe you have changed son!" said Mike finally giving in and crying with Andrew.

Within a minute later, the door opened, and Andrea came in.

"Hello, Mom!" Andrew said looking at Andrea who was shocked at the scene of her husband crying.

"It *is* you!" said Andrea as she closed the door behind her as she started tearing while walking up to Andrew happily hugging him.

"I thought it was you, but I couldn't be sure, it's been at least fourteen years," said Andrea as she was hugging her son and tears were coming down from her eyes.

"He has come home for good now," said Mike through tears looking at his wife Andrea.

"You must tell me everything that has happened!" said Mike cleaning up his tears as they sat down in chairs in the dining room.

"Well, it all started with Eladius almost a week ago," said Andrew as he quickly caught up Andrea and Mike.

"So, are you going to the school?" asked Mike looking at Andrew.

"I'm sorry, I am not sure, they are keeping where we are going quiet Dad," said Andrew seriously. "Mark has done so much for us, and this family now. He has helped us all disband my son, and wife, and I, from Nerogroben's grasp. I just can't believe this is happening!" said Andrew happily and Andrea nodded in agreement the room became brighter and easier to breathe as the Grey Matter that was left in the room dissipated.

"We should get back to the others before they notice we were gone too long," said Andrew. Both Mike and Andrea nodded in agreement. They left the dining room and went into the living room when everyone looked up. Andrew opened the door as he placed both of his arms around his parents.

"We have a major announcement everyone," said Andrew still in tears "I have finally made up with my dad, who is your grandfather, Eladius! We can stay at home now."

Everyone at first was in shock and then everyone was happy and stood up hugging and applauding and even Eladius was happy.

"You have now passed our tests both for the Elven lands and for the Wizards, Mark," whispered Eggbert to me quietly.

I was shocked, I had no idea that Mike and Andrea were related to Pam, Eladius, and Andrew.

After all the hugging and congratulating everyone sat down quietly as Andrew told his story of what happened between him and his family before the Dark War.

Chapter 23
Then the World Grew Dark

"So, let me tell you about what life was like before the Dark War started and the story of what persuaded me to change all allegiances to Nerogroben in my gullible-ness and completely regretful stupidity, Eladius," said Andrew as everyone gathered around him.

"Fifteen years ago, when we lived here in the Woodland Elms," started Andrew looking around the room. "There was an elf that lived and grew up here with me. He was close with your grandparents and his name was, Tom Clanswood. His parents never supported him throughout his life they never comforted him when he would hurt himself or when he was sad growing up. They lacked empathy and they were not very encouraging to him growing up. They always put him down and they were very negative to their own son, who was my closest friend," said Andrew looking at his dad. "I was jealous of Tom Clanswood sometimes because a good amount of the time, he would get more attention than me from my own parents. Tom was a good kid he just never was lucky with his family and that impacted him greatly. Without me in his life though, he would have grown up alone, and friendless. When we both became of age, I worked closer with your grandparents with clan responsibilities. On occasion, I would have the chance to see Tom Clanswood, but he was a spy for us, gathering important information about Nerogroben as he came close to gaining power. He was good at it," continued Andrew as he put his arm around his son Eladius, who listened intently. "One day, Tom came to your grandparents and I, and said that "Nerogroben had a duel with and ended up killing the Troll leader, his wife. After that he assumed the throne, and anyone who stood up to him, or disrespected him, or who wasn't loyal to him, ended up being killed. The Troll clan felt that they had no choice, but to give in to him. Eventually leaders out of fear of being killed or their clan being destroyed bowed to him in loyalty. Others went into hiding. It was around that time that the Magical Creatures began to get kicked out of the Guarded City of Metromark. Chancellor Rain, at the time drew up a peace agreement with Nerogroben, so that they could co-exist, so long as that there wasn't an act of war brought upon each other. Nerogroben signed the agreement. Your grandparents were leaders back then and they refused to pledge loyalty to Nerogroben and his army. It was around that time that Tom Clanswood, started trying to persuade me to join Nerogroben, so that Nerogroben wouldn't attack us. I could tell at the time that Tom Clanswood was starting to change. After much talk with Tom, I was persuaded, so I told your grandparents that I was going to pledge allegiance to Nerogroben. It was then that they kicked me and your mom who was pregnant with you at the time out of the Elven realm. They had told me that they didn't want evil to penetrate their walls," Andrew said looking at Mike who had avoided eye contact. "So that same day we got kicked out of the clan, your mom and I started our journey to Valfador, Nerogroben's castle which is in the city of Creaton. Along the way, we discovered that Tom Clanswood was following us. He finished traveling with us the guards of the castle let the two of us in. Nerogroben was then let aware of our arrival. We were brought in to see him and he asked your mom and I to meet in a private audience and late meal with him. At first, he seemed like a nice guy, and had given us a meal in which we were hungry after the journey. He told us that he may be able to help us. Halfway through the meal he asked us how we knew about his name and about his rise to power. We told him we found out at our clan through Tom Clanswood. Immediately the king stood up and we stopped eating. We stood up as well, and then he asked his guards to bring in Tom. The guards opened the door and Tom came in." Andrew explained as everyone was sitting on the edge of their seats. "Nerogroben then said to me and your mom as he looked at us "You see, I have run into a slight problem now. How do I know that I can trust you and that you are loyal to me now?" Then we just looked at Tom, and Tom who said "I can vouch for them," Nerogroben said "Oh yeah" and then he put his fingers to his chin and then said, "Well since you offered, who is going to vouch for your loyalty now?" and then he turned to me and your mom and Nerogroben said, "Ok, prove your allegiance to me, kill him, kill the spy," and we were shocked. We had told Nerogroben that he was our friend," Andrew said sadly starting to tear up. "Then Nerogroben said, "Kill him since he is a traitor, or are you saying you are traitors to me and to your own kind?" Then he took a long thick sword out and gave it to me," said Andrew trembling as he was remembering it all as if it was yesterday. He then looked at his father Mike who was wide eyed and his eyes were watery. "So, I then took the sword from Nerogroben. Just as Tom stood there, right in front of me and your mom, I swung the sword and I cut hard through Tom's neck in one full swing and his head just came clean off and landed on your mom's plate in front of her, and she threw up all over Tom's head as the rest of his now lifeless body hit the floor," explained Andrew crying. "After I did that a dark red magimark appeared on me, right here," and as Andrew explained he rolled up his sleeve, I stood up and walked to him and I compared the magimark. His was a bright red on his arm like if it was a cut still fresh and when I compared it to mine, it wasn't as visibly fresh as his looked. "It was from that moment on that Nerogroben trusted us," said Andrew looking at Mike his father, who then had burst into tears and started crying. "There were conditions for us to have food, supplies, and a home. He wanted us to give him continuous information, catching spies, and we had to pledge our son's allegiance to him when he turned of age." Andrew looked over to Eladius who had crossed his arms. "It was a bad deal, but it was the only way to support ourselves," said Andrew looking around to everyone who shook their heads in disapproval. "The past is the past, let's just focus on moving forward now," I said "We should probably get some sleep. In the morning, we should head out early." I said as everyone stood up after I did. Then I looked around at everyone at the table. "I would like to have a moment with you Andrew, Pam, and Eladius."

The three of them nodded and I looked at Burgesis and nodded at him to and he stayed as well. It was then that I thought about how I healed Burgesis's broken heart, and I wondered if it would work the same way with Andrew's red magimark under his sleeve.

"Be careful Mark," said Burgesis who was reading my mind. "We don't know exactly how that kind of magic works. It's really advanced, are you sure it is wise for you to attempt to do that again?"

"Do what?" asked Andrew alarmed.

"Please sit down here in front of me Andrew," I said calmly as I thought, *"Burgesis, Andrew, and his family have been through enough, it is the least I could do to attempt to help here."*

Burgesis nodded in agreement with my thoughts and didn't protest my argument and reasoning.

"Pull up your sleeve Andrew," I said looking at him.

"What are you going to do?" He asked worriedly.

"Something that I should have tried to do a long time ago," I explained as he lifted his sleeve to reveal the dark evil red Magimark. I put my hand over it and closed my eyes as I took a deep breath and said aloud, "I command that this evil magimark to be mended in light and goodness, Precipio quod corrigendum sit in luce magimark malum et bonum." Just then a light emerged from the palm of my hand as it hit his magimark. He screamed in pain and started to cry in agony. After a minute of the light emerging from my palm he passed out as the magic from the palm of my hand stopped. I looked at Andrew who was still breathing but knocked out and then I looked at Eladius who screamed "DAD!" in worry.

"He might end up being okay," said Burgesis who had moved in to inspect the area on his arm ahead of Eladius. "The magimark in any case is gone," He then looked at Pam and patted her shoulder, who had closed her eyes during the whole process while holding her husband's other hand. She then opened her eyes and looked at me and said, "Thank you Mark for all that you have done for me, my husband, and our son,"

"No problem," I said as I stood up and quietly left the room.

"You always do that," said Burgesis who ran after me after I had left the room.

"What do you mean?" I asked.

"You leave the room after doing something like that," he said thoughtfully. "Why?"

"There is no reason to surround yourself in your own triumph all the time if you can help it. If you do, your ego grows," I said wisely as he nodded.

"Your trying to be very humble, aren't you?" Burgesis said slowly as I noticed he looked at me with a twinkle in his eyes as he smiled and gave me a hug.

"I'm working on it," I said slowly smiling.

"Good night Mark," Burgesis said.

"Good night, my friend," I said releasing his hug.

It was then that I had walked away and went into my room started to get ready for bed and changed into pajamas when a knock came at the door. I put on a robe before answering the door. It was Eladius. "You have done so much for me and my family, for all of us! How can we ever repay you? You got us out of that situation and helping my dad?" said Eladius as he pushed himself into me running into the room, hugging me firmly.

"You don't owe me anything, your loyalty to me has been enough," I said putting my hands on his cheeks. He just smiled as I then clasped my hands in front of me as I started pacing and Eladius sat on my bed.

"I can't sleep, this whole idea of going on an adventure seems exciting and to finally be away from Nerogroben and his ruthless army feels so much better," said Eladius.

"Your life ahead is going to be full of adventure, that is for certain now," I said as I started to reflect on what Andrew had talked about while pacing and occasionally glancing at Eladius.

"I believe that your parents ended up deciding to stay here in the clan with you, when I leave in the morning," I said.

"Well I am going to stay by your side, Mark," said Eladius excitedly.

"I don't think that is a good idea, Eladius," I said wisely looking at him. "Much has to be done and for some time my life is going to be difficult. I still have much learn, so much more of this world. Besides, you should get to know your new grandparents, and clan here. You haven't had the chance to get to know them yet," I said looking at Eladius who had looked down at the floor trying to hide his disappointment. He then stood up in front of me and hugged me and kissed me.

"I'm sorry Mark," he said as he stepped back suddenly aware of what he just did. "You mustn't leave! I mean, if you go, I want to go with you!"

"You are very kind, Eladius," I said looking at him and putting my hand on my cheek where he kissed me.

"You most of all have been through so much and have been loyal and have shown me great faith through your affections for me. However, I must ask you to do me this favor. Spread your love and kindness, to those who aren't in peace and who are full of negativity. The reason I need you to do this is because it is positively contagious," I said as I looked at him and wiped a tear away from his cheek as he started getting emotional. I put my hand on his shoulders in support.

"I will always be there for you if you need more people for your guard," he said to me sniffling.

"I know you will be, but for now, be with your family, at least until I am trained more. Protect them and spread the good news and help make the Grey Matter less dense around here," I said looking around smiling as Eladius hugged me.

He then said good night and left the room.

I closed the door behind Eladius and walked to my bed. I laid on my bed on my back looking at the ceiling. I started reflecting on what Eladius had said and, Andrew's story.

It was hard for me to comprehend at first why Andrew and Pam were kicked out of their clan when his parents found out that they wanted to give their loyalty to Nerogroben. I had remembered that Barty had said *"What do they do to us? We do the same, we imprison, torture, and kill them as well. They are treasonous people!"* I couldn't help but wonder why Mike decided to just disown and banish Andrew and his pregnant wife Pam at the time. Just then a knock came at the door.

Chapter 24
Wanted

This time it was Burgesis at the door.

"I wonder if I might come in?" said Burgesis looking at me as I looked towards the doorway.

"Of course," I said as I sat up in against the wall on my bed and grabbed my pillow in my hands as I sat cross legged.

"I assume you couldn't sleep," Burgesis said as he was looking at me as he walked towards me and sat on the edge of the bed. "It so happens that I couldn't either,"

"It's cool," I said rather awkwardly.

"Is everything okay between us?" he asked me seriously looking at me.

"Yeah," I said looking at him.

"I just don't think things are okay," he said "I decided to tell you that after you're done training at the school, that is when I will take you to see our prisoners," he said as he looked worried.

"Burgesis," I said. "We are okay, I understand what you meant, and that's why I apologized earlier."

"Alright, well a lot has happened since then and you have been very distant from me," Burgesis said looking around the room.

"You're right, a lot has happened and I am still processing things for today," I said.

"Yeah, a lot has, but good things," he said
"Burgesis, one thing keeps bugging me," I said looking at him and he just laughed looking at me. "Well you know, you say it's just one thing bugging you but really you mean several things at once," said Burgesis "Alright, what's really bugging you?"

"Mike Smitherton," I replied cautiously, "I want to understand something."
Burgesis kept silent and avoided my eye contact.
"Barty said "Usually we kill, torture, or imprison traitors who give allegiance to Nerogroben within our clans," I said slowly. "Why is it that Mike Smitherton didn't do any of those things to Andrew, Pam, or the unborn Eladius?" I asked still very slowly.
"Are you questioning Mike Smitherton's loyalty?" Burgesis asked.
"I am questioning why a father wouldn't just imprison his son and family instead of killing, torturing, banishing, or disowning them," I replied.
"You would have wanted Mike Smitherton to imprison his own son, wife, and future grandson?" asked Burgesis with his eyebrows raised.
"I am just questioning his judgment at the time, and yes perhaps his loyalty comes into question slightly," I stated.
"That idea is crazy! I mean could you imagine the rebellion if Mike and kept his son within the clan? It

would have been, seen as, Andrew trying to overthrow his dad! Evil Grey Matter around here spreads like a forest fire once it's sparked," said Burgesis. "Also something else to consider, if Mike imprisoned Andrew, don't you think that a hard hatred for Andrew's father would have formed? If it did it may have formed either on either Andrew's heart, or those who may have been swayed towards believing that Andrew was right to support Nerogroben?"

"It just seemed kind of harsh for his father to have done that to him," I said looking at my bed in front of me as I was hugging my pillow.

"You also have to understand that once you get in that mindset, it hard to get out of it, his father didn't have much of a choice," said Burgesis calmly. "It was the only way to hope for his son's change of heart. They still at least had kept in touch through those years, even if Mike could bare to look at his own son."

"I guess," I said still feeling unconvinced. "Eladius left a few minutes before you came in, he wanted to go with us. I told him it would have been best if he stayed here with his parents."

"Oh, that's fine, they should be safe here. But I imagine if he didn't tell you he would've tried to sneak along in some way or another," said Burgesis laughing

Just then as Burgesis stopped laughing a knock came at the door and Burgesis raised his hand to the door slowly standing up, "Who is it?"

"It's Eggbert, may I come in? It's urgent!" Eggbert said rather hurriedly.

"ENTER!" I said loudly.

"I have news from my brothers at the school," said Eggbert as he handed Burgesis an envelope and a red seal with an "N" on it and in red, in the front of the envelope it said TO EGGBERT KROMOPOLIS. "Two of Nerogroben's men came to the school with a note that my brothers sent to me just now."

Burgesis took the already opened envelope from Eggbert and lifted the flap with the seal on it and pulled out a piece of parchment letter and three pieces of folded up poster sized parchment. Burgesis opened the letter and it said the following in red letter ink:

WANTED

BY ORDER OF KING NEROGROBEN

Headmaster Kromopolis,

I have received the most disturbing intelligence that Andrew, Pam, and their underage son, Eladius have abandoned their home. I assume they have either been kidnapped, or they have run off. I would like your assistance in their capture dead or alive for 80,000 gold coins for each person or persons caught for treason/abandonment. I have also heard news of the arrival of "the one". I want it to be understood that anyone caught holding, joining, or attempting to help "the one," will be sentenced to immediate imprisonment and possible death. Those who are caught joining allegiance to "the one," for acts of war and is also treason which (under the World of the Unknown Code Ch. 115 Section 5132) is punishable by death. I would be happy with an immediate response on this matter as soon as possible.

Your King,

Nerogroben

The three poster sized papers had Pam, Andrew's and Eladius's individual pictures on it and a family picture. I was horrified to read this and hear of this news.

"They must come with us, they now have no choice," I said to Burgesis.

"How are we going to do that? Everyone is going to be looking for them now," said Eggbert worriedly looking at Burgesis.

"Well, it's only a matter of time before he tries here to look for them," Burgesis said quietly as he finished reading the parchment.

"Well, we can't take them to the school now," said Eggbert to Burgesis.

"Wait, you mean I can't go to the school now?" I asked Burgesis who started to say something.

"Yes," Eggbert interrupted and looked at me, "Nerogroben's men are literally knocking at my doorstep of that school, and how is it going to look if I just happen to have a random Magical Human elf there. Especially if they insist on searching the school," said Eggbert worriedly.

"Where do we go then?" I asked Eggbert and Burgesis feeling hopeless.

"I didn't want to take you there yet, but it seems like I have no choice in the matter now," said Burgesis quietly to himself.

"Where then," I asked Burgesis.

Burgesis gave Eggbert a look and then said: "Let me think about it and see what our next move will be."

They both left my room.

Chapter 25
The Guards Decision

The next morning it was decided to tell everyone what was going on after breakfast in the living room.

"We have some recent bad news that we need to talk to you all about," said Eggbert motioning to me to continue as Burgesis and I stood up and moved next to him.

"It has come to our attention through Eggbert, that Nerogroben's men from his army were at the School of the Unknown recently," I said calmly looking at everyone in the room. They all started talking amongst themselves inaudibly and then silenced as I continued. "They asked Eggbert to see if he can consider the recent disappearance of Pam, Andrew, and their son, Eladius Smitherton. Apparently, they are wanted by Nerogroben dead or alive for treason and desertion and there is a rumor of my arrival which has sparked chaos and worry in Nerogroben," I continued. "I know I can trust you all in this room not to turn on me or them. You all have seen yourselves have seen how much easier things could be without an enemy such as Nerogroben, even though I may not have passed your clan tests yet, I ask that you allow this family to be under your protection with me as well," I asked looking around.

"Such a favor needs to be firmly decided amongst The Guard as a whole, Mark," Burgesis said quietly. "If you, Andrew, Pam, and Eladius could step outside we will talk about this," he continued looking at Barty and then turned to me and I nodded and walked out of the room with them. Barty stood up and followed us out silently as he closed the doors after we left. As soon as we did, Eladius hugged me as we waited outside.

"I'm scared Mark," Eladius said still hugging me.

"I know, it is okay, Eladius, everything is going to work out," I said patting his head. About fifteen minutes later, the door opened and Barty came in.

"We have reached a decision," he explained, as we all then walked back into the living room and sat down. I looked at him as he continued smiling. "We have all decided it is okay to guard the four of you, until such time your lives aren't in as much danger."

"That is awesome!" I asked looking around and Eladius got up smiling and hugged me.

"I'm sorry," Eladius said noticing my look on my face, "I am just SO happy!"

Everyone laughed.

"So, we can't take you to the school now to train you," said Eggbert looking around. He then turned to Mike and Andrea and said, "What do you suggest?"

They both shrugged, and Mike said "Well they can't stay here too long because it's only a matter of time that Nerogroben's men could be here next. We can add further protection to our clan, which will protect us temporarily from his army, for a little while but not for long," said Mike looking at Burgesis who nodded in agreement. Mike got up and left the room to warn his men and clan of the possible coming of Nerogroben's men.

"My question is how did Nerogroben's men and Nerogroben himself find out about Mark's arrival? He has only been here a week and we don't even have him trained yet, this concerns me," said Burgesis. "I know none of you betrayed Mark because none of you are displaying the symptoms of the spell I casted, so I will be checking on the other clan members to see who it was who betrayed Mark."

Everyone looked around at each other.

Burgesis got up and turned to Eggbert who was standing next to his chair and said, "I need your help with that," as he patted his robes where his map and his pipe was, and Eggbert nodded and they left the room.

Now everyone in the room was looking at me.

"I don't think we have to worry," I said to Eladius "We are going to be safe here for now until we figure out where we are going and what we are going to do."

"Who do you think it was who betrayed you and told Nerogroben that you're here?" Eladius asked as everyone looked at me and Barty left the room to join Burgesis.

"I don't know," I said sadly, "Some lost soul, I guess we will find out in a moment," as Mike Smitherton entered the room again.

"What are you going to do when you find out who it was that betrayed you?" asked Eladius carefully.

"I have not thought that far ahead," I said carefully, and to be honest, it was hard for me to even consider that someone would still betray me knowing what I was capable of. Also, considering what, I have already done to improve the World of the Unknown thus far. At the same time, I was not oblivious to what could happen, and what would possibly have to be done to that person.

"My guards are aware of what to look out for," Mike said sitting down waiting with everyone else to find out who betrayed me.

Chapter 26
The Traitors

Meanwhile, in the next room, Burgesis took out the map and placed it on the table. He then stepped back away from it so Eggbert could look at it. Burgesis stood next to Barty who had just entered the room. Eggbert put his hand out and waved it across the map and said, "Revelio" and the map came to life while he looked at it.

While Eggbert continued to talk to himself, Burgesis looked at Barty who nodded as they both moved back from Eggbert.

"I have given Mark the book, but he still hasn't figured it out yet," whispered Burgesis to Barty quietly away from Eggbert's hearing.

"Give him time," Barty whispered reassuringly.

"But you heard him yourself, he says he knows that book cover to cover and yet, he doesn't know what he doesn't know," said Burgesis shaking his head.

"Are you starting to doubt Mark being "the one"?" asked Barty.

"Okay Eggbert," Burgesis said louder ignoring Barty's last comment. "I think we need to go over the leaders and check on them."

Eggbert then nodded silently as Burgesis and Barty moved closer to the map next to him. First Eggbert zoomed in to the Village of Natar to Tom's house, a moment later, Tom could be seen resting on a tree occasionally looking around.

"No, he is okay," said Burgesis shaking his head in frustration.

Then Eggbert moved the map to the north side of the city of Adornar to Jerry's house and Jerry a moment later was seen observing some passerby's and occasionally looking out his window of his home.

"Nope, he is okay as well," said Burgesis. "Check the Cunning's house in between the Village of Probar and the Beaver Valley almost close to here at the Woodland Elms."

As Eggbert zoomed in to their house, they could see Angie making tea in the kitchen and a few moments later bringing it to her husband Martin who looked sick in bed.

"That is one sick fox," said Eggbert shaking his head sadly.

"It's Martin, that traitor!" said Barty angrily.

"I have always had problems trusting the fox clan," said Burgesis shaking his head disappointedly, "Why am I not surprised?"

"Why? Because they're foxes!" said Barty smirking.

"No, it's because I have long suspected them of being spies for Nerogroben," Burgesis explained looking at Eggbert who kept quiet.

"What are you doing to do?" Eggbert asked.

"You can't seriously be thinking of doing what I think you're going to do," Barty said gruffly questioning looking at Burgesis.

"Mark needs to know. I will also now need to bring Martin the antidote for the curse that is on him, otherwise he will die. I know Mark would not want anyone to die without talking to them first," Burgesis continued looking at Barty who rolled his eyes and was shaking his head. "I will bring him here to face trial by Mark. Then he and The Guard will decide whether they are both guilty or innocent. In the end, it will be up to Mark who will be deciding their fate." Barty nodded and they left the room to meet Mark and the rest of The Guard. When they stepped into the living room everyone stood up.

"Who is the traitor among us?" asked Mike straight to the point.

Burgesis looked around at everyone and said "After looking at almost everyone on the map to see what was going on we saw Angie and Martin Cunning's house. Angie was making tea in the kitchen and had brought it to her husband Martin who was looking rather sick in bed. The curse that I used forbade anyone from mentioning to anyone outside of our circle Mark's name and his whereabouts. If they said anything of the sort even if they just said, "the one," to anyone who wasn't a part of the need-to-know group, they would be cursed with a sickness and without this antidote here the person would die in forty-eight hours," explained Burgesis as he pulled out a bottle of liquid from his robe pocket. "So, after looking at the map, we found that in the end Martin Cunnings betrayed you," said Barty angrily looking at me.

"Okay," I said looking at Eggbert and Burgesis who all nodded at Barty in agreement, "So what is your procedure now?" I asked looking at Eladius who looked worried.

"That is up to you. I would hope maybe at least a fair trial," said Burgesis looking around at The Guard who nodded their heads in agreement.

"I would like approval to talk to Martin before the trial first," I said to Burgesis.

"Of course, your job is to set precedent to see what we are to do in the future for all future traitors. Just know that what you do, and what you say, and how you handle this, will be what we will do in the future. It will be up to you and The Guard to decide whether they are guilty or innocent and it's your job to serve their punishment if they are found guilty," explained Burgesis as The Guard nodded in silence and in agreement as they looked to me.

"Who is going to get Martin and Angie?" I asked slowly.

"Burgesis has offered," said Barty quickly looking at Eggbert.

"To make sure nothing happens, Eggbert, I would like you to go instead," I said looking at Burgesis who gave me a surprised look and seemed as if he was going to argue in retort back.

I looked at him in the eyes and flashed them at him seriously and thought to myself, "I need to talk to you Burgesis," he then nodded quickly and relaxed back as everyone else followed me doing the same. They looked at Burgesis funny because he sat down before me.

Eggbert had remained standing nodded at me and then disappeared into thin air.

I looked around at everyone and said "Times are changing and Nerogroben is in fear of what he doesn't know about me. He doesn't like the idea that I can lead this rebellion again him in which I do not feel we will fail!"

Everyone in the room cheered in agreement as I left the room with Burgesis and went outside.

"Burgesis, obviously now we can't go to the school now to train, so where are we going to go?" I asked as he put his fingers to his chin in thought as Jana came outside with us.

"Barty and I talked last night," Burgesis explained, "We both agreed that it would be best to get the four of you to The Underground which is the land outside of the school, it will be safe and your rebellion army and supporters are there as well."

"The Underground?" I asked as Jana handed me a necklace.

"Well it is deep, very deep, below ground, and this is where the army practices and makes the weapons, the above ground, above that, is where they have practices, their sleeping quarters, and meeting rooms. It is so secret that the only way to get in and see the pace is if you have these special necklaces on," said Jana as I looked at the necklace and noticed that it had mahogany colored beads on it, "the beads have a symbol on them which stands for peace and harmony. If you don't have this necklace, then you can't see it and the only thing you can see is the open field like everyone else. We call these "Rebel Entry Necklaces, or REN."

"Wow!" I said very surprised.

"When we are leaving Woodland Elms to go there?" Jana asked curiously as I put on the necklace.

"First, we need to hold the trial, after the trial, then we can leave," I said firmly.

"Sorry excuse me, I don't mean to interrupt. I would like to show you where we keep the prisoners in our holding cells outside. I was thinking you could keep the Cunnings there upon Eggbert's arrival back," said Mike as he ushered us into the woods.

"This is where our holding cell is, it isn't much, but it works," said Mike pointing at them and then looked at me.

"You don't have anyone in them," I said looking ahead as we walked closer to them and no one was in them.

"We have already dealt with our issues before your arrival," said Mike.

"Oh okay," I said as I raised my hand towards one of the cells and said "lux" and as I said this my magimarks brightened and a light appeared from my hands. I looked at Mike whose eyes were wide open, and then I raised both my hands to the cell and said "confirmate corda lucem mutare esse quietum" and then a light beam shined blue from my palms and suddenly the cell seemed to light itself. "Mike, instruct Eggbert to bring them in this cell upon their arrival. Keep them there for fifteen minutes, before summoning me, to talk to Martin," I said to Mike who nodded and walked away rather quickly in fear.

"What did you just do?" asked Barty and Burgesis stood their shocked in front of the cell.

"I am tired of having to talk to people to change their hearts, and to be in peace, and have decided that I can do so while they are in their cells to save time," I said looking at the self- lit cell nodding in approval.

"No, but, do you know what you said in that spell?" asked Burgesis looking at me worriedly.

"Of course, I did, I said strengthen their hearts with light; and change them to be in peace," I responded.

"Oh okay," said Burgesis "Just making sure," as we all walked back inside.

Chapter 27
The Trial

As Burgesis and I walked into the living room, there was a lot of shouting and noise. As we walked closer inside we saw Eggbert smiling in the middle of the room and The Guard was surrounding him and two figures that were in front of him in the middle of the room. I looked at The Guard and then I saw Martin and Angie Cunnings standing in front of Eggbert muzzled and leashed with their heads down and their tails between their hind legs. Some of The Guard was throwing things at them in anger. As I moved closer to The Guard, everyone gradually noticed me and immediately moved aside as Burgesis pushed through to Martin's side and immediate was given the antidote which was in a bottle in his robes. The room had gotten quiet as they saw my presence, and I was disappointed with The Guard for acting so crudely to Martin and Angie Cunnings. I realized that it was because of a mix of being traitors but still I was frustrated at the sight of this and Burgesis noticed it.
"I have your prisoners Mark," said Eggbert proudly as he was smiling.
"I demand that you remove the muzzles and leashes off Angie and Martin immediately!" I said shaking in anger.

"Why?" said Barty looking at me to explain further. "They should be chained up!"

"You see Mark, we have a hierarchy here. We don't approve of others of lower class than ourselves, it has always been that way, and always will be. That is why we don't get along. You see that is why you are lucky to be what you are, a Magical Human Elf. You will never understand this and why some of us flinch in discomfort when we see you being gentle and kind to others who are lower than yourself." explained Eggbert smiling as he handed me a piece of paper with a chart he had handwritten out:

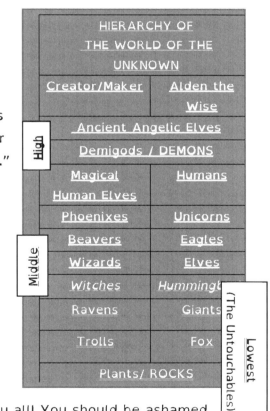

HIERARCHY OF THE WORLD OF THE UNKNOWN	
Creator/Maker	Alden the Wise
Ancient Angelic Elves	
Demigods / DEMONS	
Magical Human Elves	Humans
Phoenixes	Unicorns
Beavers	Eagles
Wizards	Elves
Witches	Hummingb...
Ravens	Giants
Trolls	Fox
Plants/ ROCKS	

High / Middle / Lowest (The Untouchables)

"How dare you all! You should be ashamed of yourselves!" I said reading the paper

Eggbert handed me. As I read, I could see that all the bold that were on top were considered Higher on the social class, then the chart showed how the witches and the hummingbrds were the middle class with the dotted line showing that the only reason why witches were considered middle class and not high class was because of the gender. Then lastly, the lower class or as the paper described, "The Untouchables" consisting of: The Ravens, The Giants, The Trolls, The Foxes, and The Plants and rocks. In complete anger, I crumbled up the paper I was handed and burned it with flames from my hand in front of him. Eggbert grew angry. My eyes turned white as The Guard stepped back a few paces. Then a good magimark burned white on me in painful heat, but I didn't care, I was so angry. "This prejudice is INTOLERABLE! I told you there won't be any hierarchy while I am here! NO ONE, can be shamed, mistreated, laughed at, or put down in this manner! Justice will be served fairly, without humiliation from everyone! ALSO, NEVER, will it be to this low level of hatred and in such disgrace and bad taste, that we treat each other with this disrespect!" I continued as apologies were said to me and everyone was in shame, "No wonder the Trolls felt the way they did, they felt unwelcomed by the rest of the Clans because they were different, I thought to myself as Burgesis nodded to me reading my thoughts sadly. He then reached down to them as he took the muzzles and leashes gently off Angie and Martin as they muttered a shamed thanks to me. I was angry with Martin, if he in fact, did betray me. I was upset at Angie if she knew of what had occurred still, but I figured I would talk to them later.

"You're Welcome. Now if you would please follow Mike, he will show you where you are going to be held for now," I said as Mike directed Angie and Martin outside. They all followed and as they neared the cell, it lit up on its own. The light could be seen from the front porch of the house. Both Martin and Angie became worried. Eggbert then pushed them into the now open cell as they went in, you could see the Grey Matter leave their bodies. They stood there weak, worried, crying, and scared. I walked out to them from the front porch, and everyone looked at me in silence.

"Martin and Angie Cunnings," I said firmly as they both looked at me "You have been summoned to a hearing to discuss your futures because of your apparent disloyalty and betrayal of me, and the rebellion of the World of the Unknown, what do you plead?"

"We plead guilty Mark," said Angie through the bars which were white "My husband Martin went to Nerogroben's men and told them about you and...

"Silence!" said Eggbert "You were the ones who told Nerogroben's Men about Eladius and his family as well!"

"NO, WE DIDN'T!" said Martin "I swear I didn't even know about them!"

"Martin is telling the truth," said Burgesis looking at me "Eggbert you mentioned Eladius and his family to Mark after the clan leaders who weren't in the guard left the room,"

I then looked to Eggbert who said looking around, "That's right, so someone else here is a traitor as well."

"Why would anyone in Mark's direct guard want to betray him if we swore to protect him," said Brittany angrily.

"Wait, no one else knew about the next location of where we were taking Mark except The Guard," said Mike Smitherton looking at me trying to be helpful.

"Why are you trying to frame us for trying to tell Nerogroben about Eladius and his family? We only told them that we have heard rumors about "the one's" arrival," said Martin to Eggbert.

"Yeah," said Angie in agreement "My husband didn't say where you guys were or where you guys were going or your names of who was part of the rebellion, unless you did," Angie suggested looking at Eggbert

"Wait!" said Eladius standing up pointing his finger at Eggbert, "I saw and heard you last night!"
Just then Eggbert's eyes changed and had a red light was coming from them as he waved his hands around. Eggbert then pointed his finger at Eladius who was standing in front of me and said, "Electro Pila!"
I realized what was going on and pointed a finger at Eggbert and said "scutum lapidem" and the electro ball flew towards both Eladius and myself as I blocked it with a stone shield. We both then flew back 1000 feet from the powerful spell.
"Eggbert tried to attack Mark and our son!" shouted Andrew who tried to retaliate with water.
Just then Eggbert whispered a few words and disappeared into thin air missing the water attack as I shouted, "Coward!" and Burgesis shouted "Wait!" but it was too late. Eggbert was gone without a trace.

Chapter 28
The Tunnel

Eladius then turned around at me and hugged me and said "Thank you, you saved both our lives!" I broke Eladius from the hug and said "Eladius, what was it that you saw and heard about Eggbert?"
"Last night, I couldn't sleep so I went on a walk. It was then, as I was coming back from my walk, I saw Eggbert leave the house. I followed him and he walked into the woods here, and he was talking to someone. I saw that he paid someone to keep quiet. I couldn't hear the whole conversation just bits and pieces of it. They mentioned you, me, my parents, Nerogroben, and the school. But I kept it to myself until now because I didn't want anything to happen to me for reporting it," said Eladius looking at me as Pam and Andrew came up to us and so did Mike Smitherton listening to the conversation.
"That means one of the elves is an informant for Nerogroben!" said Mike looking around.
"Mark, The Guard has decided that Angie and Martin are not guilty for treason since they didn't fully mention our names, our location, or our plans," said Burgesis carefully. I walked towards the cell where Martin and Angie as I observed them.

"As for you two, I am disappointed in you both. I must insist you prove your loyalty to me and The Guard. I temporarily would like both. of you to turn in your "Rebellion Entry Necklace's or REN's to Burgesis immediately. We will be adding a special enchantment to ensure your continued loyalty to me and our cause," I said

"What do you mean?" said Angie angrily. "You don't even trust us now, and we could've told them more, but we didn't!"

"This just means that you are selfish and greedy, the price for the information wasn't high enough to fully be disloyal to me," I said looking at them as they handed their necklaces to Burgesis, "I think if it was for the right price, you would put lives in danger, you lack loyalty to me, respect, and integrity to me." The guard nodded in agreement to me, some whispered, "Traitors!"

"We are sorry Mark!" said Martin pleadingly.

"For now Burgesis, keep them locked up in the holding cell until I have a chance to decide their fate tomorrow," I said looking at Burgesis who nodded.

"I will take first watch, and everyone will take turns guarding them until tomorrow morning. This will be when Mark decides what we will do in the future for traitors," said Burgesis to everyone who silently nodded in agreement as I turned and went back into the house.

"We should all get some rest," Andrea suggested as everyone nodded in agreement and went to their rooms. I stayed in the living room and sat by the fire to warm myself. Eladius and his parents stayed behind in the living room with me. A few moments later Mike and Andrea joined us sitting on both sides of Eladius as they looked at me.

Finally, after a few moments of silence, Andrea said "A lot has happened today, huh?"

"Yes, a lot has," I said slowly, while looking, into the fire.

"We have never seen light used like you used it today," said Mike looking at me after Andrea nudged him to say something. "Was this your first time?"

"Yes, it was, but, I used it to help make a difference," I said continuing to look, into the fire.

"I am worried that one of our elves in the clan is an informant. Is there something that you can do for us to help rid us of this Grey Matter from within our own clan walls?" asked Mike carefully. "We need your help and advice to ensure that this doesn't happen again."

"Yes, I was just thinking of that," I said looking up. "Do you have any archways or tunnels around here?" I asked looking at Mike.

"We have a small tunnel that is under a bridge near here," said Andrea.

"But that is a small tunnel, he asked for an archway," said Mark impatiently as he started to think.

"That's fine, a small tunnel is good, show me," I said standing up. The six of us left the living room and left out the front door and took a left to the side of the house. We then went into the woods, we traveled for only about a minute and the tunnel appeared.

"It's perfect," I said smiling at the tunnel and then to Mike and Andrea as they both beamed back at me. They then became serious as they saw me, raise my right palm and point towards at the tunnel.

I then said the following words and it had appeared around the archway in gold lettering "Numera omnes qui ingredient caveant, quia in pace sempiterna fore amicum et inimicum."

Everyone looked at it in awe, however unaware of what it meant.

"For those who don't know Latin this phrase means, "Beware all who enter, because friend and foe will then be in peace forever," I said.

"That's it?" asked Mike flabbergasted "Is this going to make any difference?

"Hang on, Mike," I continued as I still had my palm raised up. "I haven't finished, you want to change the hearts of people and help them into our rebellion from your clan and other clans? To do so, you must heal them of Grey Matter first, walk them through the tunnel at least once,"

Mike nodded and said, "How is this going to help?"

"Watch," I said as I still had my right palm at the entrance of the tunnel and my magimarks glowed again as I raised my right palm towards the tunnel and closed my eyes. The others stepped back in fear, as my eyes then opened and were glowing with white light. I took a deep breath and shouted slowly and deeply, "Cordium firmabit luce omnes eos, in pace in perpetuum," at that moment a light came from my palm and the light escaped to the other end of the tunnel. The Latin translation for what I just said," I started to explain to Mike and Andrea, "means "strengthen all hearts with light, change them all to be in peace forever."

From the moment, I said those words the woods were lit up from the light from the tunnel. The tunnel was originally made of grey cement and had Grey Matter fog flowing through it was now changed to a pure white color marble, which looked beautiful.

"Will this work?" asked Mike curiously.

"Well, you need to tell your clan to go through the Tunnel of Light. You all should walk your enemies through here, while holding their hands, and your bond will turn from feelings of evil and hatred to that similar of friends. But those of Nerogroben's army may need to go through the tunnel a few times to get rid of the Grey Matter completely," I said looking at Eladius who had run out to us with Andrew. Just then Andrew turned to Mike and said "Is it okay if my family and I go through the Tunnel of Light?"

"Of course that is fine," Mike said then he asked his men to gradually wake up the clan and place them through the tunnel twice. He directed them to one by one go once in and turn around and come out the same way they entered. Gradually the whole clan was awakened and went through the tunnel. Then they all came out the same way just as Mike ordered. We watched in awe as everyone was going in the tunnel with disgruntled and angry attitudes leave the same tunnel coming back in a single file line looking happier and with color in their faces. They were smiling and were more positive and looked as though they just had a lot of weight lifted off their shoulders as the Grey Matter dissolved from the people.

"What a miracle!" said Mike as he started touching the people who were coming out of the tunnel and he jumped in the air feeling giddy.

Gradually the clan was rejuvenated, and all the Grey Matter disappeared out from the upper ends of the tunnel off the elves. Eladius, Pam, and Andrew looked brighter and happy as well as they came back to where Mike Andrea and I were standing observing everyone.

"We are going to head to bed," said Pam looking at Andrew and Eladius who nodded feeling relaxed.

"Thank you for what you are doing, Mark" said Pam looking at me.

"You're welcome," I said looking at Eladius who I noticed did look tired.

I stayed behind with Mike and Andrea as we saw Pam and Andrew and Eladius head back towards the house and an hour later we started to see the sun rise as morning approached us. "The elves seemed more talkative to us, as they came back from going through the tunnel. Some would thank us for healing them and letting them go through, as they went passed us going back to their own homes. By early morning before mid-morning everyone in the Elven clan had gone through the tunnel. Mike told everyone in the clan to meet at noon at the holding cells as we walked back to the house.

"Do you know what you are going to do?" Andrea asked.

"I am going to take a nap," I said looking at Mike who nodded.

I went to my room and shut the door. After not sleeping all night and using that spell on the Tunnel of Light, I felt exhausted. As soon as I got into bed and laid on my side facing the door, and then I fell fast asleep.

Chapter 29
The Verdict

About six hours later, there was a knock at my door, it was Eladius and behind him was Burgesis.
"Good afternoon sleepyhead," said Burgesis as Eladius gave him a look of confusion.
"Don't worry, that's not an insult," said Burgesis noticing Eladius "it's a phrase Mark is familiar with and is used to from Earth."
"Oh okay, that's cool," said Eladius smiling as I looked at him.
"The guard needs your verdict as to what we do with traitors," said Burgesis looking at me seriously. "Again, the decision that you make, will be what we will do in the future to our traitors. Also, Mike found the elf in his clan who talked to Eggbert the other night and has him in the same holding cell as Angie and Martin."
"What is the name of the elf?" I asked Burgesis seriously still lying on my side.
"His name is Josian," said Burgesis as he left the room and closed the door.
"What are you going to do?" asked Eladius worriedly "You promised me and my family you would let us decide who we pledged loyalty to, and you said, "You wouldn't kill unless necessary."

"I know," I said as I wiped my eyes and face with my hands. I sat up, reached for the cloth next to the basin, which were both on the table next to my bed. I dunked the cloth in the water, wrung it out, and wiped my face with the cold cloth. "I know what I said, and I intend to keep the process of death, suffering, and pain as a last resort for everyone," I said looking at Eladius who smiled. "I believe in giving people at least a second chance."

Eladius started to leave out of my room and then turned around and said, "I have always known in my heart that you were a great leader, and I continue to have faith that you will be great, and won't let us down."

He left the room and I realized what I had to do, even though I didn't like this idea completely because a lot could go wrong. I tried to have faith in myself as I left my room, and slowly went outside and walked to the holding cells. As I made my way through the path to the holding cells, ahead I could hear a crowd of elves and some of the guard shouting, "Kill them, Kill the traitors!" When I got there everyone suddenly stopped shouting as I raised my arms for everyone to be in peace and they bowed and they walked a few yards away from the holding cells.

I walked towards the holding cells as The Guard stood waiting for me. The Guard stood behind me along with Eladius, his parents, Angie, and Mike. "I can tell that though this clan has gone through the tunnel twice, the Grey Matter that is still around us, is affecting your judgment as you still want these traitors' dead. But what good would come from that? I would be no better than Nerogroben himself. I want you all to reflect today on yourselves. Decide if the idea of walking through that tunnel that I made daily, would be ideal to keep your judgement clear at all times," I said looking at the crowd. "When was the last time you committed an act of treason on your clan or someone else judged you? Or when was the last time that someone's life depended on your answer, and you didn't help them and they died? We are all better than that inside. From now on I ask that you make decisions from your heart. Double check that the daily decisions you make, aren't evil, bad decisions, or only for your own personal gain, but rather for the benefit of others. Some choices that we make in life we can't change, after it's too late, and its then that we regret making them. I seriously recommend that you check your conscious consistently, because you don't want to be the cause of the Grey Matter thickening around here," I said looking around at everyone as they looked down in shame. "After much deliberation and council I have almost reached my verdict," I said to the crowd, and I noticed that many of them had red magimarks on them. "I will talk to all three of them individually at the house and if they are to be killed or die, it will *only* be done by my hand, thank you! Those of you who have Red Evil Magimarks please stay here," I said a group of people left the crowd and a huge handful of beings stayed. I then closed my eyes and took a deep breath in. I opened my eyes and they were white. Then I took another deep breath in and my magimarks all glowed white as I raised both my hands and the crowd of people stepped a few spaces back. "I command that this evil magimark to be mended in light and goodness. Precipio quod corrigendum sit in luce magimark malum et bonum." Just then lights emerged from the palms of my hands and they hit all the red magimarks on the beings in front of me. They all screamed in pain, crying in agony. After a minute of the light emerging from my palm the light stopped and everyone was silent. Burgesis looked at me from behind wide eyed and smiled. I left the crowd as they were talking amongst themselves about what I had said and some of them were looking at where their own red magimarks were. I then walked towards the house and The Guard followed me further behind. As I walked into the house, I went into the kitchen and started four kettles of water over the fire. The guard came in and everyone was applauding.

"Guys, nothing has happened yet," I said feeling rather surprised.

"You should have seen how stunned everyone is right now," said Burgesis smiling. "By the way, you are going to need a place to meet these people?"

"Yeah, I was thinking maybe I could borrow the kitchen here so that I can talk to people privately. I just need a sign placed on the front lawn stating that one-on-one sessions are at the back door," I said to Burgesis who nodded and Andrea who had overheard came in.

"Consider it done, Mark," she said looking at me smiling. The kettles finished heating up and were whistling after taking the four of the kettles off the fire and placing them on the counter. I pointed to one of the kettles and said "Serum veritate" and thought well hopefully this will be a reliable "truth serum" as the water turned a peach color and marked it with a hidden dot and did the same for one other kettle as I added the tea bags in all of them.

Chapter 30
To Mend a Broken Heart

Just then a knock came at the door, and it was Burgesis. He looked around and saw that it was only me in the room.

"I wanted you to mend my broken heart and my only red magimark I got when I was part of Nerogroben's army," he said as he looked embarrassed as he said this, and he took off his shirt and showed me his red magimark on his chest. I placed my hand on his chest, closed my eyes, and took a deep breath in. I opened my eyes, and they were white. Then I took another deep breath in and my magimarks all glowed white as I said, "I command that this evil magimark to be mended in light and goodness. Precipio quod corrigendum sit in luce magimark malum et bonum." Just then lights emerged from the palm of my hand, and it hit the red magimark on Burgesis as he screamed in pain, crying in agony. After that I noticed that the Red Magimark was gone. Then I put my hand on the magimark of his broken heart.

"What are you doing?" he asked worriedly.

"Relax, do you trust me?" I asked as he then nodded and cringed at the thought of having more pain and being unsure if this was going to work.

"Clear your mind," I said as he nodded in silence. I thought about the words of what I was going to say in English first to try to translate it, "I command that this broken heart be mended in light" I said in a loud deep voice "Quod praecipio tibi hoc in corde emendari lucem" and a sound came from my hand and a white light came from my hand and it undid his broken heart.

As I looked at the magimark light came from the palm of my hands, the magimark disappeared. Burgesis screamed in pain as tears came from his eyes. After a while, all that was on his chest was bare skin now. Burgesis blacked out and the magimark from his neck disappeared. I fainted as the magic I used was so strong it knocked us both out. An hour later we apparently were found by Eladius and Andrew who had carried us into the living room on the couches. I opened my eyes and I saw Eladius's worried face staring above me as I smiled, he backed away giving me more space.

"You nearly died, Mark," said Barty looking at me seriously.

"Did it work?" I asked looking at Burgesis who was still passed out laying on the other couch which was across the coffee table that was in the middle of the room.

"I think it worked," said Barty who had looked at Burgesis's chest and neck."

Suddenly I sat up and remembered that I had to have those one-on-one meetings with the others. "It can wait," Burgesis said as he seemed to be reading my mind as he opened his eyes and I sat up. Barty had jumped when Burgesis had said that. "Thank you, Mark," said Burgesis as he slowly sat up weakly smiling. "I feel different now, stronger in a way than before.
"You both scared us all half to death!" said Jana coming in with two wet wash cloths wiping my forehead and then wiping Burgesis forehead, neck, and chest.
"Ouch, watch it," said Burgesis who reacted as the wet cloth seemed to sear his skin where the broken heart magimark was on his chest as she jumped.
"You both should try to rest some more," said Burgesis to me as I looked at Burgesis worriedly.
"I'm fine, in fact I have never felt loads better!" as he smiled. I laid back down looking at the ceiling of the living room as I closed my eyes and rested.
An hour later, I awoke Burgesis was resting as I slowly got up, pick up the sign that was on the side of the foot of the couch and placed it on the yard outside the kitchen door.
There were a few guard members and many elves nearby. Many gradually came in as I slowly healed their red magimarks. After removing about One hundred red magimarks one by one, I grew tired as

I closed the door after the last person and picked up the sign and went back to sleep as I placed the sign at the end of the couch again.

I reflected on the pain people were feeling while the red magimarks were being removed. I realized that as the red magimarks were coming off the beings, these were given to them for various evil and immoral acts. In many ways, I thought about the process of what I did to get the magimarks removed and how it felt for them. Even though this process weakened me and had been painful in a way to me by using the light of forgiveness and peace on them, it healed them. I was thankful to have this power of the light of forgiveness and peace. Having this ability, I noticed beings changed around me. This made me feel good being able to make that kind of a difference in this world that was full of evil.

The problem I had to still deal with is the issue of the clans and their intolerance of those who differed from them and the strong presence of this "so called" hierarchy that I wanted to have demolished. It was immoral, and to judge others based on how they lived and who they were and who and how they loved, it was degrading. I was still how I was going to deal with this issue…. trying to clear my mind, I slowly closed my eyes and took a deep breath and fell asleep on the couch again.

Chapter 31
The Light of Forgiveness

I woke up, and I saw the Burgesis wasn't there on the couch anymore. I went into the kitchen to see the kettles still there. I placed them over the fire again until they whistled and as soon as they did, Burgesis came into the kitchen. I placed the kettles on metal trays which were on the counter.

"You never stop do you," he said looking at me as I poured a cup of tea out of the kettle with a dot on it into a teacup and placed it at the seat which was in front of me. I then poured a second cup of tea from another kettle without the dot on it and put it in front of me adding sugar into it.

"Nope, there is much to be done. I am a very impatient person, and am okay to admit that," I said looking at Burgesis insistently.

"Well, it just so happens that I figured that you would say that, so I took the liberty of telling Eladius to set up your sign in the front of the house again," said Burgesis smiling as I nodded in thanks. Just then a knock came at the door, it was Angie. She very shyly came into the room as Burgesis excused himself out the kitchen door leading to the living room as I locked it.

"Welcome Angie," I said "Thank you for being courageous in coming to see me," as I smiled at her.

Then I motioned for her to sip her tea which was still warm.

"You're welcome, Mark," she said as she took a sip of the tea "This tea is very good. I want to tell you that we are deeply sorry for committing treason against you."

"What I want to know is, why did you do it?" I asked.

"Things have been difficult for us," she said looking at me, "We have been having a hard time supporting ourselves. Martin believed it was the only way to get some help. I know it was wrong of us, we are so sorry. It's just at times it seems like giving in to Nerogroben and his ways is the only easy answer," she said looking down.

"Sometimes anything worth having doesn't come easy, and anything that comes easy is not usually worth having. The first step to all this is realizing you were in the wrong, and being honest and living up to your mistakes. By doing so, you ought to be prepared for the consequences of your choices, you have always had the ability to talk to me. You know that even if I am a Magical Human Elf, you can still ask me for help, or for whatever you need help for. It doesn't make you weak or any less of a being to admit that you don't know the answer to something or what to do. Sometimes we feel that when we are desperate for something in our lives, we must do something risky to get out of it, and I must insist that sometimes this is not the wisest decision to make in life," I said looking at her sternly as she shuddered.

"We are really sorry Mark," Angie said looking at me crying. "Honestly, it wasn't until you had them take the leashes and muzzles off us, that we honestly felt less shameful for being what we are. A lot of times when we are out in the community, people judge us and look at us horribly for what we are. We can't help who we are. You have made things a little easier for us within your rebellion ranks, and I just want to say, thank you for that," Angie continued looking up at me with tears in her eyes and then looked down again in shame.

"Sometimes in life, beings who don't support us for who we are, aren't worth having in our lives. Surround yourselves with beings who treat you with respect, and who are positive. Beings can't sometimes resist the temptation to be negative or opinionated and in doing that, they forget that they may violate you for who you are, and that you are a being with feelings..." I continued pausing for a moment and took a deep breath and sighed, "I can tell your allegiance is not actually with Nerogroben by your heart," I said calmly. "Please stand as I pass judgment and verdict on you."

Angie had finished her tea she stood up shaking in fear and with wide eyes. I then hugged her and said "I forgive you for all wrong doing and give my blessings to mend and rid all the evil grey matter and magimarks on your soul," I said and I translated it to Latin "placatus tibi fuero in omnibus bonis male faciendi et ministra mihi animam tuam et auferam omne malum magimarks," as I said this, in our hug, all my magimarks turned white and a warmth came over me. It transferred to Angie as she started to cry in happiness and thanksgiving. After the light disappeared from me I released our hug and she had tears in her eyes. She was snuffling and started to cry.

"I feel like an enormous weight has been lifted from me," she said as she put her hands on her face. "Thank you so much!" she said.

"It's called forgiveness, go in peace and spread the good news," I said, "Forgive those who are evil doers, and you will see them change as they themselves change their hearts!" she nodded and left the room. I started to tear up because it worked.

As soon as she left, Martin her husband knocked on the back door, I ushered him in. He was still hardened for being put into the holding cell, and he seemed rather angry coming in.

"Please sit down and have some tea with me," I said pouring him a cup of tea from the kettle with a dot on it.

"Why on Earth do you want to talk to me, just kill me and get it over with," he said grumpily.

"What I want to understand is why you did it?" I asked as he took a sip of hot tea I had poured for him, "Why did you tell Nerogroben's men about me?"

"We needed the silver," he said "We hadn't eaten in weeks, and we haven't been able to provide for ourselves with our clan."

"But you are leaders, aren't you eating better than the rest of your clan?" I asked thinking about how things were on Earth in comparison as far as food.

"In our clan, everyone naturally fends for themselves," he said

"I think you all should change that and help each other out as a community," I said. "After all how can you get much accomplished if you aren't communicating and helping each other out? Can you all not trust each other or something?" I suggested sipping my tea and inviting him to drink some more as well.

"Our clan has been through a lot since the Dark War and some of us still have alliances with Nerogroben. I just happen to also represent our clan for you," he said sipping his tea.

"How can you represent me if you can't lead like me?" I asked seriously.

"Because I don't know how to lead like you can," he said starting to tear up.

"I can show you and I can help your clan out if you let me," I said reaching out my hand on top of his paw as he nodded. I hugged him and said "I forgive you for all wrong doing and give my blessings to mend and rid all the evil magimarks on your soul," I said and I translated it to Latin "placatus tibi fuero in omnibus bonis male faciendi et ministra mihi animam tuam et auferam omne malum magimarks," as I said this in our hug again all my magimarks turned white and a warmth came over me and it transferred to Martin as he started to cry. After the light disappeared from me I released our hug. Martin looked at me and he stood up and I did as well, as we both started, to walk to the door.

I looked around and then I said, "I am going to give you and your wife a second chance. If you do betray me again, there will not be a third chance, and you will force me to kill you and your wife," he then looked at me with tears in

his eyes and nodded in understanding.

"Goodbye Mark," he said, "I understand, and I am going to go find my wife and let her know."

I nodded seriously and said, "When you are ready let me help your clan be better for each other."

He nodded and with that he left the house.
I then walked into the living room to find Andrea, Mike, Barty, Jana, Burgesis, and Eladius all sleeping on the couches. I turned off the candle by the doorway that lit the room by blowing on it quietly. I then closed the living room door quietly, and walked into the kitchen next door, and closed the kitchen door behind me. I realized myself getting tired, but I thought just one last one for now. I opened the back door and I saw two figures flying in mid-air. It was Pine and Rose, the two hummingbirds.

Chapter 32
An Issue of Loyalty

"We are here to help because we have heard that Eggbert has disappeared. We both know that you need to be trained more," said Rose flying in mid-air still next to her husband, Pine in the doorway.
"You have actually come at a bad time, everyone is sleeping, and I was about to meet with Josian," I said calmly ushering them inside.
"Who were you having tea with?" asked Pine curiously looking at the tea pots and the three now empty cups of tea.
"Angie and Martin betrayed me, so I talked to them over tea," I said happily looking at Pine and Rose who looked at each other open beaked.
"Where are they?" asked Pine looking around the room.
"Do you need help with their dead bodies?" asked Rose looking at me seriously.
"No, no they aren't dead," I said looking at Rose as she looked at Pine who was flying back to her side.
"Oh, that's unfortunate, you mean that they aren't dead yet," asked Pine looking at me and then looking at the teacups "We can fix that, you were thinking poison, eh?"
"No, no, no, you misunderstand me," I said looking at Pine and Rose putting my arms up with my

fingers out as they flew on my gloved fingers. "You both have it all wrong, they already left, and I already had tea with them."

"Oh good," said Rose confused. "But they betrayed you!"

"So, now, we can go kill them," said Pine now sounding enthusiastic.

"No, they did betray me, so we had tea and talked it over. They just left, we don't need to kill them," I explained more fully.

"But we must kill our enemies," said Pine angrily. "not have tea with them!"

"No, we need to love and forgive our enemies first," I said looking at Pine.

"So, after you love and forgive them, then do you kill them?" asked Rose

"We *only* kill if it's necessary, as a last resort," I said to Rose.

"I believe in second chances," I said coolly "I told them that if they betray me again, they will leave me no choice but to kill them."

"How can you give others a second chance," asked Rose roughly.

"Because I am not going to cause more pain, suffering, evil, and destruction if I can help it, then what is necessary. After all, how would that make me any different from Nerogroben?" I asked very seriously as I walked to the table and placed Rose on a chair next to mine.

"How do you intend to do this with little casualties?" asked Pine who flew next to Rose.

"First by leading by example," I said seriously as I sat at the table next to Rose and Pine. Just then there was a knock at the door and I said to Rose and Pine,

"Who is that?" asked Pine nodding towards the door as I pulled four empty tea cups out.

"I want you to observe, and I do not want you to say much, we are going to have some tea," I started to say looking at the door as I started to pour tea into their cups from the kettle without any markings on it. Then I grabbed the kettle with a marking on it and poured it into a separate tea cup. I then placed that tea cup and put it on the table in front of the seat in front but across the table from me.

"We are about to have tea with an elf, his name is Josian, I think he just knocked at the back door just now," I said calmly as I finished pouring out the tea, before answering the door. They both nodded silently. I walked to the back door of the kitchen and an Elf was standing there and looked at me as I ushered him inside. "Come in Josian," I said, "I have been expecting you, this is Pine and Rose they are friends of ours and they have my complete confidence that what is said in this room will not leave it," I continued looking at them as they nodded silently.

"They just released me from the holding cell and said you wanted to speak to me," said Josian slowly observing us.

"It's my understanding that you have betrayed me through Eggbert," I said calmly looking at him as he held his head down in shame. Then he lifted his head up looking at me.

"You have no right to be here in the Woodland Elms!" he shouted at me as I looked at him surprised. His face had turned a tomato red and I could see the red magimarks on him start to inflame and burn his skin more as he seemed not to react to the pain.

"He has every right to be here!" Pine interrupted angrily.

I immediately placed my hand up to calm Pine down.

"I can handle this," I said, as he calmed down. "So is Eggbert a friend or a foe?" I asked Josian who continued to glare at me in hatred.

"He is neither," said Josian bitterly "Wizards answer to no one, and they do not choose sides. This is the way it is and always has been until you came here. There never used to be sides, until the prophecy, and *you* came along. They only choose to follow what is and what isn't," Josian explained glaring around at everyone who was listening intently.

"What did you tell Eggbert or what did Eggbert tell you?" I asked.

"I refuse to tell you unless you make a deal with me instead of trying to kill me," Josian said in a changed tone of voice.

"I have made it clear that you aren't to be killed at all until we have had a chance to talk and then you decide your own fate from there," I said looking around at everyone.

"Which is more than you deserve," said Rose indignantly.

"Answer the question: What did you tell Eggbert or what did Eggbert tell you?" said Pine gruffly looking at Josian who refused to speak for a few minutes.

"Why don't you sit down," I said looking at Josian as I pointed to the table, "We were just about to have some tea anyway. You had just knocked on the door after I decided to pour a cup for you."

Josian followed me and sat at the table with Pine and Rose.

"How do I know it's not poisoned?" he asked.

"Answer Mark's question," Pine repeated to Josian as he was silent.

"I will drink from my cup first," I said slowly.

Josian looked unreceptive as I sipped my tea from my cup.

"Please," I said as I placed my hand on top of Josian's hand from across the table.

In frustration, Josian sighed, took a sip of his tea and looked at me silently. Slowly after a few more sips he said, "Eggbert told me to tell Nerogroben's men of your name and your arrival into the World of the Unknown, but not to mention him as the source of the information."

"Okay, what else?" interrupted Rose anxiously.

"Also, that you aren't trained on the elements fully yet," said Josian quietly looking at me as he sipped some more of his tea.

"How could Eggbert do that?" asked Rose looking at Pine.

"I think the more important question to ask is why Eggbert did that?" said Pine grimly.

"The problem is Mark that you're too trusting of everyone," said Burgesis from behind us as we all jumped. We looked at him and his eyes looked tired still. "Sorry I didn't think that you were meeting with people this late, Mark."

"What are you two doing here," asked Burgesis looking at Pine and Rose as he sat down on the other side of me across from Josian who looked uncomfortable as he continued to sip more of his tea.

"We found out that Eggbert betrayed Mark and so we left immediately looking around for you all," said Rose happily.

"Then how did you find us and find this out?" Burgesis asked carefully sounding very concerned.

"We remembered at the meeting who was chosen as The Guard and did process of elimination," said Pine looking at me as I had briefly zoned out deep in thought. "Then we heard the rumors along the way here."

"Actually, in reality, Eggbert didn't betray me," I said aloud.

"What!?" everyone said at once and Josian just stared at me. I poured out a cup of tea from an unmarked kettle and handed it to Burgesis who nodded his head in thanks. Burgesis then took the cup of tea from me.

"What do you mean that he didn't betray you?" said Pine.

"What I mean is that Eggbert could have told Nerogroben's men more than what he did, like my current location, The Guard, the locations of those involved in the rebellion, and our strengths and weaknesses, but he didn't," I said calmly looking at Burgesis who sipped his tea.

Burgesis had been listening intently what was going on and said "I agree with you Mark, but why leave us after Eladius said, "I saw and heard what you said last night" if it wasn't fully betrayal? Why did he not defend himself?" as he took another sip of the tea from his tea cup.

I thought about what he said as I took a sip of the tea.

After a few moments, I said, "Even though it wasn't full betrayal, it may have been guilt that made him leave. Possibly even shame for what he did. He also probably didn't think that I would listen to what he had to say. He didn't think I would listen to his explanation of what happened and was scared. I might have reacted emotionally from the situation instead of responding logically as well."

"Mark, it still doesn't excuse what he did," said Burgesis looking at me sternly. "Stop making excuses for everyone, you know what he did was wrong, and *he* knows what he did was wrong. So, in the end he should be punished for it."

"No, I don't think I am making excuses for him, and I am asking for the people in our rebellion to find him and bring him to me alive, and unhurt," I said looking at Burgesis concerned.

"Then after you have him, what are you going to do? Kill him or torture him like you are going to do to me," retorted Josian who was looking at me.

"I told you Josian, we are not going to kill you. I wished to talk to you and then I want to heal you," I said looking at Josian.

"Heal me?" he asked, as he then perked his ears up.

"He doesn't need healing Mark. We just need to hand him over to Nerogroben and his army," said Pine and Rose nodded in agreement as I took Josian's empty teacup from the front of him. I pointed to Josian and said "dormire eum" and he fell asleep in front of us.

"You're wrong Burgesis," I said as I put my arm to my side and looked at Burgesis. "I am not too trusting of people here. I put a truth serum in the tea and the whole conversation we were having with Josian right now he was speaking truth to us," I said as the three of them looked down at their teacups and put them down on the table.

"I didn't put truth serum in your teacups if you noticed throughout our conversation I used an unmarked tea kettle for our teas, but I used the marked tea kettles for Josian's teacup," I continued as I showed them the two kettles.

"Mark, you're a genius," Burgesis said looking at me.

"What are you going to do now," asked Pine looking at the now sleeping Josian.

"Now I am going to heal him. I need to remove the dark red magimarks off him. Burgesis, I need you to take him through the Tunnel of Light with Pine and Rose and then bring him back here, so I can awake him," I said as Burgesis nodded.

Before Pine and Rose could ask what, the tunnel was, Burgesis grabbed Josian by his arms and led the way out of the kitchen out the back door. Pine and Rose struggled as they grabbed his other side by his arms and vanished into the night. Five minutes later, the four of them returned and both Pine and Rose were teary eyed. "We both have never felt like this before," said Pine crying looking at his wife Rose.

"It is easier for us to fly," Rose said, "I don't feel like anything is weighing me down anymore," she said looking at me.

"Thank you, Mark," said Rose nodded her head at me as she and Pine were flying in midair in front of me happily as Burgesis placed Josian back into his chair in front of us.

"Not a problem," I said looking at Pine who nodded in agreement. "We all need to heal first before we make our decisions in life now," I poured tea into Josian's teacup and then I pointed to Josian and said to myself awake him from his sleep, and then said "a somno exsuscitem eum".

Josian then sat up in his chair and said, "What happened," looking around at us all.

"You feel asleep," said Burgesis looking at him. "I'm sorry," he said in a new tone looking kind of confused. "I didn't mean to fall asleep in front of you." He grabbed for his teacup and took a sip from it.

"We were talking to you because you had betrayed Mark to Eggbert and then we healed you and you fell asleep," said Burgesis not wanting to mention that I had put him to sleep.

"I know you were talking to me about that, I am sorry for betraying you Mark, I feel so much different now, and what did you do to me?" Josian asked me.

"We got rid of your red evil magimarks and it should change you in many ways," I said looking at Josian who was shocked.

"Josian, I told you, I am not going to kill you for betraying me. I will not kill you or your family unless it is necessary. I am going to give you a second chance, because we all make mistakes. We all go through tough times, but I will not give you a third chance, do you understand?" I said to Josian who started to tear up as he slowly stood up. He then walked over to me on the other side of the table and hugged me. I hugged him back and said, "I forgive you for all wrong doing and give my blessings to mend and rid all the evil magimarks on your soul," I said and I translated it to Latin "placatus tibi fuero in omnibus bonis male faciendi et ministra mihi animam tuam et auferam omne malum magimarks," as I said this in our hug all my magimarks turned white and a warmth came over me and it transferred to Josian. After the light disappeared from me, I released our hug and he began to cry and thank me as he left the kitchen out the back door in peace.

"Mark, you never cease to amaze us," said Burgesis smiling.

"I have to have faith that things can be done to avoid such horror," I said looking at Burgesis.

"Horror?" asked Rose.

"Yes, soon we might run into the situation where death is

inevitably unable to be avoided because it will be harder to convince others who are more hardened and full of evil to leave Nerogroben's circle," I said sadly as Eladius walked into the room and looked at me.

"You PROMISED!" he shouted at me and he ran out of the room crying.

"Eladius," I yelled and there was no response. I then looked up at Pam and Andrew who had come into the room.

"Sorry we missed everyone and heard voices," said Pam looking at Andrew and then to me.

"Eladius really does look up to you," said Andrew carefully. "What you have done for us has changed us all, and we just want to thank you again because we have noticed a change in Eladius as well."

"Excuse me, I have to go to talk to him," I said to the others. They nodded and then I ran out to find Eladius, who was on the front porch just outside the living room sitting on the bench crying.

"Eladius, I know I promised that we wouldn't kill those of Nerogroben's army. But eventually, after we give people the chance to change loyalty, we will run into the fact that no one will want to change. Then they will do everything that they can to kill everyone in this rebellion. At some point, we must protect ourselves too," I said looking at Eladius.

"You said it would be a last resort," said Eladius avoiding eye contact.

"I know that's what I said," I said looking at Eladius rubbing my tired eyes "and it is a last resort. I will only be able to do so much, and war will be unable to be avoided. I am going to give everyone the second chance to follow me, Eladius. I will even give Nerogroben himself a second chance to give up and follow me peacefully when it comes down to it," I continued looking at Eladius who turned and looked at me.

"Okay," he said as he gave me a hug and released it and he stayed sitting as I stood up off the bench and went inside to the kitchen again. Everyone was sitting around the table whispering, they stopped whispering as soon as I entered the kitchen.

"What's going on?" I asked looking at Burgesis.

"We were wondering how and when we could leave to The Underground," said Barty looking at Jana and then to me.

"I haven't slept much at all," I said noticing it was mid-day. "Can I rest before we make plans to leave?" I asked everyone at the table who looked around nervously.

"We can only give you an hour of rest because it's not going to be safe here for too much longer since we don't know if Eggbert is going to come back," said Burgesis looking at Barty.

"Ok, some rest is better than none," I said gratefully "When I get up then we can discuss my ideas and plan on our movement. I will just need your map Burgesis."

Burgesis nodded as everyone started to get up from the table. I then walked from the entrance of the kitchen and into the living room to find Eladius and his parent sleeping one of the couches and I took the one across from it. After sleeping for only what seemed like a few moments, Burgesis started shaking me.

"Mark, Mark, we need you to get up so we can figure out a plan," said Burgesis sounding anxious.

"Can I have a few more hours of sleep? I still feel just so exhausted," I said

"Mark, we have already overstayed our welcome here in the Woodland Elms. It's getting dangerous for you to be here for too much longer," Burgesis said as I finally opened my eyes and sat up on the couch.

Burgesis was standing over me and I was beginning to think that he was getting a bit annoyed with me.

"Yes, I am," said Burgesis seriously "Thank you for noticing and do you mind meeting with the rest of *your* guard in the kitchen?"

I nodded and followed him to the kitchen where everyone
was sitting they then stood up.

"Thank you all for coming," I said looking at Burgesis who walked past me and stood at the seat next to the empty seat at the head of the table which I assumed it was for me as I sat down and everyone else sat back down in their seats again.

"It is my understanding that The Guard wants me to leave Woodland Elms and go to The Underground Rebellion Station. Under normal circumstances, I would agree. Eggbert is currently absent from this guard meeting temporarily. I am not comfortable with this plan of action personally because it's something he expects. He already knows where we will be going if it wasn't to the School of the Unknown to finish my training." I explained looking around.

"But Mark, it's the only place for us *to* go, where we all know you will be safe," said Jana.

"But don't you see what we have here as an advantage? The element of surprise," I said as everyone started muttering amongst themselves.

"Mark, we have to leave here because it puts the Woodland Elms in danger with you being here, and this risks too many lives if you are found here by Nerogroben's army scouts or worse Nerogroben himself," said Burgesis calmly.

"Besides you are not even fully trained yet," said Jana looking at me.

"But exactly," I said, "Why not you all train me here?" This way if Nerogroben's scouts come we can fight them off."

Everyone started to mutter in anger with each other and then Burgesis raised his hands, and everyone quieted down quickly.

"No one more than I, wants any reason to fight off Nerogroben and his army scouts, but you only are aware of a few of the elements Mark," said Burgesis "There is much more for you to learn and understand. I think it would a mistake to send you out in a war zone with the amount of ignorance you have, it would be most unsafe. I think it would be best for you to train in safer conditions and not in the middle of a war zone full of enemies."

"I can defend myself fine," I said frustrated looking at everyone.

"Oh yeah, and what do you do if someone hits you with the darkness spells?" asked Tom the raven.

"I will use light," I said calmly.

"But you don't even understand the light," said Brittany the unicorn quietly.

"I have used it and it has worked," I said shooting a look at Brittany.

"It is one thing to use it and it is an entirely different thing to understand the elements," said Barty looking at me seriously.

"If you are so smart tell me how many elements there are," said Chris the fairy.

"There are six," I said "Earth, fire, water, wind or air, electricity, and light. You see, I know them all that is all I need to know."

"Wrong, you don't know what you don't know, Mark," said Chris "There are actually at least ten elements, not including character elements you receive for doing good, and bad."

"Character elements?" I asked now very surprised.

"Yes, as you pass the tests from our clans you receive character elements like you did when Eladius and his family joined the Woodland Elms. Also like the one you received when you arrived here and the one you received for being proud of yourself," said Burgesis.

"There are *at least ten* elements?" I asked surprised
looking at Barty, Jana, and Burgesis "Why didn't you at least tell me them of them, even if you didn't know them?"
"It's because we don't know them and understand them, that we didn't mention the others," said Jana "It's foolish to try to explain something you don't really know or understand."
"Oh," I said grasping what Jana explained slowly.
"You need to be cleverer and less foolish," said Chris "Because if you're foolish, your judgment can be off."
"Then you can become too judgmental of others," said Jana, "Which is something Barty and I are working on as well that and try to be more accepting of others.
"Okay so back on topic," said Pine impatiently "Are we escorting Mark to The Underground with Eladius and his family? Or are we going to chance training Mark here at the Woodland Elms instead?"

Chapter 33
The Decision to Keep Moving

"You are welcome to stay," Mike came into the room and interrupted "We just need extra protections placed on these woods for you to stay."

"No, we appreciate the hospitality that you have given us all. To make sure that Mark, Eladius, and his family are safe, we need to keep moving to the rest of the rebellion army. This is where we know that they will be safe," said Burgesis

"But how will we travel there, if Eggbert could possibly tell Nerogroben and his army where we are. Or for that matter where we are going?" said Barty looking around at everyone in the room carefully as everyone stayed silent.

"Is there another less dangerous route and a different place to go?" I asked everyone quietly.

"The Underground is the safest place," Burgesis insisted softly. "There is another route, but I can't say it is faster, nor can I tell you it's safer, but it is possible."

"Which way is that?" Jana asked carefully.

"It's going to involve some fighting and possibly risking all of our lives but we all swore to protect Mark and that's just what we will do," said Burgesis looking at Barty who then looked at Jana who was sitting next to him and put her hand on his in comfort.

"The only other way is through the Path of Misfortune and then across the bridge into the Village of Solotar and then enter The Underground from there," said Burgesis looking at Donna the Troll.

"Yes, I see what you are saying, we have a hidden second home by the village of Solotar that has a secret entrance to The Underground from there," said Donna looking at her husband George who just entered the room behind her.

"What is this? Is this a meeting for The Guard or a meeting of all the leaders of the clans?" asked Jack Pillowdrum the phoenix from his seat.

"We are sorry, but we snuck out here in the middle of the night because we had heard Eggbert had betrayed Mark. Then just this morning a wanted poster was going around for Eggbert. Now Eggbert is wanted by Nerogroben. I heard they are planning on setting fire to the school possibly. Apparently, he has not been found either at his home or his school," said George quickly who was standing next to Donna.

"There is a lot of unrest out there from Nerogroben's army," said Donna at the doorway and everyone started muttering.

"What other choice do we have but to do what Burgesis has suggested," said Tom the raven wisely.

"But there is a scout camp on the path on the way to Solotar, what do we know about them?" asked Brittany looking around.

"Please send in Eladius and Andrew into this meeting," I said. Within a second of me ordering this, Matt Lookings the Eagle flew out of the room above. George and Donna and returned within two minutes as everyone patiently waited in silence. Eladius and Andrew entered the room quietly as Matt flew ahead of them and took his seat at the table again.

"Thank you, Matt," I said sincerely.

"You're Welcome, Mark," said Matt as Barty and Jana got up and bowed their heads to me and got chairs for Andrew and Eladius to sit near the wall.

"Take a seat," I said as both Eladius and Andrew bowed their heads and sat down. "I am not sure if you know why I have asked for your presence during this meeting or not," I explained slowly as they both stared blankly and silently at me. "I need your willing help, and I need you to be completely honest with me," I said looking at them both "Got it?"

They both nodded and sat silently. "We are all trying to get into the village of Solotar however the only way that is the safest for all of us is through the Path of Misfortune and we realize there is a scout camp location near there," I explained watching them carefully.

"You would like information on that scout camp, huh?" said Andrew bitterly.

"Dad, please," said Eladius looking at his father.

"I told you Eladius, I knew this was going to happen eventually... yes, we

can be of help to you," said Andrew sighing slowly looking at his son's face.

"Just reminding you that The Guard promised to protect you and your family and Mark, so it's in your best interest to share what you know so we will *all* be safe," said Jana looking at Andrew who was surprised.

"What do you want to know about that scout camp, Mark?" asked Eladius.

"I realize what I am asking isn't easy, but we need to know as much information as possible about that scout camp, and you are our only resource," I said looking at Andrew.

Andrew sat quietly for a moment and then said "That location is probably one of the roughest aside from Valfador (Nerogroben's Castle) itself within Creaton. Its security is very tight, and the guards themselves are not easily fooled. They ask everyone why they are going to Solotar. They

aren't there alone, there is an underground army below that scout camp of about fifty loyalists who are not easily fought," said Andrew grumpily.
"We will go with you," said Mike Smitherton carefully.
"So will we," said Donna and George nodding in agreement.
"So will we," said Pine and Rose smiling.
"So that leaves about twenty of us in total, about two people to fight each," said Barty "Sounds like fun," he said looking around at everyone.
"This is going to be the most dangerous part of the journey," said Burgesis ominously.
"When do we leave," I asked.
"We need to leave as soon as possible," said Jana.
"We don't want anything to happen to you Mark."
Barty looked at her and then nodded in agreement.
"I just want to say that you have done well so far Mark," said Burgesis "But let's get you trained more."
"Okay," I said standing up. "Meeting adjourned I am going to go pack my things,"
Everyone nodded at me and stood up as I stood up as I left the room.
"Everyone else please sit back down so that we can get the movement of The Guard planned out," said Burgesis.
I left the room with Andrew and Eladius.

"Thank you so much Andrew for that information," I explained. "I realize that it still isn't easy doing what you did for us back there, and I will be forever in debt to you for that."
Andrew nodded silently as Eladius smiled at me and Andrew put his hand on Eladius's back guiding them slowly down the hall to another room to be with Pam. I went back into the living room and put my book into my pocket and laid down to rest. After what seemed like five minutes later Eladius woke me up and said, "Mark we are ready."
I sat up and followed Eladius outside to the front porch where everyone was lined up and placed in formation of our movement.
"Mark, you and Eladius are traveling on Brittany. I know it's a squeeze but you two should be okay because we are placing you three under invisibility. We will just have to refresh the front protection every hour," said Burgesis, "Everyone else will be invisible."
 "Okay," I said nervously I didn't feel comfortable with the idea but I realized it was the only safe option. First, I sat on the saddle which was tightly attached on Brittany and then Eladius sat behind me and grabbed my waist abruptly and laid his chin on my right shoulder which made me jump and then I looked at him and he just smiled. I looked ahead as we started moving forward.

"Easy there, tiger," he said to me jokingly grabbing my waist tighter as I grew uncomfortable. It was then that I stopped to realize that Eladius wasn't used to being around people and at times wouldn't know how to handle himself. "Your safe with me," I just stayed silent as I looked ahead at Jana and Barty and Burgesis who was looking at me and shook his head.

As we started moving ahead Burgesis placed the invisibility on me, Brittany, and Eladius in an hour we were at the edge of the Woodland Elms and the Beach of Goodness. The sun was out and was beating down on us, there were only a few clouds out, and the ocean breeze felt wonderful against my face as we heard the ocean waves crashing the shore.

"It's beautiful," said Jana looking at the ocean.

"No, you are beautiful," said Barty reaching out his hand to Jana who held his hand for a few minutes and then gave him a sideways hug. Within a half hour we were on the Path of Misfortune. It was rather difficult to follow since it started to get windy, and the clouds started to get darker and darker. A slight rain started to pour on us, and it started to storm.

Chapter 34
The Loss of a Loved One

Burgesis ordered to The Guard to stay alert along the path as we passed through the shrubbery was growing thicker, darker, and harder to see through. They walked tighter together around us, as the weather didn't show any signs of changing or improving. As we came closer to the scout camp, the trees and shrubbery around the path grew less dense. The visibility became more noticeable as we drew closer to the camp houses. We approached, a group of trolls who blocked our way on the path ahead.
"Where do you think you're going with weather as bad as this?" asked one of the grumpy trolls.
"We are going to the Village of Solotar," said Jana calmly.
"You think you are going there," said another Troll.
"Maybe we should let them pass, Grot," said another Troll.
"Oh, you think so Todd, you dope," said Grot. "No, I think that they are up to no good."
"Yeah, I think your right, Grot," said another Troll.
"Of course, I am right, Weaverly," said Grot rather rudely. "What's your business there in the Village of Solotar, Beaver?"
"It's not your business," said Barty gruffly.

"It is our business whether we are going to let you through or not," said Grot "We need a reason,"

"Our aunt is sick and needs our help to get better," said Jana.

"Do you think we are dumb?" said Grot

"No, sir, I don't think you're dumb," said Jana insistently.

"Well just in case you are wondering, the Village of Solotar is a village of Trolls, how can your aunt be a Troll if you're a beaver," asked Grot.

"That's right, she is a Troll, it's an endearment of our family friend, Donna Eubinks. We are going to her and George's house to visit," said Jana carefully.

"You see, they are up to no good, Todd. Why would Beavers want to go where they make metals in the village of Solotar?" asked Grot

"There will be no trouble here boys," said Burgesis calmly.

"Oh, it's you Frank, why we ought to kill you here and now, you traitor!" shouted Grot angrily as he raised his hands and his skin turned from green to purple.

"What are you doing with two Beavers?" asked Grot
holding up his hands at Burgesis who seemed to be trying not to react.

"It's none of your business," said Jana who was moving between Brittany, me and Eladius and Grot "Leave us alone,"

"Shut up you, or I will do it for you," said Grot as electricity balls formed around his hands.

"I wouldn't go that here Grot," said Burgesis "There are more of us then there are of you."

"What do you mean, there are only three of you, and there are like 50 or more of us here," said Grot.

Suddenly the invisibility seemed to have worn off me, Eladius, Brittany and the rest of The Guard.

"Oh, it's you!" said Grot looking at me, "Then this is an act of war!"

"No, it's not," said Burgesis looking at Grot calmly. "We are simply trying to get through to the Village of Solotar."

Just then Grot had started to throw an electricity ball towards me. Barty used his whole hand and his eyes turned white. Barty angrily shot water from his hands. With the water, he accidentally grabbed Jana and the Troll who were both next to him together. They both squirmed in the great ball of water which was floating above our heads. Grot had let go of the electricity ball and it started to head towards me. From out of the ball Jana grabbed the ball of electricity, and as she did, she seemed to be mouthing to Barty "I love you!"

While she was in the ball of water, she then closed her eyes as she curled her body around the ball of electricity. She held the ball of electricity tighter around her body as she held it between her and the Troll who looked at her in surprise in the water trying to get out. But it was too late.

Within a few seconds the great ball of electricity exploded within the water ball which then broke. After it broke, I looked at Jana's and Grot's lifeless wet bodies in front of me. Realizing what happened Barty stood in shock as I got off Brittany and ran up to Jana's body and tried to revive and heal her. Barty started crying and shouted "NOOOOO!!!" as he ran towards me and Jana. Everyone else kept fighting and Burgesis casted a quick protective shield around the three of us as many elements flew around us in slow motion.

Hopelessly, I tried as much as I could to heal her and nothing seemed to have an effect. I hurriedly pulled out my English-Latin book and tried to find the words to help her and as I kept trying everything I could. Slowly, Barty put his hand on mine, and sadly shook his head. He then used his paw and wiped the tears from his eyes. I stood up and looked around, the elements of all sorts were flying around and about thirty more trolls stormed the area and Magical Creatures of all kinds came out of the camp houses and everyone was fighting each other on the path ahead of us.

Suddenly emotions of anger erupted from me as a red magimark appeared on my forehead. Barty looked at me and at the magimark in fear. He backed several paces behind me in fear as it burned in pain. I didn't care, I was furious to see all this death and chaos around us and she was gone, there was no way I could bring her back.

I put my hands out on the path down ahead of us to see everyone still fighting and shouted "Omne quod est in nomine domini, et dimitte universa delicta commisit in corde et tota anima cum omnibus veniam lucem!" and then suddenly I rose a few feet in the air as a light so strong came out of me that it broke our shield of protection and a burst of light shined around us for miles around us in all directions from my hands, feet, and eyes. It became brighter and brighter and as it did, everyone stopped fighting and covered their eyes so that they could see. After the light stopped coming out of me, I started to feel faint. Burgesis ran up to me and caught me, as I fell backwards onto the ground. He sat us both down and everyone gathered around me. They all bowed and then kneeled on one knee around me.

I slowly opened my eyes, and Burgesis looked at me as I said, "Can everyone please stop fighting?"

"Everyone has stopped, for now," he said moving my hair from my forehead and he saw the newly formed magimark on my forehead as I closed my eyes.

"It burned red Burgesis," said Barty whispering still standing behind us in shock and afraid of me in fear still.

"What did you say?" Burgesis asked me ignoring Barty, and I opened my eyes again looking at his concerned face.

"In the name of all that is, I forgive all wrongs committed in the hearts and souls of all those present with the light of forgiveness," I said weakly and I closed my eyes and passed out. Burgesis nodded, then stood up and looked around and asked "Who is your leader of this camp?"

Then an elf pointed at the lifeless body of Grot and said, "The One" has killed our leader,"

"Then who is your second in command here?" asked Burgesis looking around as someone pointed to the Troll, Weaverly who was also lifeless on the ground.

"Then who is your third in command?" asked Burgesis looking at Todd the Troll who shook his head.

"It's Toolot, he is our third in command," said Todd nervously.

"Please have Toolot come over here, we have much to discuss," said Burgesis to Todd as he walked away silently. Two minutes later he returned with Toolot behind him who was a Magical Human elf.

"It seems to me you have caused quite a lot of troubles for me. I am Toolot, who are you all, and what business did you have starting a war on Nerogroben's territory? Oh, it's you!" asked Toolot and then was shocked as he looked at Burgesis.

"We were not trying to come through with an act of war. We were trying to just go to the Village of Solotar and we were stopped by these two," Burgesis explained pointing at Grot and Weaverly.

"Oh yeah," said Toolot "Do you have any proof or witnesses that can attest to this "incident," Toolot asked looking around at everyone.

"Yes, we do," said Burgesis calmly pointing at Todd.

"Well," said Toolot looking at Todd who remained silent staring into space and then looked at Barty sadly.

"What happened?" "My wife," shouted Barty sadly. "She is gone," as he started crying in immense heartache into his hands.

"Well, they didn't mean any harm; Grot was the first one to use electricity on this beaver here. He tried to attack everyone when they were saying they wanted to just pass through," said Todd nervously shaking at Toolot who stared at him. "Well, it looks like your story has pulled through," said Toolot turning to Burgesis. "What's going on with him? Where did all that light come from?" asked Toolot pointing at Mark as he was passed out on the ground.

"Well, the light came from him, it was the Ancient Light of Forgiveness, it's his strongest power it seems currently, and it has helped get rid of all the Grey Matter in the area. He is said to be "the one," said Burgesis calmly looking at me. "We are his guard, we just wanted safe passage to the outskirts of the village of Solotar for him, that is all. We originally were asking just for passage through, but your

leader didn't make it easy for us."

"The one" huh?" said Toolot. "I have heard that Nerogroben himself is

looking for "the one," Toolot said rubbing his fingers on his chin thoughtfully, "and I have noticed that he got rid of the Grey Matter."

"Well, it seems we have a lot of cleaning up to do around here," said Toolot "For now, please bring "the one" to my camp house, and you can stay to help heal him until he can gather strength to carry on. You can stay, if the rest of your guard, can clean up here, as for you," Toolot said looking at

Barty. "Carry her into the house as well," Barty who was in shock just looked out into the path ahead.

"Thank you," said Burgesis as he patted Barty on his back. He then calmly lifted me up and followed Toolot.

Barty noticing what was going on picked up Jana and he carried her and followed as well.

Chapter 35
A Change of Heart

A few minutes later, my weak body was placed on a comfortable feeling bed. All this time, I could hear everything going on, but I just felt too weak to open my eyes. Barty had placed Jana into another room under Toolot's instruction and stayed at her side.

I then thought to myself "Burgesis, I am up, but I can't open my eyes, since I feel so weak. Can you help me sleep?"

Burgesis was able to read my thoughts and said "Not a problem, Mark. Try to get some sleep and try not to think about what happened." he put his hand on my head and said "ut dormiunt," and as soon as he said that a warmth came over my body. I was then able to sleep soundly.

Toolot quietly entered the room and looked at Burgesis.

"Barty isn't doing well, I was just in to check on him. He is in a lot of pain; he just received the broken heart magimark I noticed. He is in the other room with her still and insists on not leaving her side. We need to talk privately Burgesis," said Toolot quietly.

Burgesis nodded while he watched me rest as he slowly got up off the edge of my bed. He and

Toolot quietly left the room and closed the door behind them. Burgesis followed Toolot to the other side of the house and into another room. Toolot closed the door behind them and added protection around the room from being overheard. Toolot motioned for Burgesis to sit in the chair across from him.

"First, I need to know something," Toolot said as Burgesis sat down. "I need to make sure that you and the guard didn't come here to try to start any war," said Toolot carefully observing Burgesis. Burgesis remained silent.

"I know since we last saw each other you are not the same guy anymore. Still, I must ask given the particularly sticky situation you are in," Toolot said.

"Trust me, if that was the case, we would not be speaking right now, and we would have kept fighting. Mark is the one that brought light to the area," said Burgesis calmly looking at Toolot who didn't seem convinced.

"Well, when "the one" awakes, I need to talk to him," said Toolot walking to the door and opened it slightly to make sure Barty nor anyone else was near it trying to listen in.

"I thought it was you Burgesis," said Toolot in a hushed voice. "I had to make sure no one knew that we knew each other."

"I understand," Burgesis nodded as he looked at Toolot.

"I don't think you understand Frank," said Toolot in a hushed voice in return. "Times are different than they were. They aren't like they were when we were growing up, in the days of the School of the Unknown. Right now, I am on a different side of the playing field than you."

"It doesn't have to be this way, I understand that you have your loyalties to follow, but you must understand that "the one" is going to make a difference in all of our lives. You must trust me," said Burgesis calmly.

"I do trust you, Frank!" said Toolot looking out the window noticing The Guard picking up the dead bodies and digging burial holes by the trees. He hesitated, "It's just to talk about "the one" is an act of treason around these parts."

"What am I to do, Burgesis? I have already been on one side thinking that is and was my only option," Toolot said carefully as he turned to look at Burgesis.

"You must do what you believe is the right thing to do. With what decision, will you have to make for it to lead you to a happier more fulfilled life," asked Burgesis looking at Toolot. "Talk to "the one," talk to Mark."

Toolot stayed quiet and nodded.

"Be right back," said Toolot as he left the room and come back a second later smiling at Burgesis handing him a cup of tea.

"Do you know why our camp was placed here?" asked Toolot sipping his tea while looking out the window from his seat.

"Because of the location of the school and it's the furthest distance of land away from Nerogroben in one direction but closest from another," said Burgesis who nodded as he took a sip of tea.

"Exactly," said Toolot "What else do you remember about the School of the Unknown?"

"I know that there were a lot of teachers there who taught the beings who had just come into their powers and wanted to learn how to use them," said Burgesis.

"What of the teachers?" asked Toolot "Do you know of the one we are looking for?"

"Yes, Eggbert," said Burgesis. "He was traveling with us and then when he received Nerogroben's message and we learned of his betrayal of Mark, he vanished. We haven't seen him since," said Burgesis

"I will let you pass through here, if I am aware fully, that you are not helping Eggbert to the school," said Toolot.

As Eggbert is concerned, we would hold him captive for questioning ourselves if he was among our ranks and we would have told you that he was with us if he was as soon as we saw you," said Burgesis carefully.

"Nerogroben is becoming more and more suspicious of the clans, even among his own ranks. He is keeping more and more to himself, and he seems to be going insane. We have heard stories that Nerogroben talks to himself and has paranoia issues. There was talk for a while that he wanted to burn down the school since Eggbert hasn't either come forth or been brought forth. We are now wondering where his loyalty lies," explained Toolot.

"Speaking about loyalty," Burgesis started. "Where do your..."

Toolot raised his hand for Burgesis to stop talking, as he heard someone at the door walking on the porch.

"Like I said when "the one" awakes we need to talk to him first," Toolot said.

Burgesis nodded his head in agreement. as he took a sip of his tea and looked at the door. The footsteps were now going away from the front door.

I was beginning to wake up slowly, and started thinking about Jana, Barty, Burgesis and everything that had happened. I was hoping it was a dream and that it all didn't happen.

The footsteps were now going away from the front door.

"You see, it's not safe for me here, even just to talk without constantly being checked on all the time!" said Toolot.

Burgesis nodded and was thoughtful for a moment.

"You know what if you left with us?" he asked Toolot.

"Because that would be too obvious," said Toolot nervously.

"The Guard would protect you," Burgesis said as he looked at Toolot who shook his head strongly.

"The Guard is to protect Mark, "the one," and even you all are stretched thin," said Toolot. "I may catch up with you all later, for now, I have to see how things go here."

Burgesis nodded in understanding as he and Toolot finished their tea.

"Well, he is awake now," said Burgesis from the other room.

I heard Burgesis and Toolot walking towards the room outside as I started thinking "Geez Burgesis, at least give me a chance to open my eyes," and I heard a laugh coming from outside the door, as I had barely started to open my eyes. I saw two figures standing in the doorway and enter the room, as a candle was turned on, which was on the table next to the couch.

"You will have plenty of time to rest later after this war, Mark," said Burgesis laughing. "This is Toolot of course, he is, well he was, third in command before Barty killed their leader. Now he is Commander-in-Chief in these parts."

"It is an honor to meet you," Toolot stated, whom I noticed was a Magical Human with purple eyes.

"You're a Magical Human," I said aloud weakly.

"I am," said Toolot "There *was* a variety of those who followed Nerogroben,"

"Followed? Was?" I asked confused looking at Toolot

"Well, you see now we need to talk privately," he said looking at Burgesis who nodded and left the room and closed the door behind him.

Toolot sat at the edge of my bed as he shook his head.

"You see, we have a problem, this is supposed to be a Nerogroben scout camp and ever since your rebels killed our leader, and you did that spell, everyone's hearts and minds have changed. Now they no longer wish to follow Nerogroben, they wish to follow you."

"How is that a problem? This is great news!" I asked
calmly still feeling weak.

"It's a slight problem because Nerogroben's men still come here and make visits and they would be suspicious of things around here as it is since there isn't any Grey Matter," explained Toolot. "We can all now finally see and feel the sun's rays and heat properly because of that powerful spell you did.

"Then maybe there is a way we can help each other," I said looking around the room, as I had sat up on the bed. I saw that there was just the bedside table with the candle on it, and across the room was another old bed and an old writing desk. On the writing desk was various pieces of parchment paper on it.

"Oh, how can that be." He asked curiously as I winced in pain as my forehead magimark disappeared.

"Please forgive me for feeling weak still, I am trying to learn my own strength when it comes to these spells," I said "What I mean is that I am giving every one of Nerogroben's men a second chance. A chance to start over, with healing and forgiveness. What I mean is maybe we can still help each other out. I built an archway in the Woodland Elms, which has a spell on it to change the hearts, souls, and minds of all those who pass through it. It cleanses the bad magimarks away, similarly like I just did here. If I built something like that here maybe you can help me spread this peace to everyone who wishes that second chance," I explained.

"I would have to think about that, Mark," said Toolot. "It would look like I am trying to spread propaganda and I don't want to run the risk of being exposed here."

"If I can do this, then maybe I could include in the spell, that as it cleanses and heals you, it allows you to forget how you got healed and cleansed so that no one else could remember it even if they saw it happening in front of them," I said

"Maybe, I will get back to you on that," explained Toolot. "For now, I am going to let you rest some more, thank you Mark for what you have done here," he said bowing to me as he placed his hand on his face and noticed that his red magimark disappeared off his face as he started to tear up.

"No, no Toolot," I said looking up at him "You mustn't feel like you have to bow to me or pay me homage. I am just trying to give everyone a second chance for those who want to follow me and my ways, to rid this world of Grey Matter, and all it is evils. Yes, I am what everyone says, I am "the one." My intention is not to rule, or be in power, but to bring peace and restore this world with all it is beauty," I said looking outside through the window.

"Have you been told how this Dark War even started? What do you expect of your followers?" he asked quietly looking at me.

"I have been told that the Dark War started because of Nerogroben and his need for control and power. I have also been under the understanding that Nerogroben is evil and an angry Troll. I don't expect anything in return from my followers, but total and complete loyalty. I want this without judgement of others and to spread the good news of love, peace, and the power of forgiveness. Everyone is taken care of by other supporters like you, me, and my guard," I said turning to Toolot. "I wouldn't ask anything of you or anyone else if I wouldn't or couldn't do it myself."

"Of course this is what you have been told… interesting…. Well although these are good sentiments, the direction of this scout camp will now fall under a new, newly elected leader by the totality of the clan that's already here, which meets tonight in this area," he explained looking out the window nearest me as he pointed to a fire in the middle of the camp houses. There is an issue of equality and the lack there of, around here," he explained looking at me.

I stayed silent remembering the hierarchy Eggbert had told me about.

"I have told that The Guard that there won't be a hierarchy while I am here," I explained firmly.

"You don't understand because you are not of this world, but there is an unsaid hierarchy here in the World of the Unknown, you can't change that. It is just the way it is. Even amongst us trolls within each scout camp and it is ranks," Toolot said avoiding my gaze at him.

"People here treat each other differently. Magical Human Elves and Humans are on the top of the rank. No one questions them and their judgement. Then the Phoenixes and the Unicorns for they cannot die, and they are pure. Then the Beavers and the Eagles are on the same ranking. Then the Wizards and the Witches and then the Fairies and the Elves and then the Hummingbirds. Those ranking creatures are the top of the reputations of the World of the Unknown they are known as the higher ranking, and they are rulers in their own rights and feel they own the World of the Unknown." Toolot continued as he then pointed out the window as I watched outside. I shook my head in frustration, noticing Britany put her nose in the air and held her head high as she passed a Troll who was carrying heavy shovel away from the grave sites by the trees.

"There are those of us left who are known as below and beneath social rank. They include the Foxes, Giants, Ravens, Trolls, and then finally the plants. The creatures that are below and beneath social rank are thought of us stupid, ignorant, and untrustworthy, more so than those above the social rank. They are not wanted by the upper ranking social elites in this World. If you associate yourself with someone beneath the social ranking then you risk being judged by your own clan and beaten by others," said Toolot sadly.

"But you're a Magical Human, it's better for you in this society?" I spoke.

"Is it better now?" he asked me with eyebrows raised.

"Well in this world as it is now, with that said, it ought to be better for people like you, those who are on the upper class of the hierarchy," I clarified.

"As a Magical Human, I am known as the highest in the land in rank socially, even at that, I can't have friends in the lowest classes of society. If I do, then I am looked at and treated differently by my peers," Toolot explained as I shook my head.

"This shouldn't be so," I said. "Why are the trolls and the plants considered part of the lowest value in society?"

"The Trolls are evil in general, easily corruptible and flexible. They are known to be untrusted.

Plants are known as the lowest in society because they are trampled on when we walk the Earth. There is no respect for each other, that is why Nerogroben wanted to change the very fabric of nature, and how we treated others. He thought that by coming to power, he could change the way we are perceived by everyone," Toolot explained.

"But your wrong," I said. "The Trolls clan has just made everyone scared to know a Troll, now they don't even respect trolls now, just because they know what they are capable of. People fear all Nerogroben's men in general. You can't just automatically assume people are going to treat you better just because they fear you. Beings here seem quick to blame Nerogroben since he is currently in power for all the chaos and this divide. It also should be ourselves that we switch the blame to for having these prejudices in the first place. The creatures and beings of the World of the Unknown, need to understand that there isn't a hierarchy. If there is, there shouldn't be. Equality is better than being treated in-equally. They shouldn't see you as a clan member but as a creature of goodness in heart first before they assume that you are evil. We are all capable of doing great things, but whether they are with good intention is up for us to decide. The creator wanted our worlds to exist but whether you realize it or not both our worlds have had similar issues of in-equality going on for years. The only way we can avoid this is to avoid prejudices and not see just one person for who they are but look at them for what they have done and could do for the betterment of our worlds. We need to love and spread peace to each other."

Toolot stayed silent for a while and looked out the window before looking at me. "I am surprised that you hadn't noticed the "hierarchy" beforehand."

"What do you mean?" I asked

"You can't see that your wizard that you know, Eggbert, he is treated better than the trolls or the Ravens?" he asked

"No, I haven't seen that," I said.

"There is disrespect from the Unicorns, and the Wizards, and the Witches,
and the Eagles. You can't see that out of all the jobs here in the World of the Unknown that the Trolls are used to go into The Underground caves and do all the dirty work. You can't see the Unicorns aren't doing our jobs, etc. You can't see the civil war within our own World of the Unknown? You can't see the tension between the clans?" he asked as I saw that there was an Eagle who was watching over a Raven and his clan members as they avoid contact with each other. "There is favoritism here Mark, you just need to open your

eyes and do something about it. My opinion doesn't matter anyway, but you can address the various members left here in a few hours. You can add your sentiments, opinions, and comments which would possibly influence what kind of leader that they elect." Toolot continued looking at me.

"What could I do?" I asked. "It's up to them to make that decision."

"The clan as a whole will elect a leader and then that leader will lead us here at this scout camp," Toolot said looking at me.

"But I thought you were leader?" I said now confused.

"I am a leader for now, but the third leader in line never really leads they just hold the position until the clan as a whole can decide their new leader and I can submit a request to run but then it would be up to the clan to decide who they deem suit to lead them," he explained.

"Oh okay," I stated nodding in understanding.

"However, it has been brought to my attention that you wish to keep moving to your destination safely, so it is entirely up to you if you wish to stay or not and have your voice of the rebellion heard before they cast their votes in and by tomorrow morning we should have the results in," Toolot said as he opened the door to let Burgesis in the room.

"Okay Toolot, I will think about it and decide," I said looking at Burgesis noticing that he wanted to talk to me, as Toolot left the room and Burgesis closed the door behind him.

"You had scared us," said Burgesis quietly looking at me as we both sat down back on the bed. "We thought you were gone,"

"How long was I out?" I asked quietly wondering where everyone else was.

"A few days," said Burgesis apparently reading my thoughts as he nodded "Everyone is out there cleaning up, they were ordered to leave you alone until Toolot could talk to you in private and check our stories," he said shaking his head.

"I see that my elements haven't done much to change people's trust in each other," I said sadly.

"I'm sorry I scared you, I guess it took a lot out of me." Burgesis placed his hand on my head and said "Sanai Eum," and a golden light came out of his head and shined over me as I started to feel a little stronger,"

"Thank you, Burgesis," I said smiling at him as he nodded

"Don't take this the wrong way, but you can't change the world on your own, forget the prophecy, use it just as a guide. Yes, you have the powers and the capabilities to change this world, but at some point, people must learn to trust each other on their own. The first steps that they need is to not only know you, but they also need to be able to know that they can trust you, and that you keep your word. Trust is like the ripple effect, once it's started right, it continues, but also, if something else within the same contingency effects the ripples, then it's harder for the original ripples to continue their original effect," said Burgesis.

"I kind of understand," I said "So what you're saying is help them start to change their hearts and minds but don't push them to make them trust me. Have them learn to trust me on their own?"

"Exactly," Burgesis said.

"Was anyone else hurt badly besides me?" I asked thinking about Jana. Burgesis knew what I was going to ask and avoided eye contact, and I could tell this was affecting him too.

"Jana still couldn't be revived even by Mike and Andrea Smitherton with even their ancient healing powers," said Burgesis quietly.

"Where's Barty," I asked

"Barty is alone right now, yesterday we had a private burning ceremony that Toolot prepared for us for Jana and only members of The Guard were able to go. We would have invited you as well but you have been out for a long time. As far as Barty is concerned, he hasn't talked or eaten or anything in the past few days since Jana," Burgesis said as his voice trailed off.

"Okay," I said carefully thinking and was starting to worry about him more.

"He is going to be this way for a while, believe me, I am still going through what it's like to lose a fiancé of my own accident of magic," said Burgesis as I looked at him and saw his face turn white as he stared into space. "You should get some more rest so you can gather some more strength before we leave to the Village of Solotar," he said as he stood up and walked out to the doorway.

I tucked myself under a sheet on the bed, and he then left the room still avoiding eye contact and looked like he was about to cry. I couldn't stop thinking about Barty. I was worried about him and I couldn't imagine what it was like losing someone you love. I felt bad that I had missed the burning ceremony for Jana which I would have liked to see how that was and granted she wasn't my wife but even I couldn't help but miss her and how welcoming and protective she was of me. As I ran through scenes of her in my head and of her last moments, I realized she was protecting me. I thought that Troll was going to attack me and Brittany and Eladius, remembering his angry voice and his skin turning purple as he started to throw the ball of electricity at me, and I awoke with a start.

Chapter 36
The Path of Fortune and Misfortune

I didn't realize that I had been dreaming about what had happened to us. Out of my own fear I had awoken with a start, rubbed my tired eyes, and felt a magimark that had appeared on the back of my palm. It seemed only yesterday that I had awoken in Jana and Barty's house and learned of the World of the Unknown. It was as soon as I woke up my door to the room, I was resting in opened, and it was as per usual, Burgesis, who had let himself in. He stood there looking at me and smiled seeming to be reading my thoughts.

"I heard you wake up and you got that magimark just now because of fear," Burgesis said sadly as he smiled and commented about my crazy looking hair. I just laughed; I couldn't help but to laugh. It was the only thing that seemed worth doing after the events that had occurred thus far. It was relieving to be able to joke around and be silly and foolish around Burgesis. He had made things that were more serious, easier to deal with. In many ways, he was my coping mechanism.

"I know it's early, but we are leaving soon to the Village of Solotar. We are meeting George and Donna Eubinks who are already there. They already left as soon as you passed out," Burgesis explained.

"It was just so that they can let the rest of the rebels know of your arrival. We sent word to them so that they know that you are okay and are already aware of what happened to Jana," Burgesis explained "They left early to do this, but they were not trying to be rude by doing this."

"Oh okay," I said looking at Burgesis "What is going on with Barty?"

"He is still very depressed and even with Andrea, Mike Smitherton, and me talking to him, he still isn't coming around to his old self again," Burgesis explained.

"Do you know if he has eaten, or talked to anyone?" I asked.

"No, he still hasn't eaten since it all happened," said Burgesis calmly. "I think he has a broken heart magimark because he is showing all the signs,"

"I would like to talk to him before we leave, I think maybe I can help him if he wants me to," I said looking at Burgesis.

"That might be possible on the way to The Underground," said Burgesis "But I think you should wait to talk to him until then where you will have some notion of privacy,"

"I imagine that The Guard is still trying to figure out the best way and time to leave this Path of Misfortune," I said to Burgesis.

"Actually" said Burgesis "the name of the path is now renamed; it is now called the Path of Fortune. Toolot renamed it after the faith that Jana had in you, and the rebellion. Now everyone who walks this path with now be able to enjoy it without as much Grey Matter!"

"Wow," I said, "Please tell Toolot I said thank you," I stood up and followed Burgesis out into the living room area where the rest of The Guard was sitting in a circle.

"We should leave as soon as possible just in case people left before Mark did his spell and went to Nerogroben," said Brittany worriedly looking around at The Guard.

"Yeah, I agree with you Brittany," said Mike looking at Pine who also nodded in agreement.

"When are we leaving?" I asked The Guard as they looked up at me and had jumped not realizing I was there. I couldn't see Barty within The Guard meeting.

"We are leaving as soon as possible," said Rose as I watched her packing up and nodded my head.

"How will I find out about the results of who is the new leader here at this scout camp?" I asked looking at Burgesis.

"I am staying above and behind," said Matt Lookings, the Eagle. "I will keep an ear and my eyes out for news here at this scout camp."

"Oh good, so you can let me know what happens to the leadership here," I said smiling at Matt who nodded at me.

"So, we can leave immediately," Burgesis said looking around at everyone.

I glanced at Eladius who had kept his eyes on me smiling the whole time observing me as I tried not to act like I noticed. Everyone then got up as we all started to gather our things and file outside. Toolot who seemed like an incredibly wise Troll had been waiting outside of his camp home so that we could all talk in privacy and seemed to know that we were leaving even before anyone said anything to him.

As Burgesis walked up to him to shake his hand Toolot said "Don't worry, you just try to keep him safe, we will be okay here,"

"We intend to keep him as safe as possible," said Burgesis looking at me. "Good luck," he said to me as I walked up to Toolot and shook his hand.

"Thanks, and thank you so much for housing us until we could gather strength and thank you for helping us with the burning ceremony for Jana," I said

"With hope and a little faith, maybe we all can finally see things from a better perspective, perhaps we shall see each other again soon," said

Toolot wisely looking at me as I slowly walked away with the rest of The Guard.

We continued down the path away from the scout camp and started our journey. I sat on Brittany and Eladius did as well, but he stayed silent as he grabbed my waist and we moved on.

"Mark, do you remember why I told you Whiskers had picked you?" Burgesis asked me slowly.

"Well, I just figured you saw a lot in me in comparison to other guys my age," I said, "and because you noticed Whiskers had passed."

"Ah, Whiskers, I was beginning to wonder if you had remembered about him," said Burgesis quietly. "Do you remember how you felt when he passed away?"

"Yeah," I said quietly "I felt like the world was over, like there wasn't any more point to moving on forward."

"Well, not to put this so dramatically but, Barty feels like this right now," explained Burgesis as we walked along, and I noticed Barty was behind us slowly walking sadly and not paying attention to what was going on. "When you lose someone, you love, you begin to regret things that have happened in the past as you reflect on them, and things that have happened. Things that were done that you realize you can't take back, things that you wish you handled differently. You start to regret certain things, certain memories, and it hurts. It becomes harder to get by day after day, because you long for that loved one to come back. Just so you can say "I love you, or I miss you! Or I'm Sorry."

"The loss of a loved one is so difficult to deal with at times, even for me, and it has been ten Earth years, since I lost my own fiancé," Burgesis explained.

"So can someone, ever really heal from these feelings?" I asked

"Now the pain is only temporary like the newly burned magimarks. We still feel the loss, but it becomes easier to deal with as we surround ourselves with other people and things to do. We get the broken heart magimark and the loss of magical powers happens here in the World of the Unknown when you lose a loved one. When you are grieving and if your grieving, you're at your most vulnerable state of mind mentally, emotionally, and physically," Burgesis explained carefully.

"Remember I said how your magic is never as strong as it once was, once you are in that grieving state of mind, and have the broken heart magimark."

"Yeah, I remember, but it just stinks, because I wish there was something I could do for Barty," I said looking behind us at Barty who seemed to be talking to himself and wiping tears away from his eyes.

"There is something you can do for him," Burgesis said looking at me, "You can be his friend, and be there for him and support him,"

"Burgesis, I would like to go to Barty and walk with him," I said making up my mind "Brittany can you please stop so that I can walk with Barty," "Sure," said Brittany as she stopped and I got off her, and walked up to Barty and held out my hand for him to hold on to as we moved forward on to the Path of Fortune.

He had grasped my hand as everyone in The Guard was staring at us as I looked ahead and walked with him at my side.

"Wh-Wh-Why?" said Barty "You're "the one." You are Mark. You should be on Brittany being protected, I ca-ca-can't protect you,"

"We are all here for each other," I said, "You're right, I am Mark, and I am "the one." I am also your friend, you don't deserve to be in pain," I stopped in front of him to wipe his eyes. "Here, stop right here Barty,"

We both stopped on the path and before anyone could say anything to me, I said "This might hurt a bit," he cringed at the thought of pain but nodded as I thought about the words of what I was going to say in English first to try to translate it "I command that this broken heart be mended in light" I said in a loud deep voice "Quod praecipio tibi hoc in corde emendari lucem" and a boom came from my hand and a purple light, came from my hand and it undid his broken heart as I looked at the magimark as light came from my palm. I looked at the broken heart magimark and nothing happened as Barty screamed in pain and tears came from his eyes and Barty blacked out.

I fainted as the magic used was strong it knocked us both out. Immediately, The Guard saw what was going on and tried to catch me. I opened my eyes, and I saw Eladius's worried face staring above me and knew I was okay, and then I closed my eyes again.

Burgesis saw what happened and ran up to Barty and to me and tried to heal us, and immediately The Guard moved to the side of the path.

As soon as we did, a figure was seen in the trees and was walking towards us. It was Eggbert, the wise. at the thought of pain but nodded as I thought about the words of what I was going to say in English first to try to translate it "I command that this broken heart be mended in light" I said in a loud deep voice "Quod praecipio tibi hoc in corde emendari lucem" and a boom came from my hand and a purple light, came from my hand and it undid his broken heart as I looked at the magimark as light came from my palm. I looked at the broken heart magimark and nothing happened as Barty screamed in pain and tears came from his eyes and Barty blacked out.

I fainted as the magic used was strong it knocked us both out. Immediately, The Guard saw what was going on and tried to catch me. I opened my eyes, and I saw Eladius's worried face staring above me and knew I was okay, and then I closed my eyes again.

Burgesis saw what happened and ran up to Barty and to me and tried to heal us, and immediately The Guard moved to the side of the path.

As soon as we did, a figure was seen in the trees and was walking towards us. It was Eggbert, the wise.

Chapter 37
Friend OR Foe

Immediately as soon as The Guard saw who it was, everyone got in front of me and around me and even the birds above swooped down to the ground to protect me.
"WHAT ARE YOU DOING HERE!!!" said Brittany who had immediately ran in front of me and Eladius who was still at my side and was laying over me as I didn't have the strength to keep my eyes open for too long at a time.
"I have heard a great deal of news, and wanted to make sure you all were okay," said Eggbert calmly holding his walking stick in one hand and a pipe in the other. "Seems like I arrived just in time!"
"You weren't wondering about Mark's well-being when you told Nerogroben's men about him were you," said Tom the Raven indignantly eyeing him beadily.
"Or when you betrayed him and attacked him and Eladius!" said Matt.
"I believe that it has been brought up that I have not betrayed Mark at all, and I am entitled to, at least a second chance. Seeing how you all are short handed in guarding "the one," I thought I would stop by," said Eggbert who was trying to get a glimpse of me through The Guard.

The guard had never been put in this situation and both Barty and I were not in any fighting condition. I could hear the dilemma arising, even though I still didn't have the strength to keep my eyes open. I thought to myself, Burgesis please tell The Guard that I am okay with Eggbert coming along. He could help by conjuring up a cart or means of transport for Barty and I, until we have enough strength. I knew Burgesis should be able to catch on to my thinking.

"It is Mark's decision to let you travel with us," he said looking at The Guard as he put his hand on Brittany.

"The Guard is going to be keeping an especially close eye on you until you have earned our trust back. We would like you to conjure some sort of cart or means of transport for us, so that we can pull Barty and Mark to safety. When we reach our destination, they will hopefully have gathered their strength back," continued Burgesis.

"It would be my pleasure," said Eggbert and very quickly he put his pipe in his mouth, held his walking stick with his right hand while using his left hand and said some words that were unable to be translated and properly heard by my ears. A covered cart appeared there in front, and it enabled The Guard to attach Brittany to the cart, and pull it with ease. A few moments later I was carried into the cart and so was Barty who was laid out next to me who also seemed to be passed out.

"So, can we carry on with this journey?" asked Eggbert sounding a little impatient.

"Yes," said Burgesis "Let's go, before we are caught by any of Nerogroben's men, and it gets too dark."

As we moved along the path, I could feel the gravel start to get rough and I was worried about how far and how long Brittany would be able to go without getting tired of pulling the two of us. Eladius was in the back of the covered cart as well with us.

"It's okay Mark," Burgesis said from outside of the cart. "You're safe, that's all that matters,"

True I thought. I looked over to Barty to see him still passed out and faint. I reached out my hand to him and he had grasped my hand softly and I smiled. I didn't want to wake him. I needed to make sure that he was still alive at least, and that he knew that someone was there with him, even if it wasn't Jana.

"It's good he is sleeping," said Eladius quietly looking at my hand reaching out to Barty. "He hasn't slept since Jana..." and his voice trailed off quietly "You scared us all, you know that, right? Why do you keep doing that?" he asked me.

"I'm sorry Eladius," I said softly in a whisper.

I laid there and nodded in silence. I could tell everyone was still dealing with the loss of Jana. I even wished I could have done something to have helped her and it just felt so horrible that nothing more could be done. At least maybe Barty is healed I thought.

"I am not so sure of that," said Burgesis from outside of the cart quietly. "The way in which you tried to heal Barty might have delayed the healing process if anything and I don't think you were able to fully heal him completely. It was too soon! You should have known that! These things take time to get over! You can't rush the healing process of grief! Maybe he will at least have his elemental magic back. Possibly, it's too soon to tell."

I could tell I had made things more difficult for The Guard, "I'm sorry Burgesis," I thought

"It's okay Mark, I should've realized that you would have tried to do the same thing you did for me for Barty. It was far too soon for that," Burgesis repeated. "It worked for me because I have had the broken heart magimark for years. No I am not over the loss, but I have mentally and physically come to terms to it is effect. So, when you healed me, it felt like you were naturally trying to heal me, as if I had any other bruising or scratches," Burgesis scolded.

"Oh okay," I whispered still feeling weak.

"You will feel like this for a while, it's going to take some time for you to get your strength back," Burgesis said to me. "You can't heal everyone! The good news is we are almost ready to make camp for tonight and by tomorrow early afternoon, we should be at the rebellion camp."

I nodded and rested in peace.

Ten minutes later, we stopped the cart in a clearing that seemed to be surrounded by trees and The Guard added various protective enchantments around the camp to protect it from intruders, etc. After that, they started making the campfire and placed five blankets near the fire for me, Barty, Eladius, Pam, Andrew, and Burgesis.

Barty was still not awake yet as I sat next to him observing him and wishing he would wake soon so I could talk to him.

"He will be resting for some time, perhaps by later this morning he will awake," said Burgesis quietly as the rest of The Guard gathered around the fire which started to feel warm after being hit by a cold breeze from the night air.

"You mentioned Whiskers earlier, and I wanted to

continue that conversation we were having earlier with you," said Burgesis quietly as the rest of The Guard seemed to take turns being on guard as the rest of everyone started to get some rest for the night after making soup by the fire.

"Yeah, Whiskers was a great companion to me," I said softly considering the fire.

"He spoke highly of you, and he saw a lot in you, every night he would meet with me and tell me what had happened the day before, and he would get excited every time you would prove how pure you were," Burgesis explained.

"But Burgesis, Whiskers always stayed home," I said looking at him as he shook his head.

"No, we wanted you to think he was always home. In reality he was always there at your side," said Burgesis smiling.

"He was invisible, he was able to make himself invisible and walk-through fences and gates. He saw you while you were in school, in class, at recess, at the stores, in the car, everything," Burgesis explained looking at my confused face. "His mission was to find someone, not just anyone, but a person who was, "the one," the person who would be Nerogroben's match, and he chose you."

"He was there the whole time?" I asked amazed.

"Of course, he was, this was his mission," said Burgesis "In fact, in the morning, you are meeting, his wife, Gretta."

"Whiskers had a wife?" I asked

"Of course," Burgesis said "Whiskers *is from* the World of the Unknown. How else would I be able to talk to Whiskers? Do you think I would trust any tabby cat from Earth, no sir! Or perhaps do you still think I am mad for talking to a cat on Earth?"

"No, no, sorry, I didn't mean anything by what I said," I said worriedly.

"Relax," said Burgesis laughingly. "I am just joking completely! But it is clear, that he chose you, nothing but that could have given us the sign you were "the one.""

I laughed and thought about what he said and then slowly asked "So, you are saying that because he died, this was the sign that I was "the one"?"

"Well, to be honest, he didn't actually die," said Burgesis quietly. "I must apologize for misleading you. I above everyone else knows how important truth is to people. You see, what I didn't explain to you, is that if you die on Earth, you actually have the choice of either moving on, or coming to the World of the Unknown, as any creature or being."

"So, Whiskers is alive?" I asked surprised and angered.

"Yes, it's just that, he can never return to Earth as you know it," Burgesis explained.

"But you said, "If I died here in the World of the Unknown, then I would cease to exist on Earth, how could you, lie to me like that," I said sadly.

"Yes, this is true," Burgesis said "If you die here in the World of the Unknown then you can't come back to the World of the Unknown. It's at that point that you can either, go to Earth, or Heaven, or Hell. Let's say for example that Whiskers dies here in the World of the Unknown, since he has already died on Earth, he can't go back to Earth, so he would just move on,"

"Oh, so will I also get a chance to meet Whiskers again?" I asked.

"Yes, I daresay you will!" Burgesis said smiling. "In fact, he has been bugging me our entire trip here in the World of the Unknown to meet you."

"Really," I said "How? I miss him so much! I would love to see him!"

"Well, he can read minds, and he is the only other one who can do that and on top of that he can talk to you through your mind, if he chooses to do so. In the morning, you will be able to see him," said Burgesis "now try to get some rest, we have a big day tomorrow!"

I laid my head down on to a pillow and went to sleep excited about the opportunity to finally meet Whiskers again.

Chapter 38
Whiskers and his Wife Gretta

The next morning, I awoke to hear a chopping noise. I opened my eyes out of well rested curiosity to see Barty, chopping at wood. Everyone else was gathering their things and loading them up on the cart preparing to leave.

"Sorry Mark," said Barty looking at me noticing I had awoken to noise made by him. "Burgesis said we need to bring as much wood with us as possible since there is a chance, we should be camping next in the Field of Dreams. It's about a half days' journey there before we arrive to the George and Donna's house. That is on the outside of the Field of Dreams."

"Oh okay," I said rubbing my eyes "How are you feeling? What is in the Field of Dreams?"

"I am doing a lot better! I think the question you need to ask is not what, but who is in the Field of Dreams," Barty said looking around at Burgesis to continue the conversation.

"Who," I asked looking to Burgesis, as Barty immediate started to chop the wood again into small circles.

"Exactly, who" said Burgesis from behind me as I jumped.

"You see, the Field of Dreams is literally that, just bubbles of happy and exciting dreams of people from Earth. This is where they are all stored. Whiskers and his wife, Gretta, have lived secretly next that field for a long time," said Burgesis.
"Wait, won't people like Nerogroben easily find them in an open field like that?" I asked worriedly packing up my pillow and blanket and putting them in my pack.
"No," Burgesis laughed, "You see they are protected by ancient magic. Magic that one couldn't even begin to dream of understanding, and they can never be found by those who don't know them. Therefore, it will look like just an open field to someone just looking at it from the distance."
"How are we all going to be able to find them then?" I asked
"Well, actually only me, you, and Barty will be able to find and see Whiskers and his wife," said Burgesis.
"Really?" I asked looking around as Barty walked up to the side of us with a bag full of wood.
"Yeah, they are a very private people," Barty said "We used to go there all the time, Jana and me," Barty continued and suddenly sadly standing there with his head drooped.
"What about the rest of The Guard?" I asked "What will they do?"

"They will be there at the campsite waiting for our return," said Burgesis as he passed me and placed his hand on Barty's shoulder as Barty looked up and nodded with a slight smile at Burgesis.

"The Field of Dreams has a different effect on everyone," said Barty slowly.

"The guard is going to have to wear special goggles and ear plugs to avoid losing control around the field."

"Goggles and Ear plugs," I asked, "Why do they need this if they aren't coming to see Whiskers and his wife,"

"Because the Field of Dreams isn't exactly a safe place for many beings. Beings and creatures of all types have gotten so mentally and physically disabled from the field that, if they don't wear the protective gear they die if they leave the field," said Barty quietly.

"What happens to people when they don't wear the protective gear exactly?" I asked looking at Burgesis as I started to fold my blanket and sleeping bag.

"There are things called lost and unaccomplished dreams, they are yellow looking bubbles," said Burgesis mysteriously.

"Yeah, I know about those kinds of dreams. I have had them before," I said.

"Well, what happens is that when those things are lost and unaccomplished and they see you there in that field, you can literally be attacked by them again. Your brain can only handle so many memories and dreams that it gets on over load and you fall asleep and eventually you forget to wake up," explained Barty.

"Why is that such a bad thing?" I asked curiously.

"The dreams consume you and well you never wake up and if you were to be taken out of the Field of Dreams while you were sleeping," said Burgesis "Your dreams kill you."

"How can my unaccomplished and lost dreams kill me?" I asked.

"It's because of the combination of the dreams and the evil Grey Matter," Barty said looking at me seriously.

"It's just evil that affects them, and they go bad after they mix with the Grey Matter, they turn into a nightmare," said Burgesis.

"So, am I to understand that the Field of Dreams is the only place where Grey Matter can't go? I thought that there is only one Field of Dreams," I asked.

"Yeah, the one by our house is called that as well, but this Field of Dreams is above The Underground it's so bright to go through. You have to wear the goggles to protect your eyes, so you won't go blind," Barty said

"It's like walking into an area like the sun and keeping your eyes open while looking at it, you go blind because it's so bright," said Burgesis. "So the area just outside of the Field of Dreams is so dark because the Grey Matter has been trying to penetrate it for years."

"So how far is The Underground from the Field of Dreams?" I asked

"The underground is literally right underneath the Field of Dreams," Burgesis said.

"Are you going to be okay going through the Grey Matter?" I asked worriedly.

"The Grey Matter is thick, but it doesn't attack when there are three or more people holding hands walking through its thickness, its focused on trying to build up so it can push through the Field of Dreams but its impenetrable!" said Burgesis confidently.

"So, Whiskers and his wife live in the Field of Dreams?" I repeated

"Well, they live just outside of it just after the Grey Matter," Barty said

"It is incredibly beautiful there at their house," said Burgesis "Their home is just like yours on Earth actually,"

"It's the same?" I asked

"Yeah, it was changed that way once Whiskers was on the assignment to find "the one," he made it his second home away from home. He wanted it this way so that when he visited here, in the World of the Unknown, he wouldn't forget the layout of your Earthly house. He wanted to be prepared so that if circumstances forbade him being able to go to Earth, he could still enjoy something similar here in the World of the Unknown," said Burgesis

"Oh wow," I said, "That makes things a lot easier for me,"

"Yes and no," Burgesis said carefully. "You have to understand how difficult it's going to be for you both to get used to each other again. It's going to be difficult to say goodbye to him again especially since you don't look the same."

"As this is all touching and everything," said Eggbert walking towards us. "We have to focus on trying to get to the result which I am assuming now is The Underground and not my school,"

"Yes, Eggbert," said Burgesis.

"So, since we are going to eventually be passing the school would it be wise to give him a tour of the school as we pass it," asked Eggbert looking at Burgesis and then to Barty and was apparently forgetting my presence at the time.

"Well, we have heard that Nerogroben is going to burn down your school," said Barty "We after all

don't know if this is true or not, but it can only be assumed since we have only heard about this through word of mouth. In fact, Toolot from the scout camp, back on the Path of Fortune, wanted to talk to you and find out where your loyalties lay,"
"Is that so, well it might interest you to know that my school is perfectly well protected from the likes of Nerogroben and his wretched army," said Eggbert through gritted teeth.
"Can you two not fight so much for once?" Burgesis said looking at Eggbert and then to Barty and then looked at me and shook his head out of frustration. "We don't know what's going on at the school, and we won't know until we get there," said Burgesis "Besides, it is up to Mark if he wants to see the school or not at that time. He doesn't have to give an answer now," Burgesis insisted as the two of them had automatically looked at
me for a response as I kept quiet.
We started to walk towards the cart and Brittany was standing there already hooked up to the cart by The Guard.
"Good morning Mark," said Brittany pleasantly
"Good morning Brittany," I said.
"How did you sleep last night," asked Brittany conversationally
"I slept okay," I said

"Are you going to be okay to walk or do you want to ride in the cart?" she asked

"I want to ride in the cart today," I said

"Oh okay cool," said Brittany unconcernedly as I had gotten into the cart.

Eladius was already in it looking out the window of the cart to see his parents behind the cart talking.

"Good morning Eladius," I said

"Good morning," Eladius said.

"Are your parents riding with us today in the cart or are they walking it," I asked

"They are walking it again but they will be behind us," said Eladius. "The guard is moving around everyone since that Wizard Eggbert is with us now,"

"Oh well that's good, right?" I said

"Yeah, I guess," said Eladius as he went quiet and looked down.

"What's the matter Eladius," I asked

"I really shouldn't say," he said looking down at the floor of the cart and avoiding eye contact.

"Tell me," I said

"The guard is worried about whether we should trust Eggbert," Eladius said quietly.

"Eggbert is a wizard, we should be able to trust him," I said. "Look at this cart, he made its quite sturdy, and it's worked this far past the Path of Fortune."

"Yeah, your right but I am just not sure whether my family and I can trust him or not," Eladius carefully whispering in my ear.

"We, The Guard, and myself, gave you and your family a second chance when we didn't need to, you just need to trust me, trust my decisions that I am making," I said "If I felt unsure about something, I would tell you and your family, and the rest of The Guard immediately."

"Okay, Mark," said Eladius looking up at me. "I will trust you then."

"Good," I said confidently.

As we moved on forward silently, I signaled Tom to come down to us at the window on the cart to talk to him.

"Hey Tom," I said, "Thanks for coming down to talk,"

"No problem Mark," he said, "Is everything okay?"

"Yeah, I was just wondering if you could just make sure that there is some water near our next campsite that is drinkable."

" Yeah sure," said Tom the Raven in a low tone, smiling.

"Thanks Tom," I said calmly looking at him "How far are we from the Village of Solotar and the Field of Dreams?" I asked.

"We are almost there," said Tom as he took off.

"What exactly is in the Village of Solotar?" I asked Eladius who looked at me as I asked him the question.

"Well, you heard what that Troll said on the Path of Fortune," said Eladius "It is a metal village, there they have most the trolls in Nerogroben's army making metal swords, and armory."

"Are they all Nerogroben's followers?" I asked

"Most of them, the ones that aren't, are friends of the Eubinks, and they tend to help them out around their scout camp house. I have only been there once," said Eladius.

"Wait, they are spies for Nerogroben?" I asked surprised

"Well to Nerogroben, they are, at least that is what he thinks. The information coming from that scout camp is not to be trusted by any means," said Eladius. "They give out false information to Nerogroben and his army. In fact, I wouldn't be surprised if that is why they think Nerogroben's men were going to burn down the School of the Unknown."

"How do you know that it's false information?" I asked

"Well it's because it's in code isn't it," Eladius explained in a whisper, he took out a piece of paper, "take the whole sentence of information for example, "Nerogroben's men are going to burn down the School of the Unknown," then change the first positive word in the sentence which is the word "are" and make it the opposite so now the sentence reads "Nerogroben's men aren't going to burn down the School of the Unknown," then delete the sixth and the seventh words of the sentence, and it changes the whole entire sentence meaning to "Nerogroben's men aren't going to the School of the Unknown. You see?"

"Oh wow," I said "So the whole message was Nerogroben's men aren't going to the School of the Unknown? But why worry Eggbert like that?"

"It's because they wanted to test him," said Eladius quietly.

"Where did you learn to decode Nerogroben's messages?" I asked

"My parents taught me at a young age, and whenever they left to work and found out information, they would leave me a coded message for me to figure out," Eladius said as he crumpled up the paper and burned it in a bowl that was in a cupboard in the cart.

About an hour later, we arrived to the outskirts of the Village of Solotar. I looked out the window to see Burgesis knock on the door of George and Donna's house. Donna opened the door quickly and was whispering to him as he leaned over her to hear what she was saying. He then straightened up and walked away towards me and the cart as Donna closed their door.

"We must leave immediately to the Field of Dreams where they will meet us," said Burgesis to me quietly. "It is not safe here anymore."

"But wait," I said looking at Eladius. "I thought that the Field of Dreams is by Barty and Jana's house. That's a long distance away."

"Oh you must mean the grasslands. They call it the Field of Dreams as a nickname because it reminds them of the other," said Eladius smiling.

Immediately Burgesis led The Guard towards the Field of Dreams, and about an hour later in silence we were heading finally towards a great light. I noticed that everyone started to wear their protective gear as Eladius, and I put mine on. As we got closer to the campsite, we could tell that everything was lit by the plants within the Field of Dreams, and we arrived at our campsite.

"What are these plants called?" I asked Eladius

"Steph flowers!" Eladius said as I admired them.

I got out of the cart as the rest of The Guard started to prepare and secure the area. Once we were certain everything was set up, Burgesis looked at me expectantly through his goggles which I couldn't help but laugh at him. He looked funny.

Burgesis walked up to me with Barty smiling and said, "Are you ready to leave the camp to meet Whiskers and Gretta?"

"Yeah," I said

"I need to talk to them and give them an update on things here," said Burgesis.

"Do you think we could get some wine juice from them
and maybe some supplies?" asked Barty as he looked at me.

"Yeah, that shouldn't be a problem," Burgesis said.

"Do you think they could come with us to The Underground?" I asked.

"I don't think that it's a good idea Mark, not with Captain
Koda there," Barty said quietly.

"Who is Captain Koda? What's wrong with that idea?" I asked, "Well nothing is wrong with the idea particularly. It's just that, Captain Koda is what you would call a Dog, on Earth. They generally, don't get along with cats here in the World of the Unknown, just like on Earth. At times, they get on each other's nerves. He oversees The Underground which is under George and Donna's house," said Burgesis looking at me smiling.

"Oh my goodness," I said "They both have issues here too?"

"Yeah, unfortunately," said Barty smiling

"But they are on the same side, they are against Nerogroben," I said.

"Yeah, I mean it's not that they are as bad together, as they are on Earth, like fighting wise. It's more like they like to insult each other, and it can be bad," said Barty.

"Well, I insist that Whiskers and his wife come with us," I said "It's been a long time since I have had a chance to see Whiskers. I don't care what Captain Koda must say, he is going to behave, they both are."

Both Barty and Burgesis smiled but kept quiet as they both led the way to Whisker's house. We walked to the edge of the campsite clearing and then we went through dark woods. Burgesis grabbed my hand trying to lead the way as I grabbed Barty's hand. I had never seen woods this dark before. Burgesis seemed to be reading my mind and said "These woods unfortunately are darkened by pure Grey Matter. It's very concentrated here because it can't enter the Field of Dreams. We should have brought the Steph flower with us Barty."

I looked at Barty and he nodded as he looked at me.

"The Steph flower is called the flower of light," Barty explained "It works based off goodness and happiness, and it can be a very dependable light source,"

"Well, it's too late now, we can't go back," said Burgesis

"Wait a moment," I said

"Don't you try any magic that you can't handle right now Mark," Barty said "It would be an easy time for the Grey Matter to attack you when you are at your most vulnerable."

"I was just going to try making light," I said

"The darkness will try to consume the light," said Burgesis as we walked on.

I just kept the idea to myself and didn't pursue it. After what seemed like a considerable amount of time, we got through all the Grey Matter and we finally saw it. My house, the front porch light was lit up as I ran up to the door and rang the doorbell excitedly. Burgesis and Barty ran to keep up with me.

The door opened and there was Whiskers and his Wife standing on their hind legs.

"Well come on in, Mark," said Whiskers "You shouldn't have to ring the doorbell for your own home. I came into the house, and I turned around and picked up Whiskers and gave him a huge hug as he put his head on my shoulder and started patting my head. Burgesis and Barty came in as well laughing and greeting Whiskers Wife, Gretta and then Whiskers.

The room seemed to brighten on it is own around us as we all were just so happy to see each other as we all followed Whiskers and Whisker's wife into their sitting room.

"We are so happy you have come to our home, Mark," said Whisker wife as she motioned for us to sit down, "My name is Gretta, I am Whisker's Wife. I was so sad to hear of his death on Earth and I had to wait three days to figure out if he was coming here or moving on," she explained as she sat down and motioned for us to sit down.

"Why did you have to wait two days?" I asked as Burgesis seemed curious about something on his own but decided not to mention it now.

"It's a process for our creator and The Ancients approve and help us transition," said Whiskers.

"What do you mean?" I asked.

"Well not everyone can live in the World of the Unknown after they die," said Whiskers "Those who lived a moral and good life on Earth and didn't break any of the commandments in the bible would be able to make the decision of heaven, hell, or the World of the Unknown."

"So, you didn't get to pick the World of the Unknown, heaven or hell?" I asked looking at

Burgesis and then to Whiskers who had stayed silent.

"Mark, I think we need to explain this a little deeper than you think," explained Burgesis carefully looking at Whiskers who nodded at Burgesis.

Chapter 39
In the Beginning: The Seven Guardians, Seven Virtues, and Seven Deadly Sins

I looked up at Burgesis who had looked at me and nodded as Whiskers looked at me and started to explain. "There is an ancient story that I want to tell you. In the beginning, as you possibly may know, the Creator made Earth in 6 days and rested on the Seventh day. This Seventh day is the Sabbath day on Earth," I nodded, and he continued. "Well while the creator may have been resting on the seventh day per Earth's perspective, it wasn't actually resting. It is said that it was working and making the World of the Unknown, that is why you haven't heard from the Creator since the sixth day. The Creator saw that what he made on Earth was good but there was something more that he was hoping for to happen. A world without as much error. That is when the fallen Angel wanted to be like him and tried to claim dominion on Earth and in heaven until the Creator kicked him out and banished him to hell. The Fallen Angel was to blame for starting the evil on Earth through the snake with Adam and Eve, the first humans. It was from then on, that Grey Matter was created inside the human body, but didn't take over the Human soul or in a physical from like Grey Matter. It was at that point that the Creator realized that it wanted this change in it is judgment with regards to allowing evil to take over a body to this internal extent. So, on the seventh day, The World of the Unknown was created, and it was beautiful and was full of Magical Creatures and Magical Human Elves. This World was supposed to be it is masterpiece and it didn't want this world to be full of Grey Matter/Evil. The Creator also didn't want to allow the magic that was in the World of the Unknown on Earth with the humans. So, the Creator also created a powerful Necklace. The Necklace was symbolic of the Creator, and it is power, which allowed the wearer to be immortal and only if you took it off and held it in your hand you could you use it as a portal to get onto Earth. This Necklace was to be kept in secret and under the protection of the Seven Guardians from the World of the Unknown. NO ONE was to know of it is existence and NO ONE was supposed to know of the Guardians and their purpose. They were given powers only many of us could dream of. The Guardians were referred to in conversations as "The Ancient Seven." To allow a balance of the two worlds, the Creator hand selected the Seven Guardians of the Necklace of Erdemleri. "Erdemleri" is Turkish for Virtues. There are things that can create evil Grey Matter in the World of the Unknown and Seven things that can cause catastrophe on Earth with any Human being. These are Seven temptations that the humans have issues with at times. They are what they call the Seven Deadly Sins, have you heard of them?" explained Whiskers looking at me as I shook my head. "The Seven deadly sins are: Pride, Greed, Lust, Anger, Gluttony, Envy, and Sloth. You must keep in mind that each of these sins have a corresponding Virtue. Each one of the Guardians was to use their Virtue to guard the Necklace of Erdemleri no matter what. These corresponding virtues were Humility, chastity, patience, temperance, kindness, and diligence. They were to use the seven deadly sins on those who were too close to the necklace or too close to the discovery of the exact existence of The Ancient Seven themselves. No one and you may never even ever find out, who The Ancient Seven are. The Seven are an old ancient people, and they are aware of what is occurring and apparently, the necklace is lost. It was lost in the Dark War. Stolen some say, I don't know what to think of that, just that I have a worrying feeling about it. But the Creator and the Seven decide what happens to each one of us. We don't always have a say, but they take our consciousness into consideration as to what we would have wanted. The Guardians were to never allow the Necklace into the hands of evil and were to elect how it was to be used. I was made by the magic of the creator's own hand, and it has not been seen in years. The Council of Foreign Affairs knows of one of the Ancient Seven Guardians. The Guardians still exist today but whom they are is a much-guarded secret. In fact, they only find you when they want you to find them. It is just never a shared fact to know of them and who they are. The Cycle of death is something that the guardians also set up with the Creator. It was decided that it was the creator's choice, and it's also the choice of the Creator if *it* wants to accept our decision or not," said Whiskers "So you are kind of in limbo until the decision is finalized and it's on the third day it reaches his decision."

"Interesting," I said "So my parents for example, they will have the choice and heaven and hell or the World of the Unknown as well? But the Creator might decide he wants them in heaven instead of the World of the Unknown?"

"Well, you're partially correct," explained Burgesis looking at me, "You're under the assumption that the Creator is a he, it's a common mistake,"

"It's a mistake?" I asked, "I always though the creator was a he."

"Well, the Creator is, an "it," explained Whiskers "We shouldn't assume genders in the spirit world."

"Interesting," I said looking at Gretta who was seemingly calm.

"What are you two doing here in the World of the Unknown then?" I asked

"What do you mean?" asked Whiskers

"Well, do you have any goals here?" I asked.

"Goals?" asked Whiskers "We just want to live on peacefully."

"Not to sound rude or anything but have you seen the chaos and disorder out there in the World of the Unknown?" I asked

"Yes Mark, we have seen it," explained Gretta "But we are just two cats and in fact we are the only two cats here in the World of the Unknown, so we don't have a clan yet, it's up to the Creator to decide when "it" wants that to happen, if at all."

"All because you don't have a clan you don't think you have enough influence to make a difference, am I, right?" I asked

"Yes, Mark," explained Whiskers sadly. "Things are going to fix themselves."

"Your wrong Whiskers and Gretta," explained Burgesis

"You were right to die on Earth Whiskers," explained Burgesis "It wasn't in vain, this is "the one," Burgesis said pointing at me and looking at Whiskers seriously.

"How can he be "the one" he is just a boy!" said Gretta.

"No, he is more than that, he is extremely powerful," said Barty looking at Burgesis.

"We have a lot to catch up on," said Burgesis

"We have not even heard so much of a rumor of anything changing out there," said Whiskers.

"That's because of that Grey Matter out there, it's made you live in the shadows of ignorance," Barty said giving Whiskers a paw-shake as we all sat in the sitting room.

Burgesis looked around and he seemed surprised at how similar things were. He and I sat exactly as we did the first time we met in our living-room back on Earth.

"So, catch us up," said Gretta looking at Burgesis and Barty. "What's been going on out there? We know something has been happening because it's been too quiet for something not to be going on out there."

"You are right," said Burgesis looking at me, "A lot has been occurring,"

"So where is Jana?" asked Whiskers looking at Barty who just busted into uncontrollable tears, stood up, and left the room.

"Did I say something?" asked Whiskers surprised at Barty's reaction after he left the room then looked to Burgesis who put his fingers together in mid-air in front of him.

"Well, it's just one of the many updates that we needed to give you," said Burgesis sadly as he stood up walked out of the room and brought Barty back into the room and gave him a cloth to wipe his tears away and patted him on the back as he sat Barty back down into his seat. "Jana died trying to save Mark and some of The Guard," explained Burgesis looking at Gretta who immediately got up and started to comfort Barty.

"Died?" asked Whiskers blankly.

Burgesis looked at Barty at first who was still crying and started to recount everything that happened to Jana and the rest of The Guard on our journey between the oohs and ahhs of Gretta and Whiskers. After Burgesis explained the incident of what happened to Jana, Whiskers said "I'm sorry for dragging things out like this but this boy is not hardly "the one" yet." Suddenly Barty stopped crying and said, "What do you mean he isn't "the one"!" as he looked at me and then to Burgesis.

Chapter 40
The Book of the Known

"He technically all he has only proved to those here in the World of the Unknown is that he is no more than a normal boy who happened to be able to change into a Magical Human Elf while coming here," stated Whiskers sounding harsh.

"Now hold on Whiskers, we agreed upon the sign that you would give me if you found "the one," Burgesis said as he pointed his finger at Whiskers who had his hands up.

"Now Burgesis," Whiskers said, "You didn't hear me correctly, I said he is not, *hardly* "the one," Mark still must prove himself to all the clans that he is worthy to be followed, not just me. *If* he beats Nerogroben, then *maybe* he will be called "the one," explained Whiskers looking at Burgesis sternly.

Burgesis turned to look at me calmly and said, "Mark's magic abilities have been truly remarkable."

"Oh really?" said Whiskers looking at me and then looking at Burgesis.

"Yeah, Mark can use the power of Light and Forgiveness to clear the Grey Matter, heal the broken hearts of those of whom he has touched, and clear away the evil red magimarks of those around him as well with that light," said Barty pointing out Burgesis magimark as Whiskers looked at it as he shook his head in disbelief.

"The light of healing broken hearts... What!" stammered Whiskers. "How is he able to use such ancient magic? Even the most accomplished Magic have problems with such things, who has taught him the magic of The Ancients? Who taught him these things?"

"He is able to fully use the powers and they work and he uses them of his own volition, no one has taught or told him of such powers," Burgesis said sounding proud.

"Does he even know the basics?" asked Whiskers sounding flabbergasted.

"Of course, he is aware of the basics, how else could he learn to defend himself?" Barty said.

"Defend himself?" asked Gretta looking at Whiskers with her eyebrows raised.

"Humph, he's going to need to know a lot more than that when he meets Nerogroben," said Whiskers looking at Burgesis frustrated as he crossed his arms and avoided eye contact with anyone in the room.

Burgesis and Barty stayed quiet as Gretta stood up and left the room and came back two minutes later.

"So what else has been happening out there?" asked Gretta as she came back into the sitting room with glasses of fruitade. I grabbed the fruitade from the tray as she placed it in between Burgesis and me. She grabbed two glasses for Barty and Whiskers and she took the last cup.

Burgesis looked at me quietly as we both took a sip of the fruitade in silence. As I finished drinking I looked at Burgesis and thought "You were right Burgesis, I have to try to get used to Whiskers and how he is, just like he is trying to get used to me and how I look," as Burgesis smiled at me from across the coffee table and nodded in agreement.

"So I see Mark figured out the most silent way to talk to you Burgesis," Whiskers said noticing our faces.

"This of course is the best way to talk to each other in private," said Burgesis looking at me and still smiling.

"And it can be maddening," said Whiskers, as he and Gretta started shaking their heads.

"It's so rude," said Gretta looking at Burgesis as I just smiled.

"Grot, the Troll is dead" explained Burgesis looking at them.

"We aren't sure yet, but the scout camp along what used to be called the Path of Misfortune may have changed allegiances," said Barty looking at me.

"Used to be called? Switched allegiances?" said Whiskers looking at Barty and Burgesis as Burgesis explained what happened.

"Now it's called, The Path of Fortune, due to Mark and the light of forgiveness, which essentially has weakened, and in some cases, gotten rid of the Grey Matter along that path," said Barty.

"Oh my," said Gretta looking at Whiskers who crossed his arms.

"I don't believe it," said Whiskers "Do you honestly think that one spell of the light of forgiveness is going to have a lasting effect on the likes of Nerogroben's men? They have been in this Grey Matter for decades!"

Then Burgesis explained the story of the Woodland Elms with the changes of the hearts of everyone including the

Guard and Eladius and his family.

"Well there are no guarantees in either worlds Earth or even here Burgesis, you know that," said Whiskers skeptically.

As Burgesis continued to update Whiskers and Gretta they began to listen more intently. When Burgesis told them of how Nerogroben was looking for Eggbert the wizard, Eladius, and his family, both Whiskers and Gretta looked fearful.

"Don't worry, they are being protected in the Field of Dreams with the rest of The Guard," explained Barty as he interrupted Burgesis who then continued to explain how The Guard agreed to continue to protect Mark, Eladius, and his family, under Mark's request.

"How ever did you get The Guard to agree to work together like this?" asked Gretta looking at Burgesis who pointed at me.

"Yeah," said Whiskers thoughtfully. "I don't believe what you are telling us."

"Well the truth will be out," said Barty smiling proudly. "You will begin to believe *if* and *when* you see Mark in action...."

"What do you mean *if* and *when*?" Gretta asked looking at Barty who then cupped his hand over his mouth realizing he shouldn't have said anything about it yet until Burgesis had a chance to talk to Whiskers privately. Burgesis shot Barty a look who responded with a face of apology as Burgesis hesitated.

"Well, to be honest, it is Mark's request that you come along with The Guard to the Underground," explained Burgesis looking at Barty rather harshly who shrugged it off.

"THOSE DOGS!" said Whiskers looking at me.

So carefully I then thought about what I was going to say and before I did say anything Burgesis laughed as he seemed to be reading my mind.

"Yes, I am requesting that you and Gretta to get out of your comfort zones and come help me train to fight better. Obviously, you think I am inadequately educated in matters regarding the basics, maybe I could learn more from more people like yourselves," I said looking at Whiskers who sat their open mouthed and looked surprised by my attitude as if I just smacked him in the face.

"That was harsh considering I went to Earth to find you and be your pet for all those years," explained Whiskers sounding hurt.

"Well it seems to me that you have already prejudged me even before you have seen what I can do during a fight," I explained looking at Whiskers defiantly as Barty and Burgesis looked at each other and seemed to be impressed with my retort back.

"You know already that if it is not our abilities that shows who we truly are it is our choices and what we choose to do that defines us Mark," said Whiskers wisely as he drank the last of his fruitade and Gretta nodded in agreement and got up to collect the empty glasses from everyone and place them on the tray. "You have a lot to learn boy," Whiskers added looking at me.

"Yeah, well maybe I do," I said roughly, "But I can't be trained if your holed up here, while the rest of the World of the Unknown is being torn apart." Burgesis nodded in agreement with me.

"He may have a lot more to learn, but it's up to those around him to at least give him a chance, to be a good influence on him. Otherwise, he will fall from his

errors here," said Burgesis calmly looking at Whiskers.

"Good," said Whiskers crossing his arms seemingly offended by the ongoing conversation. "Let him fall, he's just a boy, maybe he should fall so he can learn to get back up again."

"Well, it's sort of the point to help him mature, and grow up, these tests aren't exactly for fun are they," said Barty quietly.

"Wait, wait," I said looking around. "Hold on, you guys know what the clan tests are?"

"Yes, we do," said Whiskers softly.

"But why can't I know them?" I asked

"You should have already known," said Whiskers frowning at Burgesis and Barty who remained quiet as they looked at each other quickly.

"You mean you haven't shown him the book?" asked Whiskers.

"Of course he has the book," said Burgesis looking at Barty.

"He should have figured it out already," said Burgesis looking at Whiskers and then he looked at me and said, "We have already given you all the information you need to be helpful and successful here in the World of the Unknown,"

"All you have given me is this stupid old English-Latin dictionary and basic training," I said indignantly as I was looking impatiently at everyone as they all stared at me in astonishment. Even Burgesis looked at me surprised with my attitude.

"It's not a stupid old English-Latin dictionary," he cautiously.

Whiskers slapped his paws on his forehead in frustration. "It's more than what it is Mark," said Whiskers.

"I thought we aren't supposed to help "the one," said Barty looking at Burgesis and then to Whiskers.

"*According, to prophecy, we aren't supposed to help "the one" complete his tests or when it comes down to it, to fight Nerogroben himself,*" said Whiskers. "It doesn't mean we can't show him the way and how to use the book or train him."

"Oh come on," I said looking at everyone as I pulled out the book and slapped it on the coffee table loudly in front of them "I know this book from cover to cover already, there isn't anything else that you can show me that I haven't already read in this stupid book!"

"You know what your problem is?" said Whiskers frowning at me. "Your problem is that you lack patience and you think you know everything, are very conceited."

"BUT I ALREADY KNOW THE BOOK!" I said slowly and loudly as I started to feel myself getting angry and frustrated with Whiskers.

"Knowing isn't understanding and there is more to this than just a simple book in front of you," said Burgesis carefully looking at Whiskers.

"You need to learn to not just see with your eyes, but also you need to learn to see with your heart," said Gretta.

"What do you all mean? Can you all just speak plainly and not in riddles," I asked looking at Burgesis who cleared his throat.

"You know everything about this book cover to cover huh?" said Burgesis looking at Whiskers who just smiled.

Burgesis moved the book so it faced him on the coffee table. Then he waved his hand over the book and said "Revelio". As soon as he said that and put his hand over it, the book became thicker in size and larger and Whiskers laughed as he looked at my surprised reaction.

"I remember that look, it is the same look you would give if you knew you were going to be getting into trouble," Whiskers said as he continued to laugh as he covered his mouth with his hand in happiness. "What's the matter, I thought you knew the book cover to cover?"

Just then Whiskers, Barty, Burgesis, and Gretta just laughed.

"You don't know what you don't know, child," said Gretta smiling as she looked at my surprised face. Then Burgesis grabbed the book in front of Whiskers and him. and turned the now bible thick, coffee table sized book, around to face me right side up. He then nodded to me to open the book. I opened the book and was surprised by how much the page shined and made my face glow as I held the book closer to me. I closed my eyes and enjoyed the smell of the pages of the book. The book smelled as if it was freshly printed. After I opened my eyes again, I observed the first page. The first thing I noticed was that it was ancient, the text looked medieval.

In the middle of the page was the following which I read aloud, "*This book is written in dedication and memory to those who have lost faith. As a guide, may this keep you on the path of the light, and may it not lead you astray into the darkness. – Signed A Friend.*"

I looked up and everyone in the room, just smiled and nodded for me to continue. At the bottom of that same page was a quote that just appeared. "This just appeared out of no-where," I said looking at Burgesis showing him the quote amazed.

"It looks like the book wants you to read a quote more," said Barty wisely as I looked at it, and read it aloud.

"Strength of Character means the ability to overcome resentment against others, to hide hurt feelings, and to forgive quickly," –Lawrence G. Lovasik, Earth. I then turned the page, it read, "*Table of Contents,*" Which I started to read the chapter titles aloud one by one:

"*Map of the World of the Unknown, 17 Character Magimarks,*" and then under it tabbed slightly more to the right with their corresponding page numbers, and read the following: *Empathy, Determination, Faith, Acceptance, Forgiveness, Cleverness, Happiness/Joy, Hope, Patience, Humility, Honesty, Kindness/Generosity, Loyalty/Honor, Bravery/Courage, Order/Responsibility, Hospitality, Positivity,*" I stopped reading and looked around.

"But these are the Character Magimarks aren't they?" I asked Burgesis who nodded and said, "Continue reading."

"*Basic Elemental Magic, Ancient Advanced Magic (Prerequisite: Basics),*" I then tried to turn to the

Ancient Advanced Magic Page, but it wouldn't let me turn to the page, the section was closed off. "Burgesis I think the book is broken, it won't let me turn to the Ancient Advanced Magic pages."

"It's because the book knows that you haven't read through what it wants to tell you about the Basics first," said Burgesis laughing. "My goodness boy, have you ever not read a book? I thought you were reading high school level books?"

He finished shaking his head.

"Yeah, I do read, and I do read at that level," I said embarrassed.

"If you want to read ahead to the other chapters, its best to endure the beginning otherwise you may not understand the middle and the end of the story," said Barty wisely as I nodded and looked back at the table of contents.

Symptom spells," I then read aloud frowning at Barty as I looked underneath it to read on as I saw that there was tabbed over subsections for this subject as well. "*Magic the Strengthens, Weakens, or is Physically, Emotionally, or Mentally Impairing.*" There are spells that do that to you?" I asked allowed after reading the subsections looking at Burgesis who nodded sadly.

"Some have even gone mad by using this magic," said Burgesis quietly to me.

"Lessons of the Clans, People not to trust, Natural Powers of the Clans, History of the World of the Unknown, Clan Histories, Rivals, and Family Histories, Foreign Councils of Earth and the World of the Unknown, Magimarks and their meaning, History of this book, Index" Then suddenly I looked up under the Lessons of the Clans, lettering appeared slowly as I said, "That's funny, this just appeared, *The Secret Story of the Beginning,*" I stopped reading and looked up at Whiskers who reacted and looked up at Burgesis who nodded and he then looked at me.

"This book updates as you incur more knowledge as well as shows you information that you should learn," said Whiskers now smiling wisely.

"Wait, how can this book contain history of the clans? How far is it updated from? How can this be an updated list of people to trust?" I asked pointing to the table of contents. Just then a light appeared around the book pages that were closed as I jumped in surprise and read. "This book updated every five minutes and contains Clan history as of five minutes ago."

I looked in shock at Burgesis who laughed at me, "Yes Mark, this book talked back to you and no it doesn't have a name."

"What you have Mark, is a very Ancient Book...This book can gather information that dates back as far as the beginning days of the World of the Unknown and how it was created, as the book feels your ready you will be able to read more of it. But some parts of the book are closed off until the book feels you are ready to know and sometimes things appear that it wants you to know," stated Whiskers interrupting Burgesis who was about to explain the same thing else but stopped to let Whiskers finish. "The book itself never lies and was started by the Creator itself who formed the World of the Unknown, it's meant to help the beholder to be successful," said Burgesis "But in the wrong hands it can be dangerous."

"This English-Latin Dictionary is a disguise for what this book actually is, it is the Book of the Known," said Barty carefully. "No one can know that you have this book, do you understand? This book is said to have been lost in time, and it was recovered by Burgesis. That is how we know about the prophecy."

"Yeah, I understand where is this prophecy that you spoke of earlier to me that is supposed to be in here exactly?" I asked trying to open ahead to the pages the book would allow me to open to.

"Well actually," said Barty looking at Burgesis

"I pulled it out of the book," said Burgesis calmly as he looked at me, "In the future from now on though, you are never to pull anything out of that book. I pulled it out because it is up to you to make your own destiny. It isn't for anyone else to tell you what you do, how to be "the one," or even to tell you that you don't need to be successful. We all can only be your guide from here on."

"There is a section that is just for the History of where this book has been and who has had it in the past," said Whiskers matter-of-factly.

Just then there was a loud crack outside the door and in a flash Burgesis stood up and said "Et in fide" and the book went back to normal. There was a knock at the door and immediately everyone stood up in defensive positions as Gretta timidly started to answer the door.

As soon as Gretta slowly opened the door it burst open with a flash of light and as the light dimmed it slowly dimmed to what disappeared to on a walking staff being held by a figure that was standing at the doorway. It was none other than the Great Wizard Eggbert himself.

Chapter 41
The Nightmare of Dreams

"Pardon for breaking up this gathering but, you are all needed back at the camp," said Eggbert quickly. "There has been a disturbance."

"How dare you barge in here into our home!" shouted Whiskers angrily.

"No problem, Eggbert," said Barty calmly trying to calm Whiskers. "We will be there soon," Eggbert then bowed towards me and teleported away in a flash of light at the doorway. I then looked at Burgesis who seemed to be reading my mind. I had looked at the book, and wondered, what did he say in English, for the book, to change back normally.

"Ah, that's right, sorry Mark, what I said in English, it meant "I have faith," but it can't be said without meaning," Burgesis said quietly in my ear as I smiled.

"So where did The Guard set up camp exactly?" asked Whiskers

"The camp isn't far, it's just outside the Grey Matter," said Barty as he, Burgesis, and I grabbed out protective goggles and ear plugs. I grabbed the book and put it in my pocket as we started to leave the house. One by one we started to leave the house with Barty and Burgesis leading the way closely followed by me as Whiskers and Gretta left the lights on and locked their house up behind them.

As we walked to the campsite, there were flashes of colored lights ahead as we ran faster to there and in minutes we arrived just in time to see yellow bubbles that turned red and black clouds followed them as they moved.

"This looks like a nightmare," said Barty looking at me and shaking his head with his hands up in case one of the nightmares attacked us, we put on our protective gear. In quick action, I used gusts of wind to push the floating dreams away from The Guard and then I looked around to see Matt being attacked by a dark red dream bubble in mid-air. I realized that he didn't have on any protective gear as he fought the best he could. I thought to myself I need to control this, this time as I could hear Eggbert's voice in my head "It is one thing to know and it's another thing to understand." I closed my eyes as I heard Gretta's voice in my head next, "You need to learn not just to listen in your head, but you also need to learn to listen to your heart." I started to concentrate on my feelings and emotions that I was feeling. I was angry because Matt was being attacked but I then changed perspective, and thought "Why are the dreams attacking? I asked myself. As I started to try to understand what was going on, I allowed that

understanding to fill my heart and I thought about the ancient words in the English from, "In the name of all that is, I forgive all wrongs committed in the hearts and souls of all those present with the light of forgiveness," and suddenly I felt those words should be whispered. So, I whispered them calmly by responding to the situation and not reacting to the situation with emotion. As I raised my hands up and breathed in a deep breath before I said the following words in a whisper, as a different kind of peace came over me, "Omne quod est in nomine domini, et dimitte universa delicta commisit in corde et tota anima cum omnibus veniam lucem!" as I said it in a low whisper my magimarks lit up and my eyes glowed as the power radiated from me. "That's it Mark!" Burgesis said smiling and then the dreams changed from red to yellow again and started to float around freely again and the Grey Matter and clouds of negativity cleared the area and dissipated. I slowly opened my eyes, and as I did I noticed even Whiskers and Gretta were affected by the Ancient Magic I used. They had started to cry. Everyone started applauding and Eladius ran up to me and hugged me. Burgesis walked up to me and patted me on the back.
"You did it Mark!" said Eladius
"I am very proud of you Mark," said Whiskers as he started to tear more. "Your Magic is starting to get

stronger, and more powerful. You will need to have more control, so you can keep your eyes open, but that was excellent!"

"Thanks," I said looking around for Matt. I walked up to where I last saw him and found him lying on the ground with his wings outstretched on the ground as he was taking deep breaths.

"Are you okay Matt?" I asked worriedly

"Yeah, I am okay just trying to catch my breath," he said looking up at the sky above us.

"What happened?" I asked, "What made them attack?"

"These dreams followed me here, I just got back from the scout camp on the Path of Fortune, and since I didn't have my protective gear on at the time they attacked me," he said.

"How did the results go from the voting?" I asked curiously

"Well they unanimously decided to switch the camp loyalty to you because of the impact you left on the trolls

there," said Matt as he looked at me smiling.

"Well that's awesome!" I said looking at Burgesis who then nodded in agreement.

"But, they didn't choose Toolot as the leader," said Matt "They picked a different Troll, who is bigger in size in comparison to Toolot, I am not sure what kind of leader he will be, but his name is Luke,"

"Maybe there is hope since they changed their loyalty," said Barty quietly as Matt stood up again. "Toolot is not nearby there anymore either! They don't know how he left or where he is!" Matt continued.

"Hopefully," said Whiskers as he had walked up to us to overhear our conversation.

"Hey Whiskers," said Matt looking at Whiskers and nodded his head at whiskers who also responded with a respectful nod.

"Where are you all headed?" asked Matt "It's weird seeing you out, around here."

"We are all headed to The Underground," said Whiskers as we all started walking and The Guard had gathered their things and followed around us.

"It's long ways away," said Barty looking at Eggbert.

"We should teleport to the Eubinks house," said Eggbert as he motioned for everyone to gather closely to him and around him.

"But how are we going to do that?" asked Barty "There is only a few of us who know how to teleport here and not everyone knows how."

"I have a plan," Eggbert said smiling

Eggbert pulled out a long tarp that was rolled up in his robe. "Everyone, hurry up, under here, hide under this tarp," he said as he placed the tarp over all of us and he whispered a few words from the

English-Latin dictionary and all of us where lifted off the ground. We felt a whoosh underneath our feet, about a minute later we all landed on the soft ground again.

"How did you do that?" I asked.

"We wizards have many tricks up our sleeves," he said quietly as he took the tarp off me and the rest of The Guard and Eladius and his family looked at me wide eyed as I tried to give them a look of reassurance. They seemed to calm by this. When we looked around there was a house in front of us, it was a normal Earthly looking house with sunflowers growing along the pathway.

Chapter 42
A Weakness of a Great Leader

As we walked up the pathway that lead to the front door suddenly the door opened, and it was George and Donna Eubinks smiling.

"We thought that was you all," said Donna smiling as she walked out the front door to start hugging and greeting everyone. "Come on in,"

Everyone seemed relaxed as we gathered single file inside the house. It was larger inside than it looked outside. The house was cold in feeling but homely none the less. There was a fire that was burning in the fireplace in the sitting room where we all gathered.

"You all must be hungry and thirsty from your journey here," said George as he motioned for them to go to their dining room.

"We have already prepared for your arrival," said Donna. "If you want to sit by your place cards our servants have already started to set up the dinner plates."

We all sat in our respective formal place cards. The dining room was very large and fancy there were three huge, beautiful crystal chandeliers that were lit up along the long dining room table from the ceiling. I stood at my sitting and noticed Burgesis was sitting next to me on one side and Eggbert was on the other. Both George and Donna Eubinks sat on opposite ends of the table. Which was weird for the guard as we all sat down, I noticed one of the servants give me a worried look at the table. Burgesis seemed to take notice of how my reactions to things that were going on around the room as wine was poured around the table from the various Troll servants. He seemed to be feeling uneasy, as I was. "A toast," said George as he and everyone took their glasses stood up and held them up "To a great and powerful leader, who will overcome all evil and Grey Matter, to Mark!" he said hold his glass up to me as everyone took a sip of their wine. As I took a sip of my bitter tasting wine, Burgesis said "NOOOO!!!" as Burgesis noticed how George and Donna Eubinks and Eggbert were all observing me, but it was all too late; Burgesis pushed the glass out of my hands. I started to feel weak, and faint and I fell over into his arms.

TO BE CONTINUED...

Grey Matter Series Volume 2

Is already out...

Contact the author via email for further information regarding the Grey Matter Series.

authoraparker@gmail.com

OR

Follow us on Facebook:

https://www.facebook.com/greymatterthestoryofmarktrogmyerintheWotU/

Sources/ References

1. All Latin Words – Google Translate
2. Turkish Translation – Google Translate

Meet the Characters Illustrated by Brendan Alicea:

Mark Trogmyer, Earth 3176

Frank Burgesis, Earth 3176

Mark Trogmyer,
Magical Human elf,
World of the
Unknown form

Frank Burgesis, Magical Human elf,
World of the Unknown Form

Eggbert the Wise,
Wizards Clan
Leader
for the World of
the Unknown

Grey Matter Series
Character Clan Chart
and the Clan Lessons DRAFT

Name	Clan	Lesson
Mark Trogmyer	Human from Earth	"the one?"/ needs to learn all clan lessons below and all the elements
Frank Burgesis	Both Worlds	Integrity – standing up for what you believe in no matter what others feel. Ref.– Mark does this on his own... Healing takes time...
Barty & Jana Burgeons	Beaver Clan from Beaver Valley	Trust/ Respect of Life
Andrea & Mike Smitherton	Elven Clan from Woodland Elms Harmony Meadow	the importance of loyalty and family -Andrew, Pam, Eladius making up with Mike and Andrea. Ref Ch21
Alice & Jack Pillowdrum	Phoenixes	Immortality
Chris & Elizabeth Ersal	Fairies of the West	the importance of forgiveness of others and the ability to harness that power
Angie & Martin Cunnings	Fox Clan	Knowledge is like a double-edged sword ...Teamwork and the importance of working together as a clan - Ref.
George & Donna Eubinks / Toolot	Troll Clan	The importance of equality

John & Terry Popper Chancellor Rain	Magical Humans	Charity/ Generosity
Pine & Rose Plantoligong	Hummingbirds	Patience
Danny & Jamie Fortesque	Giants of the East	Humility
Britany & James Figwiggins	Unicorns	Pure in heart/ importance of honesty
Tom & Jerry	Ravens	Pride
Eggbert & Jenny Kromopolis	Witches & Wizards	importance of love, friendship, and sacrifice/how to handle situations rationally and responsibly ref. Ch. 18 (Eladius and his family)
Bubba Joe & Captain Koda	Dogs	Security VS Insecurity
Whiskers & Gretta	Cats	Getting along with others/ Friendship
Matt & Shirley Lookings	Eagles	Bravery VS Courage

Earth 3176:

Mark Trogmyer was born with the traditional morals and values that sets him apart from his own peers. Mark is brought into the World of the Unknown by the unlikeliest of people, Frank Burgesis an old man who randomly appears on his doorstep. Burgesis tells Mark that the World of the Unknown is full of magic, magical beings, and Evil or Grey Matter and that it has been prophesized that he is "the one," the last pure child on Earth. Within the prophecy, "The One," is man kinds last hope for the Earth and The World of the Unknown. If Mark is "the one," then he is the only one, who can change the evil hearts of many. Mark is also then informed that while learning lessons along the way, from the various clan leaders, to gain their loyalty, he must defeat the evil troll Nerogroben who has taken over the World of the Unknown, as supreme leader.

A force to be reckoned with Nerogroben has a powerful army of loyal followers, and his powers and influence are spreading and darkening the realm. With the help of his guard and the various clan leaders, will Mark be able to unite these clans, who don't get along because of a social hierarchy, and prove himself worthy as "the one"? Or is he doomed to suffer and fail because of the growing evil dark forces of distrust that have already started to plague over both these worlds?

Grey Matter Series

"Where everything is not what it seems."

Volume 1: The Story of Mark Trogmyer in the World of the Unknown

ISBN: 9781723022494

Now available on amazon and bn.com

Volume 2: The Wrath of Nerogroben

ISBN: 9781534993518

Released Fall 2017

appvis.wixsite.com/ greymatterseries

Made in the USA
Middletown, DE
07 February 2025